With love, for Leona Judy
In whose kitchen I hid from my mom when I was three.

Acknowledgments

Those familiar with Old Town may be surprised to learn that Sophie and her friends reside on Duchess Street. Throughout the series I have taken pains not to pinpoint the exact location of Sophie's house because I don't want to inconvenience any residents of Old Town. According to The Connection Newspapers, citing *Walking with Washington* by Robert Madison, the street now known as Oronoco Street was originally called Duchess Street, completing the procession of Queen, Princess, and Duchess Streets. Apparently, a tobacco inspection warehouse was located on Duchess Street. A favored tobacco called Oronoco was processed there and it became Oronoco Street. As I searched for a name appropriate to Old Town but not currently in use, I stumbled upon Duchess. And so, after all these years, Sophie and her friends live on Duchess Street, but I'm still not telling exactly where it is! I also made up a high house number for Natasha that I don't think exists as well.

I also took some liberties with the "quiet" fireworks. They do exist and are mandatory in some places around the world. I have no idea what fireworks regulations are in Old Town, but this is fiction, so I get to make up that part!

Many thanks to Susan Smith Erba, who assisted me with information about my athletic characters and their muscle cream in this book. And special thanks go to Amy Wheeler, who so kindly set me straight on many restaurant details. Thanks also to Betsy Strickland, who has informed me that she looks for thanks in each of my books and expects to see her name! So thanks for being a great friend, Betsy.

Also heartfelt thanks to Karen Hines, Tammy and Bill Nash, and Kim and John Edwards for patiently taste testing endless cheesecakes!

As always, this book wouldn't exist without my editors, Wendy McCurdy and Elizabeth Trout. And most special thanks to my agent, Jessica Faust, who always sees the bright side and keeps me going.

And last, but most certainly not least, thanks and kudos to my cover artist, Teresa Fasolino. I always think she can't possibly top the previous cover, but amazingly, she does.

Cast of Characters

Sophie Winston
> Nina Reid Norwood—Sophie's best friend
> Mars Winston—Sophie's ex-husband
> Bernie Frei—Sophie's friend and manager of The Laughing Hound
> Francie Vanderhoosen—Sophie's neighbor

Natasha—local domestic diva
> Austin Sinclair—her tenant

Wolf Fleishman—detective

Bobbie Sue Bodoin—the Queen of Cheesecake
> Tate Bodoin—her husband and owner of Blackwell's Tavern
> Rebecca Josephine Bodoin (Jo)—her daughter
> Spencer Carver—her son
> Pierce Carver—her ex-husband

Coach Jeff Cosby—Spencer's track coach

Blackwell's Tavern
> Marsha Bathurst—assistant manager at Blackwell's Tavern
> Liddy Albertson—waitress
> Eli Dawson—bartender

The Laughing Hound
> Eva Rosales—assistant manager
> Shane Hasler—bartender

Eddie Bigalow—fish purveyor

Chapter 1

Dear Sophie,
My mother-in-law hates my guts. After announcing
to everyone within 100 miles, that I was a deadbeat,
she showed up with a cheesecake. Is it possible to
poison cheesecake?
                                    Suspicious in Loafers Station, Indiana

Dear Suspicious,
Happily, I have never tried to poison a cheesecake,
but it's my guess that you can poison almost any-
thing. Before you throw it out, remember that giving
someone cake is often a form of apology. Invite her to
join you. But don't eat any until after she does.
                                                        Sophie

I stood under spotlights outside of a closed car dealership
waiting for my ex-husband Mars to arrive and feeling like I
had been through the wringer. I had spent a long weekend
with my parents at their home in Berrysville, Virginia. On the
way back, in the dark of night, my beloved car conked out on
I-81. I called for a tow truck and while I was waiting, my ex-

husband Mars, who had been staying at my house to dog and cat sit, had texted to find out why I wasn't home yet. After what seemed an eternity of giant trucks barreling by me in the dark, my car had finally been towed to the dealership where Mars had promised to pick me up. I was initially leery when an alpine-white BMW rolled up and came to a full stop, the engine idling.

Bernie Frei stepped out and opened the passenger door for me with a playful bow. My hound mix, Daisy, leaped onto the pavement and danced around me in circles, pausing twice for a smooch.

"May we give you a lift?" Bernie asked teasingly in his delightful British accent.

"Thank you, kind sir," I said, playing along. Daisy vaulted into the back seat and I settled on the leather passenger seat, relieved to be on my way home.

Bernie tossed my bags in the back. He slid into the driver's seat and handed me a strawberry milkshake and a wrapped disposable spoon. "I thought you might be hungry or thirsty. I figured this would cover both." Turning onto the road, he asked, "What happened?"

The milkshake was so thick I had to use the spoon. "The shake is perfect, Bernie. Just what I needed. I don't know what happened to the car. The engine started sputtering and slowed. Thankfully, I was able to pull over and it just plain died on me. Thanks for picking me up. I thought Mars was coming. How did you get dragged into this?"

"No problem. I'm happy to pitch in. Mars was going to come but he got a last-minute call, so here I am."

Bernie had been the best man at my wedding to Mars. Born and raised mostly in England, he had met Mars when they wound up as roommates at university. Bernie's mother had married more times than Elizabeth Taylor, dragging him around the world when he was a child. At some point he'd had enough and returned to live with husband number three, who by all accounts was a wonderful father figure to Bernie, if a bit too outdoorsy and devoted to country life for Bernie's mother's taste.

No one expected footloose Bernie to settle in Old Town but he'd landed a job managing an upscale restaurant called The Laughing Hound for an absentee owner and had been enormously successful at it. The same absentee owner had purchased the mansion in which Bernie resided to keep an eye on it. Far too large for one person and three cats, when Mars ended his relationship with Natasha, he had joined Bernie in the mansion, which was beginning to resemble a comfortable man cave.

Bernie now guided the car over backroads to Old Town and we were home in no time. The lights were on in my house, and it had never seemed more welcoming. Bernie insisted on carrying my bags inside.

Mars held a phone to his ear as he opened the kitchen door for us. He had spent the weekend there while I was away.

My ocicat, Mochie, who had bullseyes on both sides of his body and fur that looked like necklaces and bracelets instead of the spots he was supposed to have, mewed like I had been gone forever. I swept him up into my arms. He tilted his head and rubbed it against my chin. All was well again in my world. If there was a second stroke of bad luck, it would likely come in the form of the repair bill for my car.

I thanked Bernie profusely, and Mars, too. The two of them left for home in Bernie's car, which made me smile because they lived, as my grandfather would have said, within spitting distance.

Tuesday morning loomed early but I was eager to get back to work. I had just finished my breakfast of a soft-boiled egg and toast when the car dealership phoned. It was great news. The part that had failed could be easily replaced for a reasonable amount of money and the car would be fine. The requisite part was being shipped to them as we spoke.

By eleven thirty, I was at Blackwell's Tavern for a business lunch with Mrs. Hollingsworth-Smythe, which rhymed with tithe with a long I and a silent E, and her daughter, Dodie Kucharski. I had organized several major charity events for Mrs. Hollingsworth-Smythe and found it difficult to turn her down when she asked me to arrange a very large Fourth of July party overlooking the Potomac River.

Old Town Alexandria, Virginia, where I lived and worked as an event planner, was a hot spot for visitors because we were located across the river from Washington, DC. Old Town was a destination itself, with lovely historic homes, and charming shops and restaurants.

Favored by Mrs. Hollingsworth-Smythe and her friends, Blackwell's Tavern was an upscale place, which had been around for many years. The food was good, but their cheesecake selection was outstanding. I happened to know that they were Bobbie Sue's Cheesecake, the same cheesecake served by many restaurants in the DC area and across the country for that matter. But most restaurants offered only one flavor. Tate Bodoin, the owner of Blackwell's Tavern, happened to be married to Bobbie Sue Bodoin, whose cheesecake baking business had grown into a small empire. She didn't have a restaurant of her own because she sold directly to restaurants, but it did mean that her husband offered little else on his dessert menu.

Tate, a slightly pudgy man with graying light brown hair, glasses, and a substantial white mustache, stopped by the table to see how our lunch was and pitch cheesecake for dessert.

To my complete horror, Mrs. Hollingsworth-Smythe declined dessert because she was on a diet, and informed her fortyish-going-on-fifty daughter, Dodie, that she would not be having any cheesecake if she wanted to fit into a certain dress for their big bash. I couldn't exactly pig out on a slice of raspberry chocolate cheesecake in front of them!

I gave Tate an apologetic look. "I'll take four slices of cheesecake to go. You know Nina will want some. Surprise me."

He patted my shoulder in a friendly way. "They don't know what they're missing," he joked before ambling off.

"He's such a gentleman," said Mrs. Hollingsworth-Smythe. "Sophie, darling, please be sure that we offer an ample assortment of cheesecake on the dessert table at the fete."

"Mother . . ." prompted Dodie.

"Oh, yes, Dodie. How could I possibly forget? Sophie, dear, I understand that you are friends with the man who runs The Laughing Hound. Please be sure that he receives an invitation. Dodie has her eyes on him. You know, after my first divorce, I went after a working man, too. He was something else. The love of my life!"

"Mother!" Dodie's tone admonished her mother.

"Am I embarrassing you, Dodi? You know I was quite the looker in my day."

"Mother!"

"Yes, well, perhaps enough said about that. But there is something very sensual about men who toil for a living."

Well, well. Bernie would be surprised to hear about this!

Except for the lack of dessert, something *I* never turned down, the meeting had gone well. When I paid the check, I noticed an envelope in my purse. With two clients looking on, it wasn't the time to empty my purse and examine the contents. After the requisite goodbyes, I collected my takeout cheesecake and headed straight to my home, which bore a coveted plaque next to the front door that designated it as a historic dwelling.

Mars and I had inherited it from his aunt, who had been an extraordinary hostess in her day. She had enlarged the dining room and living room to accommodate her parties. Mars liked the house but wasn't particularly sentimental about it, so I had bought him out when we divorced. The mortgage put a mighty kink in my budget, but I loved the old place with the high windows and creaking floors.

After greeting Daisy and Mochie, who dutifully met me at the door, I hung my purse where I always did—on a hook in the coat closet, where I could grab it in an instant. My mother always emptied her purse entirely when she came home. I supposed that made it easier to switch purses to match her outfits, but it seemed like an extra chore to have to locate wallet, car keys, house keys, tissue, comb, and whatever else I needed.

Before I settled down to work, Nina Reid Norwood, my best friend and across-the-street neighbor, stopped by with her dog, Muppet, an energetic little white floof-ball whom she had adopted.

Nina flopped into a chair by my fireplace, holding a box in her hands. She was generally energetic and upbeat. But today, she seemed glum.

"Tea and cheesecake?" I asked.

She perked up. "I *need* cheesecake right now. How did you know?"

I grinned and opened the box that I had set on the counter. Each of the four slices of cheesecake looked different. "I think you'd better choose."

Leaving the box in the chair, Nina rose and looked at the selection. "Cherry topping is just boring. What do you suppose this one is?"

I examined the dark crumble on top. "Oreo?"

"I'll have that one." She walked over to the bay window and looked out. "Have you heard of early dementia?" she asked.

I nodded, placing her plate of cheesecake on the table and adding a napkin and fork. "Yes, it's terrible."

"I think there's something seriously wrong with my husband." She turned toward me, her expression grim.

A forensic pathologist, Nina's husband traveled constantly and was rarely home. "Did something happen?"

She retrieved the box and heaved a great sigh. "Last week, a package arrived addressed to him. Naturally, I opened it." She flicked open the box and pulled out a rubber chicken. "He ordered a chicken slingshot."

It was hard not to laugh when she held up the limp rubbery form of a chicken.

"When I asked him about it, he claimed he never ordered it. I stashed it in the closet so I could show him when he came home. Today, this arrived." Nina withdrew a plastic bag, prominently marked, INFLATABLE UNICORN.

I stared at it and tried very hard not to laugh. The picture on the bag showed a multicolored unicorn that might be a big hit at a children's party but had no real function that I could see. "Clearly there has been a mistake."

"My husband denies having ordered it. I thought the first one was an error. When the second one arrived, I thought they must be for someone with a similar name. Another person named Norwood, maybe. They came from the same company and we have an account with them, so I called to let them know. The man on the phone was very nice, but insists the shipment was to my husband. But he has no recollection of ordering *any* of these things."

I brought our tea and my cherry cheesecake over to the table and sat down. "I don't think that's a sign of dementia. You know how easily things get mixed up. Unless there's something else . . ." I hoped there wasn't.

The cheesecake brightened Nina's spirits and she was in a better mood when she left with her chicken and unicorn. But I knew she was still worried. Who wouldn't be?

The rest of the day was spent outlining a schedule for the week-long conference of a research chefs organization, including tours of Washington and a night at the Kennedy Center. Consequently, my purse hung in the closet until Wednesday afternoon, when Nina popped in and asked if I felt like a stroll with the dogs down to our favorite coffee shop.

Daisy and I were ready for a break. I checked on Mochie, who was lounging in the sunroom, then suited up Daisy in her halter, and grabbed my purse off the handy hook. I didn't always take the whole purse. Often, when I walked Daisy, I only tucked a cell phone with cash in my pocket. But for some reason, I took the whole thing, maybe because the turquoise color was so summery and happened to match my sleeveless blouse.

Consequently, it wasn't until I took my wallet out to pay for my caramel latte that I noticed the envelope again. I frowned at it, upset with myself for forgetting about it. I paid for my latte and Daisy's pup cup and joined Nina at a table overlooking the Potomac River.

I pulled out the envelope. It was lilac, the kind that came with a card or stationery, but it wasn't addressed to anyone. It was sealed shut, though. That was odd. I didn't recall placing it *in* my handbag.

"What's that?" asked Nina.

"I have no idea." I ripped it open and slid out a sheet of matching lilac paper. Daisy whined softly and touched my leg with her paw. "Sorry, sweetie, I didn't forget you." I held her pup cup in one hand and unfolded the letter with the other.

I read it to Nina in a soft voice, so no one would overhear.

Dear Sophie,
My aunt says you have solutions for all her problems. I hope you can help me, too. My friend and I landed great summer jobs. They pay well and the work is fine. But I think something illegal is going on there. Can my friend and I get into trouble, even if we're not involved?

Worried in Old Town

"Poor kid!" she said. "There's no name?"

I handed her the note and the envelope. "They match," I observed. "The kind of thing you buy to write thank-you notes."

"The violet color would probably indicate a girl," said Nina.

"Could be. Any kid could have this or might have swiped it from a family member. But I'm betting on a girl. Summer jobs. Fourteen and over," I mused.

"It doesn't sound like she knows you," said Nina.

"Good point. She's probably not in college. A college student would have looked me up first and wouldn't have bothered writing to me about a legal matter."

Nina groused, "It's so difficult with printers. If it had been handwritten, we might have been able to deduce something from the handwriting. Where did you get this?"

"It was in my purse. I saw it when I paid the check at Blackwell's Tavern. But I was with clients, so I didn't want to take it out in front of them. And then I forgot about it until just now."

Nina gasped. "Worried in Old Town must work at Blackwell's Tavern. Who was your server?"

"A man in his thirties." I mashed my eyes shut and tried to remember the name tag on his shirt. "Antonio Hirsch."

"We're seeing Bobbie Sue Bodoin tomorrow night. Maybe we can think of a clever way to ask her."

"There's a good idea," I said sarcastically. " 'Bobbie Sue, one of your husband's employees thinks something illegal is going on at his restaurant. Could you put us in touch with a server named Antonio Hirsch so we can talk to him about it?' "

Chapter 2

Dear Sophie,
I'm planning a Midsummer Night party. I would like
to serve dinner, but it starts at eight o'clock and I'm
afraid people will eat before they come.

Host in Fairylawn, Idaho

Dear Host,
Let your guests know what to expect. Call it a Mid-
summer Night Dinner Party or a Midsummer Night
Dessert Party. That will clear up any doubt!

Sophie

That afternoon, I pondered how I could help Worried in Old Town. I phoned my editor, who confirmed that we should not treat it like letters about recipes and entertaining. I decided to take it to Sergeant Wolf Fleishman of the Alexandria Police, and with his permission, in my next column we would ask Worried in Old Town to contact me, without printing the letter.

That straightened out, I headed to the police station.

Wolf came down to the modern lobby. "To what do I owe this unexpected visit?"

Wolf liked to eat and usually carried a few extra pounds, but they did nothing to detract from his good looks. Silver glinted in his sideburns as the summer sun shone on them through a window. We had dated for a time and I was pleased that we continued to be friends. I handed him the letter.

He slid it out of the envelope and read it. Then he flipped the envelope, examining it, and read the note again. "Where did you get this?"

I told him about it mysteriously being in my purse after eating at Blackwell's Tavern. "I've talked to my editor. We're putting a request in my column tomorrow for her to get in touch with me."

"You're not going to print the letter, I hope?"

I tilted my head. "C'mon, Wolf. I'm not that stupid."

"I can't stop you from doing that, but I have concerns. Keep it very neutral. I don't know of anything major going on in Old Town right now, but I don't want you or Worried in Old Town getting tangled with a bunch of thugs. May I keep this?"

"Yes. I made a copy."

He met my gaze. "I want to know when she contacts you." He held up the letter. "This could be anything from a mistaken impression to some kind of retaliation or prank. But it could also mean something sinister is going on."

The letter went out of my head again the next day as I tackled Bobbie Sue Bodoin's Midsummer Night dinner party for her employees. Fortunately, she had decided to rent the outdoor terrace of a restaurant located on the Potomac River where her guests could enjoy Old Town's Midsummer Night festivities on the water.

It was early evening when Bobbie Sue Bodoin examined the massive assortment of desserts and asked, "There's no cheesecake, is there?"

I assured her there wasn't.

Nina had come along on my job so she would get a premier seat for the fireworks on the Potomac. She blurted, "I *love* cheesecake! Why aren't you serving it?"

Bobbie Sue, who was about five and a half feet tall with a voluptuous figure that she didn't mind showing off, promoted her cheesecake business by calling herself the Queen of Cheesecake. "Those words are music to my ears," she said. "But Nina, darlin', this is for my employees and I want it to be very special. Cheesecake is what *we* eat every day. There's always at least one in the lunchroom. You should come by sometime when we try out new flavors. On those days, when I go home, the last thing I want to see is cheesecake!"

"Maybe I should sign up as an official taster," Nina suggested.

"Nina has a unique palate," I said. "She can taste all kinds of subtle flavors that other people don't even notice."

Bobbie Sue smiled at Nina. "I'll keep you in mind. We're going to be testing cheesecakes like crazy. To celebrate our expansion, we're having a cheesecake contest to find a new flavor. The prize is ten thousand dollars. You should think about entering." She studied the Apple watch on her wrist for the fourth time in the last few minutes.

"Don't worry. We'll be ready for them," I said. Most of her two hundred guests were on their way to see Shakespeare's *A Midsummer Night's Dream* at the park nearby. It would end at twilight, giving them just enough time to walk over to the riverfront restaurant where they would be seated outside to enjoy a late dinner followed by a dessert buffet, and watch the fireworks over the river.

"Hmm?" she murmured. She looked over at me. "It looks

wonderful. I'm so glad you talked me into including cheeses and fruit for those who don't feel like anything too sweet for dessert." Her gaze fell to her watch again.

"Is something wrong?" I asked.

"There's just so much going on. Months ago, when I scheduled this party, I stupidly thought Midsummer Night would be boring. Then someone decided to put on the play, and my daughter Jo's ballet class agreed to be fairies."

"Jo? I thought her name was Rebecca. Do you have two daughters?" Nina asked.

Bobbie Sue waved her hand. "She's ten now and is in her *Little Women* phase. Her name is really Rebecca Josephine—"

Nina interrupted her. "That's beautiful!"

"I think so! But I guess it's a lot for a little girl. I told my husband that in a couple of years, she's going to tell us to call her RJ. But for now, she's Jo."

She took a long sip of iced tea. Even though it wouldn't officially be summer until tomorrow, the heat and humidity hadn't gotten that memo.

"Anyway," she continued, "then the merchants association decided all the stores and restaurants would be open until midnight, so my husband, Tate, is busy, and our son, Spencer, wants to run in the Midnight Madness 5K, and I feel like I'm going in circles keeping track of everyone. I've been trying to remind Tate to catch at least part of Jo's performance, but I'm getting his voicemail. I hope he doesn't forget. She would be devastated. After the performance, I'll bring Jo and some of her friends back here with me. They're going to a slumber party tonight, but I promised them dinner, dessert, and fireworks first." She took a deep breath and threw her shoulders back. "All I need to know is that *you* have everything under control here."

I shot her a smile. "Go take care of your family. Nina and I will make sure everything is ready for your guests on this end."

"You're an angel." Bobbie Sue took off at a fast clip.

"Did you follow any of that?" Nina asked. "She's a crazed micromanager! Do you think she ever sits down and re-laxes?"

"I hope so." I focused on the job at hand. Anyone who has spent time around water knows that breezes can waft through without warning. I had made sure the florist knew we needed weighted vases for our centerpieces. In addition, with the Fourth of July in two weeks, Bobbie Sue had asked that we stay away from traditional red, white, and blue, which unfortunately were also typical nautical colors. She had okayed my idea of a watermelon-pink theme with shades of green to cool it down. White tablecloths already hung on round tables. I carried a centerpiece to one. Seafoam-green sea glass pebbles weighed them down. Shiny dark green Monstera leaves and curling fronds of ivy provided the base for a mound of lush watermelon-pink peonies and softer pink peonies with fluffy brilliant golden centers. The arrange-ments were kept low so the guests could interact across the tables and the flowers wouldn't block anyone's view of the river and the fireworks.

When Nina and I had placed all the arrangements, we moved two heavy urns of tall flowers in the same color scheme to flank the ends of the dessert buffet. I made a quick check of the door inside the restaurant. As I had asked, they had posted a tasteful sign that read PRIVATE PARTY.

I glanced at my watch. Sunset would roll in around eight thirty-seven. Ten minutes to go.

The waitresses provided by the restaurant to take drink or-ders and serve dinner checked in with me. Everything was ready.

Nina shot me a sideways look. "If you would like to enter the contest, I would be happy to taste test for you."

I laughed aloud. "I can see right through your feeble at-tempt to get me to bake cheesecakes for you to eat."

"Aw, come on! You're always baking something. Why not

cheesecake? Ten thousand dollars isn't chump change. We could take a nice vacation on that kind of money."

"We?"

"Well, as your official taster, I think I would be entitled to something when you win."

Five minutes later, people began to arrive. Drinks and dinner were served, and everyone appeared to be enjoying themselves.

Bobbie Sue returned with Jo and a few other fairies in tow. Jo wore oversized translucent silver fairy wings and a sweet periwinkle-blue dance outfit with a gauzy tulle skirt. A floral wreath of ivy leaves, tiny fresh white roses, and purple statice sat on her head. She was adorable.

But Bobbie Sue looked out of sorts. Was she clenching her teeth? A muscle twitched in her jaw as she scanned her guests.

"What did Daddy say?" asked Jo. "Is he coming here?"

Bobbie Sue looked a little queasy. "Honey, he thought you were the best fairy of all!" she said enthusiastically.

Jo beamed.

"Jo, sweetie, would you get mommy an iced tea? Just ask that waitress for it. And then maybe you and your friends can eat dinner? I think that table over there is reserved for you."

Jo nodded and the fairies flitted off. Guests stopped them to admire their outfits. The fairies added a magical touch to the party.

Bobbie Sue's lips pulled tight. "Tate didn't show up," she whispered. "I could just kill him for letting her down. This meant so much to her."

A woman approached us with a huge smile. "This was such a wonderful idea, Bobbie Sue. I love seeing everyone's spouses and catching up on their families. And your Rebecca is darling in that fairy outfit!"

Bobbie Sue managed a smile. "Is Steve with you? I'll come by your table to say hi."

"Are you going to make a speech?" asked the woman.

Bobbie Sue's eyes widened in horror. "Good heavens, no. That's so . . . plastic. I plan to stop by each table. It's much more personal. I don't want anyone to feel like they came to a meeting. This is supposed to be fun! Let's go see Steve." The two of them headed for the farthest table and Bobbie Sue engaged her guests.

"Look at her," murmured Nina. "You'd never know Bobbie Sue was angry with her husband."

Half an hour later, the soft sounds of a band playing Mendelssohn's *A Midsummer Night's Dream* tinkled through the air, and fireworks began. The music morphed into the *1810 Overture* as the fireworks grew bolder, bursting softly in the sky until the music reached a crescendo and the sky lit up with cascading sparkles.

"I didn't hear any booming," I said.

Nina grinned. "They were quiet fireworks. It's easier on dogs, horses, and humans who are sensitive to loud bangs. There's a town in Italy that forbids noisy fireworks. Old Town is so dog friendly that when some of the rescue groups proposed we follow suit, the town readily agreed."

"I'm all for that. Poor Daisy gets hysterical about fireworks. I dressed Daisy in her Thunder Shirt before I left today."

The party continued until after midnight. The fairies were picked up and like a proper host, Bobbie Sue remained until the last two couples straggled out.

"Any word from Tate?" asked Nina.

Bobbie Sue ran her fingers across her forehead. "He was supposed to stop by here, too." She pulled out her phone and made a call. Shaking her head, she said with disgust, "Voicemail again."

"When is the last time you saw Tate?" I asked.

She blinked at me. "This morning at breakfast. There was a problem at my cheesecake factory, Spencer overslept, and

Jo's sitter canceled because she was grounded." Bobbie Sue shot me a sideways glance. "Honestly, I was so rattled that I barely paid Tate any attention. I'm such a bad mother. I left chocolate cheesecake for Spencer's breakfast. Then I dropped off Jo at her best friend Esme's house, and rushed to work." She closed her eyes. "I don't know if poor Tate or Spencer ever even left the house." Her eyes widened. "Spencer! The run started at eleven thirty. If I hurry, maybe I can be at the finish line when they get there." She started to leave and turned around. "Thank you for making tonight special. Everyone enjoyed it. And thanks for listening to me complain about Tate, too!"

She was off before I could respond.

Nina hissed, "I like Bobbie Sue, but she's so rattled she probably doesn't know what her husband is up to. That's a woman who has a serious problem on her hands. Bet you a chocolate cheesecake that she's at your door in the next seven days asking for our help."

I am not a very picky eater. But chocolate cheesecake was quite high on my list of preferred indulgences and I hadn't had any in a long time. It was better than a foot massage or a long soak in a bubble bath. If I lost, I would have to bake one for Nina, of course. But that was unlikely. Chances were that Tate's phone died and he was at home, having forgotten all about his daughter's performance, his wife's party, and his son's race.

"You're on," I said.

Chapter 3

Dear Sophie,
My perfect grandson wants a New York Cheesecake
for his birthday cake. I'm happy to oblige him. How
does it differ from a regular cheesecake?
     Angel's Grandma in New York Mills, Minnesota

Dear Angel's Grandma,
New York Cheesecake is the height of indulgence.
Loaded with cream cheese, eggs, and heavy cream
or sour cream, it's often taller than the average
cheesecake. It's dense and plain, no fruity flavors,
candies, or cookies. It's most often served plain or
with a strawberry garnish. Happy birthday to your
grandson!

                                        Sophie

A special note to Worried in Old Town: Please con-
tact me immediately at Sophie@SophieWinston-
Events.com.

Nina won the bet at four o'clock in the morning. I woke to the ringing of my landline not two feet from my ear. I felt for the receiver and murmured, "Hello?"

"I can't find him. I can't find him anywhere."

It took a moment for my brain to engage. "Bobbie Sue?"

"I'm so sorry. I know it's the middle of the night but I'm just desperate. I'm at the restaurant. Could you and Nina come down here? I don't know what to look for."

"Have you called the police?" I asked.

"No!" She said it loud enough to shake me fully awake. "I . . . I don't want to involve the police." In a much smaller voice, she added, "Not yet."

A big part of me wanted to roll over and ignore her. But I wouldn't be able to sleep now anyway and I liked Bobbie Sue. She was competent and smart, which made me think something was up. "Okay. Give me a few minutes."

I let Daisy out, and back in, while I called Nina, then went upstairs to change. It was chilly outside in the wee hours, so I opted for stretchy jeans, a periwinkle mock turtleneck without sleeves, and a matching periwinkle jean jacket. I gave Daisy and Mochie a little midnight snack and met Nina just as she emerged from her house.

The streets were quiet, with not a soul to be seen. Not even a car purred in the distance.

"Have you heard anything about Tate on the grapevine lately?" I asked. Nina volunteered at the animal rescue and had loads of chatty friends.

"Not a word. Neither he nor Bobbie Sue ever come up in gossip. As far as I know, they've always looked like the perfect couple. To the public at least. It's hard to know what goes on behind closed doors."

We reached the restaurant. The gaslights on either side of the glass double doors flickered. But the lights inside were dim like it was closed and no one was there.

When I knocked on the glass, Bobbie Sue emerged from the shadows to unlock the doors.

My heart sank when I saw her. Eye makeup had smeared under her eyes and she wore the same vividly colored dress she had on the night before. The only difference was her shoes. Sneakers had replaced heels.

"Tate never came home last night," she blurted, locking the door behind us. "I have awakened half a dozen of our friends. No one has seen him. They don't have any unidentified patients at the hospitals. His car is in the garage. It's like he vanished."

She was going to have to call the police. Maybe we could talk her into it. "You still can't reach him by phone?"

"No! Yesterday morning when I left the house is the last time I actually saw him. He phoned me around noon to find out if the problem at the factory had been resolved. It was a perfectly normal conversation, just checking up on the situation."

I had been so hopeful, but the circumstances were beginning to sound far worse than I had imagined. "Have you checked his calendar?" I asked. "Do you have a password for his computer?"

Flicking on lights as we went, she led us through the dining room and upstairs to a second-floor office in the back where a brass lamp shone on a highly polished antique desk with claw feet. "He kept a hand-written calendar. Both of us do that. Old-school, I guess, and the fear of computer hiccups." Bobbie Sue plucked a book-style calendar off the desk and opened it at the ribbon marker. "There are just notes about meetings and a charity dinner that's coming up."

I held my hands out for it. On yesterday's date, there were no entries, but there were dots. Ink dots. As though Tate had tapped his pen on the day several times. Had he meant to write something? Had he thought better of it? Or had he been on the phone talking with someone and tapping the date that was open?

While Nina asked questions of Bobbie Sue, I studied Tate's desk. A green leather blotter lay on top of it, no doubt to protect the surface. I lifted it and noted Bobbie Sue's frown.

There was nothing underneath. "Is there a safe here somewhere?" I asked.

She shook her head. "Not that I know of." She hurried to add, "I have never been involved in the management of the restaurant, but I think I would know if there were a safe."

I pulled out the top drawers and felt underneath them for envelopes or papers that might have been taped to them but found nothing. I crawled under the desk and looked up. Tate hadn't affixed anything he meant to hide.

I stood up, brushing off my clothes.

Bobbie Sue stared at me, her jaw twitching. "You think the police are going to get involved."

It was a good bet. I answered carefully, trying not to upset her. "Why don't you want to report him missing?"

She didn't respond right away. "I am so scared that I can hardly breathe. Tate is older than me. I suspect he fell or may have had a heart attack. The police won't help with that."

"They could help you find him," I pointed out. "They might be able to ping his phone. What if he needs medical help?"

"What if he's been kidnapped?" asked Nina.

Bobbie Sue's expression changed to one of horror. She could barely speak. "There . . . there's been no ransom note. No phone call. Why would you think that?"

I shot Nina an annoyed look. "I'm sure you're right, Bobbie Sue. If Tate had been abducted, you would have heard from the kidnappers. Maybe we should look around here to make sure he wasn't taken ill, and no one noticed. You two check around up here and in the attic. I'll take the dining room and the kitchen."

I probably should not have left Bobbie Sue with Nina, who might put ideas in her head. I suspected the real reason Bobbie Sue hadn't notified the police yet was publicity. She and Tate were prominent in Old Town. Neither the cheese-cake business nor the restaurant needed lurid headlines about one of them having gone missing. Especially if another woman was involved. It might come to that, but she was probably being prudent to look around first. I trotted down the stairs and into the large kitchen.

A refrigerator issued an annoying hum. The faint scent of bleach lingered in the air and the stainless-steel counters gleamed. I left the kitchen. A door in the rear led outside. I opened it and peered into the alley behind the restaurant. I couldn't see much in the dark, but I didn't notice anyone lying on the ground. There weren't even many cars parked there. A high brick wall acted as a barrier to the houses that backed up to the alley.

I closed the door and locked it. As I turned, a spot on the floor caught my eye. Probably a drip from garbage that had been taken out, I thought. It was dark cherry red. From a sauce, perhaps. Or maybe it was blood. Just in case, I didn't dare touch it.

A nearby door opened to stairs that led to a dank base-ment. It was creepy, even when I flicked on the lights. Boxes of wine, spirits, and supplies were stacked on top of each other. Some had been opened. Along the wall to the right, bottles stood in a commercial wine rack that ran from the floor to the ceiling.

I edged slowly through the stacked boxes. Something crunched under my shoe. I stepped back to see what it was, but it had embedded itself in my sandal. Balancing on one foot, I bent my knee and examined it, expecting to see a pebble. But a piece of glass had stabbed the sole of my thong. I cautiously wiggled it out and realized there were more on the floor. Wine bottles probably broke down here on a regular basis.

The trail of scattered glass shards led toward the wine rack that ran along the wall. And in their midst, an arm lay outstretched on the floor.

Chapter 4

Dear Sophie,
My new husband is hosting an extremely important business dinner. I'm having it catered, of course, but they don't seem to know what pairs well with the exquisite cheesecake that will be served for dessert. They recommend sweet wines! Can you please help me?
                    The New Wife in Sweetwater, Tennessee

Dear The New Wife,
Sherry and other after-dinner wines are conventionally served with cheesecake. If you would prefer a sweet wine with a hint of tartness, then a Riesling would go well. In my opinion, the best drink of all to go with cheesecake is champagne.

                                        Sophie

I screamed. I hadn't meant to. It was a reflex. I could hear hurried footsteps upstairs and Nina calling out, "Sophie? Where are you?"

My focus was on the hand. Trying to avoid the glass and

liquid on the floor, I stepped carefully toward the hand and found Tate. He lay on his abdomen. Shards of glass gleamed around his head and had scattered on the floor in a very light amber liquid. His hair appeared wet and sticky. Not daring to kneel on the glass, I squatted next to him. "Tate? Tate?" There was no response, and I reached out to feel for a pulse. His arm was cold and stiff. There wasn't a chance of a pulse, yet I tried anyway. I was fairly certain that rigor mortis had set in, which meant he'd been dead for at least two hours, if not more.

Footsteps clattered on the stairs. "Sophie?" Nina called out. "Back here."

Bobbie Sue screamed and launched herself at Tate. "No! Tate! Tate, can you hear me?"

She would cut herself on the broken glass. I stepped toward her, but it was too late to stop her. Besides, I knew a little glass wouldn't keep me away from someone I loved.

Nina nudged me and pointed upward. A space that had probably accommodated two large bottles was empty on the top row of the wine rack. A step stool had fallen nearby.

I pulled out my phone and was somewhat surprised that I was able to call 911 from the basement.

"Alexandria Police Department," said a man's voice. "What is the nature of your emergency?"

I stepped away, mindful of the glass. "It's Tate Bodoin. He's . . . dead."

I told him where we were and that it would probably be easiest if everyone parked in the alley behind the restaurant. While I spoke, I walked up the stairs, opened the back door, and found a doorstop to hold it open.

Dawn was breaking. As alleys went, this one was fairly pretty. In spite of the darkness, I could make out large leafy trees lining both sides. The tall brick fence that ran along the opposite side had, no doubt, been built to provide privacy for the homes that backed up to the alley. It was a beautiful morning with a clear sky and birds chirping happily in the trees. I could hardly believe that Tate was dead.

I sat down on a step for a moment and picked bits of glass from my sandals so they wouldn't be driven in deeper as I walked. Only then did I realize that I was shaking. Not just my hands, my entire body quivered. A shard immediately pricked my finger, and a dot of bright red blood sprang to the surface. Bobbie Sue would need towels and hydrogen peroxide.

I rose and returned to the kitchen, where I located paper towels and a first aid kit. Carrying them, I returned to the cellar, where Bobbie Sue still clung to Tate's lifeless body, sobbing. As I'd anticipated, tiny beads of blood dotted her pretty face.

"Bobbie Sue," I said gently. "I think you're bleeding. Can you stand up?"

"Nooo," she wailed.

Tires crunched and the purring of an engine reached us. I ran up the stairs to meet the emergency medical technicians and led them into the cellar.

"Ma'am," said an EMT to Bobbie Sue. "We need you to stand up so we can help this gentleman."

Bobbie Sue didn't move.

He gently placed his hands on her upper arms. "Ma'am, I need you to stand up now."

He helped her to her feet, and I saw the faces of his co-workers as they got a look at her. "Is she injured, too?" asked one of them.

Blood was smeared on her forehead and left cheek. I wasn't sure if it belonged to Tate or to Bobbie Sue. She held her hands out, her fingers bent stiff, like hawk talons. Blood dripped from them. "Tate," she whispered.

The EMT asked, "What's her name?"

"Bobbie Sue Bodoin," said Nina.

His face brightened. "The Queen of Cheesecake?"

Nina nodded, and he steered Bobbie Sue toward the door. She stumbled along as though her brain had disconnected.

One of the remaining EMTs asked Nina and me questions about Tate. Beyond his name, we weren't much help. We didn't know anything about his medical history.

We were sent upstairs, out of their way. I couldn't blame them. With all those boxes stashed in the cellar, there wasn't much room for people, not to mention that it could be a murder scene and we were trampling all over it. Nina and I headed for the dining room, where Bobbie Sue was being treated by an EMT.

I was relieved to see Wolf Fleishman of the Alexandria police force arrive. Always competent and usually reasonable, he was often a calming influence when people had to deal with the worst thing they had ever experienced—the murder of a loved one.

He gave Nina and me a quick nod before disappearing into the cellar.

The EMT finished with Bobbie Sue. Her hands were bandaged and her face had been wiped clean of blood, although a few small cuts from the glass were obvious. Rivers of tears stained her face. She appeared to be in shock. She hadn't uttered a single word. She stared straight forward as though she didn't know any of us were there.

"Her vital signs are okay," said the EMT. "I'll be downstairs. Give me a shout if you need me."

I picked up her bandaged hand and held it gently in mine. "Do you want me to call anyone?"

Her eyes finally broke their fixed stare. She shook her head slowly and sobbed softly. "Jo is at her friend's house and Spencer is at home. They're probably not even up yet. What time is it?"

"Seven thirty," said Nina.

Bobbie Sue jumped out of her chair. "Employees will start arriving in half an hour!"

Nina spoke softly. "We'll send them home. I suspect the restaurant will be closed for a couple of days."

Bobbie Sue relaxed. "Yes, of course. Of course. I'm sure Tate's assistant, Marsha, could handle it but I couldn't. Closing is the right thing to do." She sat down. Numbly she muttered, "How could this have happened? Do you think he slipped?"

"Looks that way," Nina said softly.

At that moment, we heard a scream from the kitchen, followed by a loud thump.

Chapter 5

Dear Sophie,
My husband and I love cheesecake. But really, there's only so much cheesecake two people can eat. Can I freeze cheesecake?
Cheesecake Fan in Baker, Florida

Dear Cheesecake Fan,
You most certainly can freeze cheesecake. Place it on a freezer-safe dish or disposable cardboard cake base and freeze about one hour. When firm, wrap it in plastic wrap. Then wrap it again, this time in aluminum foil. It should be good for about one month. After that the texture will likely change.
Sophie

Nina and I ran into the kitchen. One of the EMTs had just broken a vial under the nose of a woman in her forties. She sputtered as she came around. Curly dark hair framed her face. She had used a light hand with makeup and wore a navy-blue skirt. Blue polka-dots decorated her white blouse that tied in a bow at the neck.

She sucked in air and tried to sit up. "What . . . what?" Her eyes widened. "Tate!" she screamed.

Bobbie Sue had followed us and now wedged between Nina and me. I thought she was going to help the woman stand but instead, she collapsed to the floor, tears streaming down her face. The two of them embraced and sat there, sobbing.

After a few moments, Nina and I helped them to their feet. Sniffling, Bobbie Sue introduced us to Marsha Bathurst. "Marsha is the assistant manager of the restaurant. Tate's right-hand woman, for sure."

"I can't believe he's gone!" Marsha wailed. "Oh gosh, it just shows how unpredictable life can be. Just yesterday, he was fine and walking around the restaurant greeting diners." Her jaw quivered. "Did he have a heart attack?" She clapped a hand over her mouth in horror. "He must have been down there when we closed last night."

For the first time since the discovery of Tate's body, Bobbie Sue stopped crying. She stared at Marsha.

I suspected she was trying to get a grip on exactly what had happened, because I was having thoughts of that sort myself. If Tate went to the cellar to retrieve a bottle, wouldn't the server or customer who was waiting for it have wondered what was taking so long?

"He could have been alive. He might have lived if someone had gotten help sooner," Bobbie Sue said.

Marsha sobbed even harder. She gasped for air and said, "I thought he went out. I didn't know he was here."

Just behind them, EMTs carried Tate's body out to the ambulance. I was glad Bobbie Sue and Marsha had their backs to the door and didn't see what was transpiring. Wolf emerged from the cellar but instead of going outside, he approached Bobbie Sue.

"I'm very sorry about your loss, Mrs. Bodoin. Your husband is being transferred to the medical examiner's office.

That's required by law in Virginia when someone dies who isn't currently in the care of a physician because of a terminal illness. Due to the irregularity of Mr. Bodoin's death, we'll be sealing the restaurant off for a day or two, pending the medical examiner's investigation. I imagine you'll be closing the restaurant for a few days in any event, so that shouldn't present a hardship. Now, if I could escort you ladies out?"

Bobbie Sue retrieved her purse, and we all filed out the back way, into the alley. The ambulance had left, which I thought was probably for the best. Bobbie Sue and Marsha didn't need to be confronted with Tate's shape in a body bag.

When Bobbie Sue locked the back door and handed the key to Wolf, he asked if there was an alarm system.

"This is a pretty safe area. Anyone breaking in the front would probably be seen. Tate put up a camera in the back"— she pointed at a tree—"but it was constantly being triggered by cars driving through the alley, bicyclists, even birds, so he turned it off. He said the mere presence of a camera would still help deter crime. Someone scouting the place with intentions of breaking in wouldn't know if it was working or not."

Wolf thanked her and took her aside to make private inquiries.

When they returned, Marsha asked if there was anything she could do.

Bobbie Sue shook her head in the negative. But then her eyes widened. "What am I thinking? Marsha, would you notify the employees of the restaurant? That would be such a help to me. I don't have a list or contact numbers. Tell them we'll be closed at least two days if not longer."

Marsha nodded. "Don't give the restaurant another thought. I'll post a sign on the front door, too. Consider it done."

Bobbie Sue forced a smile. "Thank you, Marsha. I know how much Tate relied on you."

Marsha took off, sniffling and wiping her eyes.

"I need breakfast. How about a back booth at Biscuits & Gravy?" asked Nina. "Would you like to come, Bobbie Sue?"

"Hmm?" Bobbie Sue stared at Nina blankly. "Um, no thanks. There's a lot to do. I don't know how I'll tell the children."

We offered to walk Bobbie Sue home, but she declined, saying she wanted to be alone. I couldn't blame her. She needed time to grieve.

Nina and I headed to her new favorite diner. Biscuits & Gravy was as down-home as the name implied. The lady servers wore pink uniforms with 1950s-style circle skirts and aprons. The gentlemen servers wore white shirts with matching pink trim on the short sleeves and breast pockets. The walls had been painted a soft turquoise, and the atmosphere was pure happy retro. But it was the food that brought people in, from authentic gumbo to banana pudding, and old-fashioned chocolate sundaes that had been an instant hit. Nina passed the long counter and led the way to a booth. The benches were covered in turquoise vinyl just a shade darker than the walls.

The diner had a cheery vibe. I was fairly certain that Nina was craving ham biscuits for breakfast, but after the grisly discovery of Tate's body, the comforting diner was a good choice.

We placed our orders and were quietly relaxing with coffee when Bobbie Sue dashed in with all the fury of a tornado.

Chapter 6

Dear Sophie,
My husband grew up in the country and he cannot
bring himself to dispose of rusted items. We must
have five rusted rakes with broken handles. How do I
convince him to throw them away already?
                    Stainless Steel Wife in Rust, Michigan

Dear Stainless Steel Wife,
Maybe if you use those rusted rakes, hubby will be
happy to buy a new one. Take off as much of the han-
dle as you can. Mount the rusted end on your garage
wall with the prongs toward you. Now make a twine
loop on the ends of small tools and garden imple-
ments and hang them from the tines.
                                        Sophie

Bobbie Sue slid into the booth next to me.

Our server poured coffee for her, and Bobbie Sue ordered three Biscuits & Gravy breakfast specials to go.

"I have to feed the kids. And me, too. I doubled back when I realized I needed food. The last thing I want to do right now is cook. You said you were coming here, and I wanted to talk to you." Coffee in hand, she leaned in and whispered, "Tate was murdered."

Nina started to speak, but Bobbie Sue held up her palm and continued in a hushed voice. "You were there. You heard Wolf. He didn't call it an accident. He used the word *irregularity*. If he thought Tate had been killed by a bottle of champagne that accidentally fell on his head, he wouldn't have closed the restaurant down pending the outcome of the medical examiner's report."

I had picked up on Wolf's carefully chosen words as well. "I'm not sure it means he was murdered. But Wolf probably wants to rule out that possibility."

Bobbie Sue turned and looked me straight in the eyes. "Tate had a brachial plexus injury from a car accident a few years ago. He couldn't raise his arms over his head. There's no way he would have been reaching for a bottle up near the ceiling."

My eyes met Nina's as Bobbie Sue's revelation sank in.

"If he had really wanted that bottle of champagne, he would have asked someone to get it for him or used a taller ladder that would have enabled him to grab the bottle at shoulder height." She shook her head. "Even then he would have had trouble with it. And I don't recall seeing a tall ladder. Do you?"

Our breakfasts arrived. We waited in silence while the server refilled our coffee cups. "Could I have the check, please?" asked Bobbie Sue.

When the server left, Nina said, "There was no tall ladder."

"Just that short one," I said. "If a tall ladder had fallen, we would have noticed because it would have crashed into the boxes of wine that are stacked up."

Nina tucked into her biscuits and gravy. "Mmm," she murmured. "Just like my nana used to make."

I had opted for sunny-side-up eggs with bacon and toast. I

could easily have made them myself at home, but after everything we had been through that morning, I felt the need for something simple and comforting.

Bobbie Sue set down her coffee cup, stole a piece of my toast and slathered it with butter and raspberry jam.

I broke the yolk on my egg and Bobbie Sue blurted, "Did he have his phone with him? Did either of you see his phone? He didn't answer my calls yesterday evening."

"We'll have to ask Wolf," I said.

"All these wild thoughts are running through my head," said Bobbie Sue. "Could he have been down there, alive, while they served dinner upstairs?"

It *was* a horrific notion. And unfortunately, not impossible. The clatter of a busy kitchen could easily have hidden the crash of bottles, not to mention Tate's calls for help if he didn't die right away. But I didn't want to add to her pain by speculating when we didn't know yet exactly what had happened. "Marsha said she thought he had left," I said.

"So what's the deal with Marsha?" asked Nina.

"She, um"—Bobbie Sue twisted her hand in the air—"has a thing for Tate. I don't think Tate was ever interested, but she acted like he walked on water."

Bobbie Sue turned toward us. "Okay, look. I'm about two inches from a major meltdown. I"—she swallowed hard—"have to tell the children." She took a deep breath. "So many people to call. So much to do, and all I want is to crawl into a corner and cry." The muscles in her face did a strange dance like she was trying hard not to burst into tears. Her fingers rolled into a tight fist and her hand shook. "I need you to take care of this for me." Her voice broke as she struggled to speak. "Find out who killed Tate. I don't care what it costs. I have to know who took him from us. It's the least I can do for him."

I was about to tell her that Nina and I weren't private investigators and that she needed to rely on the police, but

Bobbie Sue deposited money on the table on top of her check and fled before we could stop her.

We stared at the three takeout containers she had forgotten and left behind.

"I suppose we should give her time to pick up Jo before we bring her the food," I said.

"I'd like to ask her questions, but this obviously isn't the time. It might have helped if she had given us some leads," Nina grumbled.

I sipped my coffee. "Well, we can start with the one person we know had a key to the restaurant, and"—I twisted my hand in the air like Bobbie Sue—"who had a thing for the dearly departed."

"Rigor mortis kicks in two to four hours after death. So he was probably killed before two in the morning. Maybe last night. That doesn't help much," Nina said. "What time was it when he stopped answering his phone?"

"We'll have to ask her. Certainly when we were setting up her party. And during the play. He missed Jo's performance, so maybe he was already dead then," I speculated.

"Or maybe he turned it off because he didn't want to be interrupted," said Nina, raising her eyebrows.

We ate quietly for a few minutes.

"Do you think the champagne was symbolic?" asked Nina.

"Symbolic of what?"

"That's what I'm wondering. Wouldn't it have been easier to grab one of the wine bottles at hand? Why champagne from the top shelf?"

"Because that's what the killer was getting when Tate walked in?" I postulated. "His killer was on the small step stool fetching a bottle of champagne and saw the opportunity to whack Tate on the head with it?"

"That would narrow it down fast. It would have to be someone who worked there."

"Or someone who sneaked into the basement to steal a bottle of champagne. So it could have been a diner," I said. "But there's one thing that bothers me. The reason I ventured down the stairs was because I thought I saw a little drop of blood near the back door."

Nina blinked at me over the rim of her coffee mug. She set it down. "So someone could have knocked him off somewhere else and brought him to the restaurant?" Nina gaped at me. "That changes everything."

"Or the killer could have had an injury that was bleeding. Or it could have been from a restaurant employee. I'd like to see his phone, too," I said. "What if he was meeting someone?"

"You know," said Nina, "we're thinking of Tate as the innocent victim. But what about the letter from Worried in Old Town? Maybe he was doing something illegal, and someone caught him in the act."

"More like the other way around, I think. Maybe Tate caught someone in the restaurant doing something illegal and that person knocked him off."

"There you are!" Natasha smiled at us wanly. In spite of the warm weather, she wore a long-sleeved white blouse with the collar turned up for drama and a pair of gray trousers, intentionally cut mid-calf. They flared around her slender legs that looked even longer perched on strappy high-heeled shoes. I never understood how she managed to wear three-inch heels on Old Town's brick sidewalks without breaking an ankle. I couldn't do it!

Natasha and I had been classmates when we were growing up. My mother claimed Natasha pushed me to excel because she was always trying to compete with me. By nature, I wasn't particularly competitive. But Natasha had a way of getting under my skin. We were rivals at everything except for the beauty pageants that she loved so much. Tall, and thin enough for her collarbones to show, clothes draped on her beautifully. She was a natural beauty with lush raven hair and big brown eyes. In contrast, I was short and leaned to elastic-waist pants because I liked to eat.

I never dreamed she would still be a part of my life when we were adults. But when I divorced, or maybe a wee bit before, Natasha had moved in on my husband, Mars. He had come to his senses after a few years and left her, something she still struggled with. Mars, on the other hand, had bounced back with renewed vigor. She still lived on our street, though, and we wrote competing domestic advice columns.

At the tender age of seven, Natasha's father had disappeared, an event that had scarred her for life. She still searched for him, and a recent DNA test had turned up a half sister, whose mother was just like Natasha's mom, a free-spirit from the hippie generation. Her dad hadn't been located, but the man certainly had a type. His two wives had become friends and opened a new age–type store that sold healing herbs and stones.

Natasha slid into the booth next to me and stage whispered, "I have reached the bottom. My life cannot get any worse."

Our server promptly arrived with a coffeepot and a mug in hand.

"Just black coffee, please." Natasha slid off her oversized Jackie O–style sunglasses.

"We have fresh from the fryer doughnuts," suggested our perky server.

"Fried food?" Natasha asked in a derisive tone.

Our server threw me a wide-eyed glance of disbelief before leaving. I assumed that few of their patrons acted repulsed by their fabulous food.

"What happened?" I asked.

"I thought I would be the Martha of the South by now. Instead, that Magnolia woman beat me to it. I can cook. I can decorate. I have dark hair like she does. It's Mars's fault. If he was into knocking out walls and building houses, I would be a star."

It was always someone else's fault. I raised my coffee cup to my lips and didn't say what I was thinking.

Nina didn't hide her thoughts. "Oh, I *love* them! He's adorable and she's so talented. Uh, Nat, you do realize that she has a completely different style from yours."

"I know!" Natasha whined. "I would never decorate with all those grungy, scuffed-up items that belong in the trash."

"But that's what people like," Nina pointed out.

"Tell me about it. My own home is almost unrecognizable. Now that my mother and my father's second wife have moved in, there are stinky old antiques everywhere. They rave about them! I have suggested they take them to their store, but it's already getting too small. People love that junk. I grew up with my mother's remedies, cures, and the rusted signs she collects, but I thought I was done with them when I got my first apartment. Now she has placed crystals and other fussy things all over my house to bring good fortune. Well, it hasn't worked for *me*. I counted on my half sister, Charlene, to be on my side, but noooo. She loves all that stuff. And now she has taken over my pristine kitchen to make her My Personal Chef meals. Every day she's in there whipping up dishes while Dolly Parton and Elvis Presley croon in the background."

"My Personal Chef?" asked Nina.

"It's the name of her company. We had to have the kitchen inspected. Of course, it passed. She makes huge batches of mashed potatoes, salads, mac and cheese, roast beef, whatever is on the menu for that day, and delivers them to people, so they have a full dinner waiting when they come home." Her mouth twisted in dismay. "She's had to hire a delivery guy because she has so many orders. I can't even get in my own kitchen to bake cheesecakes for Bobbie Sue's contest."

"You're entering?" asked Nina.

"Of course. Frankly, I could use the money and if there's one thing Bobbie Sue knows how to do, it's publicity. I could use a boost from the Queen of Cheesecake."

Natasha shot me an annoyed look. "You're the one who told me to buy out Mars's share of the house. If you hadn't done that, I would still be in my perfect, quiet home."

I didn't bother arguing. It wasn't my fault, of course. Natasha had made her own bed so to speak, with my ex-husband! I had nothing to do with the situation in which she now found herself. The two mothers and her half sister had graciously moved in to help pay the mortgage. Without them, Natasha would have lost the house and had to move elsewhere.

"I have nothing," she whined. "My house is overrun, I'm still not married, and even though I have been trying so hard, I'm not a star and don't have any idea how to get there anymore."

She sounded so pathetic I almost felt sorry for her. *Almost.* "You have your TV show and syndicated advice column," I pointed out.

"It's not enough. My TV show is local. I can't interest any of the streaming companies in it. I have no sponsors. Everyone else has moved up in the last years. But not me." She patted my hand and gazed at me briefly. "Not you, either, Sophie. You still have that sad little job."

I knew I should be offended, but I found it humorous that she felt compelled to put down my job at every opportunity. Maybe it made her feel better about herself.

She gazed at Nina. "Not you, either, but you have a husband." She wistfully murmured the word again. "*Husband.*"

"Natasha, instead of trying to be a star, why don't you do what you love? That way you'll be happy each day."

"That's right, Sophie." Nina smiled at Natasha. "Pick something you're passionate about and make it happen.

There are so many opportunities and you're always tuned in with what's new and on the cutting edge."

"I am, aren't I?" Natasha sat up a little straighter and looked from me to Nina. "Thank you for your help. You two are just the best!" She stood up, slid on her sunglasses, and strode to the door as though she thought every person in the restaurant was watching her make her exit.

"Uh-oh. What did we say?" Nina groaned.

I shrugged.

"I have a bad feeling she'll be blaming us for something soon," said Nina.

"I fear that you're right."

We paid the check, collected Bobbie Sue's three takeout orders, and left for her house.

Chapter 7

Dear Natasha,
I have met the man of my dreams but he hates my coffee. I don't know what I'm doing wrong. I put coffee in the machine and add water. Help!
   Hoping for a Ring This Time in Coffee City, Texas

Dear Hoping for a Ring This Time,
There are so many ways to slip up when making coffee. First, stop buying pre-ground coffee. Buy coffee beans and grind them fresh for each pot.
                                                    Natasha

Bobbie Sue's home was on a small side street loaded with shady trees, not far from the Potomac River. It sported a historical plaque but appeared to have undergone a good deal of updating.

I hoped we weren't interrupting at the exact moment Bobbie Sue was telling her children that their father had died. If the food wouldn't have spoiled, I'd have been happy to leave it at her doorstep.

Orange impatiens bloomed profusely along the front of the house. The door knocker was shaped like a pineapple, known to be the sign of hospitality.

Nina clanged it and a man opened the door. Neatly trimmed coffee-colored hair topped an attractive face. He wore jeans and a blue and gold T-shirt with a team logo on it. He assessed us quickly. "Wow. Food already? That's great. I know Bobbie Sue will appreciate it."

Nina introduced us and handed him the food containers. "You would be . . . ?"

"Sorry. Jeff Cosby, but everyone calls me Coach. I coach Spencer. I was supposed to give Spencer a ride to work this morning and Bobbie Sue told me what happened." He stepped aside. "Come on in."

He led us to a huge kitchen that screamed *a professional chef lives here.* The double refrigerator had see-through glass doors. Someone had organized it beautifully, with milk bottles standing in a row like little soldiers. Red and green peppers nestled in a glass bowl next to strawberries. A coordinating freezer stood beside the refrigerator. The stove was restaurant worthy with eight burners and a griddle. Spacious and airy, the kitchen boasted two dishwashers and every kind of countertop gadget imaginable. A tall window and French doors overlooked a generous and well-landscaped lawn in the backyard. A kitchen table and cozy nook by a fireplace provided plenty of room for noshing and family time.

"Bobbie Sue is in the living room with Spencer and Jo. I think she wanted me here because I work with kids. She's worried about how they'll react and thought I might be able to smooth the way for them. It's hard losing your dad." He gave us a sad smile. "How did you hear about it? I didn't think people would start coming over with food until tomorrow."

Nina explained that we were there when Tate was found.

"That must have been awful. In the cellar? What do they think happened?"

Nina whispered, "I don't want the children to hear, but it looks like he was murdered."

Coach stepped back. He rubbed the back of his neck and followed her example of whispering. "Murder? Do they know who did it?"

"Not yet," she whispered. "Do you know anyone who would want to kill Tate?"

He shook his head. "In his own restaurant? That's hard to believe. Hey, do either of you know how to work this gadget? I'm more of an instant coffee kind of guy." He pointed at a stainless-steel box with its own milk frother and entirely too many buttons.

Nina stepped aside. "She's the cook. Not me."

I examined the contraption, thinking it was probably much simpler than it looked. After all, coffee was basically ground coffee and water, wasn't it?

Coach handed me a bag. "I guess we need these."

The second I touched it I knew we were in trouble. Coffee beans. At my house, I used a little coffee bean grinder. A simple thing about four inches tall. It didn't even have buttons or levers on it. It had only one function and did it well. I had a hunch that maybe the giant contraption in front of me ground the beans itself and then added boiling water. Not even the caterers whom I hired for events had coffee machines this snazzy. Besides, they were the ones who made the coffee. Not me!

I lifted a hatch on the top and peered inside. It smelled like coffee.

A commotion erupted behind us. I turned just in time to see a teenaged boy race through the kitchen and out the door. Spencer, I presumed.

Coach ran after him. "Spencer! Spence!"

Bobbie Sue and Jo stood at the French door watching, their faces wet with tears. Jo clung to her mom and asked, "Will Spencer ever come back?"

"Of course he will, sweetie. He needs some time to be alone. That's all." Bobbie Sue hugged her daughter to her. "You stick with me, all right?" She looked over at me. "Do I smell coffee?"

"Not yet," I said. "Do you know how to work this gizmo?"

"I hate that thing. It cost a fortune. Tate was so proud of it."

"Coffee on the left, espresso on the right," said Jo.

A dim smile crossed Bobbie Sue's face. "I'm glad *you* were listening to him."

Jo smirked. "He said it to you like a million times."

I examined the compartments and buttons on the left side and took a chance by dumping coffee beans into a little chamber. I pushed a button, which caused a loud racket. For a moment I thought I might have broken something, but it was only grinding the beans. I guessed at a spot for water, added it, and in a matter of minutes, the lovely aroma of coffee wafted from the monstrous gadget.

Coach returned, panting hard. He bent forward, his hands on his knees. "That boy can run!"

"Where is he?" asked Bobbie Sue.

Coach straightened, breathing hard. "Never caught up to him."

Bobbie Sue stared out the glass door.

"Give him some time, Bobbie Sue," Coach said softly.

She lashed out. "A member of my family was just lost forever. I'd feel much better right now if my children were safe at home with me. Is that too much to ask?"

She burst into tears, which worried Jo. She stood motionless, looking horrified. "I can go find him, Mommy."

Bobbie Sue wrapped her arms around her daughter's shoulders. "You stay with me, honey."

"Are you hungry, Jo?" asked Nina. "We brought the food your mommy forgot."

Jo nodded vigorously. "Mommy came to get me too early. Everybody slept late. They were going to have pancakes at Esme's house for brunch. Is this brunch?"

Bobbie Sue gasped. "I walked off without your breakfasts! Where is my brain?"

Coach, apparently not ruffled by her outburst, patted Bobbie Sue's shoulder. "Don't beat yourself up. You have a lot on your mind. And you're probably still in a state of shock."

Nina, a self-confessed microwave expert, heated the contents of two of the takeout packages. I stashed the third in the fridge and proceeded to pour coffee for the adults.

Jo helped herself to orange juice.

"Bobbie Sue, could I pull you away for a moment?" I asked.

"Sure." She led me into a family room that appeared well lived in.

Soft, worn leather furniture faced a large television and a red brick fireplace. A football lay on the floor. A jigsaw puzzle was in progress on the coffee table and a stuffed pig looked at us from the sofa. This room was where they lived.

"Is there anything I can do for you?" I asked.

She shook her head. "There's so much to do. I need to sit down and make a list. People to call, a memorial service to plan. Ugh." Tears started again. "An obituary. I can't believe I have to do that. That shouldn't have been necessary for thirty years!"

I gave her a minute to compose herself.

"Thank you for asking, Sophie, but I can't think of anything that I don't have to do personally. I appreciate the offer. What I'd really like you to do is find Tate's killer."

She picked up the pig. "I was the one who bought gifts

for the children. I guess that's the case in a lot of marriages. But one day, Tate brought home Oinky for Jo. They'd had a conversation about pigs when I wasn't home. But he remembered. There was something so sweet about it. A real bonding moment between them. And now someone has taken him from us." Her tone had grown harder.

Nina must have been listening. She was leaning against the doorframe when she asked, "Who, Bobbie Sue? Who had a grudge against Tate?"

"I don't know. When you own a business, I guess there's often a disgruntled employee or supplier, even a competitor who dislikes you. But I hadn't heard anything lately about problems with a particular person. You'd have to ask Marsha."

"What about your private life? Former friends, enemies?" I asked. Trying to be discreet, I added, "Anyone who would be jealous of him?"

Bobbie Sue must have understood my question because she swung around and gazed at me with wide eyes. "I'm not having an affair with anyone."

"Was Tate?" asked Nina.

"I don't think so. Not that I know of, anyway. We were happy together. I hate to say this, but Marsha was with him all day long. She would know if he was getting calls from a woman or leaving for periods of time." She paused and frowned at us. "His phone. The police must have his phone. I wonder if I can ask the phone company for his call records."

"If you know the password for your account, you might be able to access it online," I said. "Some companies, including some big ones, allow a person to look up the call record."

Bobbie Sue rushed to a small desk and grabbed a pad of paper and a pencil. She scribbled something on it. "One more thing I need to do." She looked up, her eyes meeting mine. "Start with Marsha. If I had the time for it, I would go to her myself." She wrote something on another sheet of the pad, ripped it out, and handed it to me. "Here's her address. Tell her I sent you."

The door knocker sounded. Bobbie Sue's shoulders sagged. "And so it begins."

We followed her to the front door. She threw it open and demanded with hostility, "What do *you* want?"

Chapter 8

Dear Natasha,
I have always loved Victorian style rooms. Over the years, I have bought a few wonderful pieces, but they never seemed right. I just got a nice bonus at my job and I'm creating my dream living room. I could use some tips to make it all work.
Ready to Redecorate in Victoria, Minnesota

Dear Ready to Redecorate,
Victorian style has evolved. Today's Victorian room absolutely requires long drapes. Instead of dark walls, go lighter but use patterned wallpaper. Bring in as much velvet as you can on furniture and pillows. And don't forget the big glitzy chandelier.
Natasha

The man at the door didn't bristle at Bobbie Sue's rough reception.

About six feet tall, he had short hair the color of mushroom soup, and a prominent brow ridge over startlingly blue eyes. He held out his arms to Bobbie Sue as if offering a hug. "Spencer called me. I'm sorry, Bobbie Sue. Really, I am."

She recoiled and backed into me. "This isn't a good time."

"Is Spencer here? I think this would be a great time to re-mind him that he still has a dad."

Nina and I looked at each other. A first husband we hadn't known about? It made perfect sense. Spencer was at least six years older than Jo.

"He's not here." She started to close the door, but the man stepped forward and held it open with his palm.

"C'mon, Bobbie Sue. Are you really going to be a jerk at a time like this? I came to help you."

"Too little, and way too late, Pierce." Bobbie Sue folded her arms across her chest. "I don't believe you, either. You're a bigger fool than I thought if you expect me to trust your sudden act of sincerity. Now if you don't mind . . ."

"But I do mind. Tell me where Spencer is, and I'll pick him up. He should be with family."

Bobbie Sue huffed, but I could see her relenting. "I don't know where he is. He ran out of the house this morning after I told him about Tate."

"See? You do need me. I'll find him and bring him home." He turned and walked out to the street. We watched as he reached into a white Jeep Wrangler with the top down. He pulled out running shoes and changed into them. With a quick glance back at us, he took off at a jog, heading toward the river.

Bobbie Sue closed the door and sagged against it. "Great. Just what I needed."

"Tate was your second husband," said Nina. "Spencer isn't his son?"

"Tate wanted to adopt him, but Pierce refused. Spencer's last name is Carver, like Pierce." She heaved a huge sigh. "It all seems so long ago now, but it's not. I will never forgive him. I know I'm supposed to, but what he did was completely unforgiveable. Pierce left Spencer and me. He walked out one day leaving me penniless with a toddler." She spoke bitterly. The wounds ran deep.

"Another woman?" I asked.

"I don't think so. Pierce wasn't ready for the responsibilities of a family. He literally ran away. And I couldn't even pay the rent. That was when I started baking cheesecakes at home. I didn't need a sitter and could make my own hours. I put Spencer in a stroller and walked the streets selling cheesecakes to every restaurant I could find. Money trickled in at first, and then I started getting some regular orders. That was when I met Tate. I walked into Blackwell's Tavern and even though it sounds corny, sparks flew when we met. I'm not joking. It was instantaneous. Love at first sight for both of us. He was everything Pierce wasn't. Mature, dependable, fun, and such a gentleman." She smiled wistfully. "It wasn't his money. After Pierce left us, I was determined to have my own career and my own money. I never wanted to find myself in that situation again. I didn't have much back then, but I was the one who insisted on a prenuptial agreement with Tate. Pierce had taught me a big lesson."

Bobbie Sue sank onto a bench in her foyer. "Tate was always supportive of me and my business. I think he was proud of the way I managed to grow the cheesecake line. He was a great dad, too. I can't imagine why anyone would have murdered him." Her voice petered out at a high pitch and the tears began again.

I hated to make her situation worse, but I had to ask, "Would Pierce have wanted Tate out of the way?"

Bobbie Sue swallowed hard several times. She grasped the arm of the bench. "I don't know. Pierce started taking more of an interest in Spencer a few years ago when he began to show athletic ability. Heaven knows he had no interest in Spencer as a child, but he started coming around again to watch Spencer in track meets."

"Does Pierce live around here?" I asked.

"He moved to a townhouse in Alexandria a couple of years ago. It's a quick drive for him."

"How does Spencer feel about Pierce?" Nina asked.

Bobbie Sue sighed. "Spencer has mixed emotions about him. Tate was more of a father to Spencer than Pierce ever was, but I suppose every child is happy when a parent shows an interest. Tate and I decided it was better for Spencer to have all three of us than it would be for us to shut Pierce out of Spencer's life. We didn't want Spencer caught between angry parents. I held my breath, afraid Pierce would let Spencer down like he had before. Turned out I'm the *only* one who is truly aggravated by his continued presence. I try not to show it in front of Spencer." She sniffled and wiped tears away with her fingers. She flapped her hand. "I can't be bothered by Pierce right now. There are more pressing things to worry about."

Nina and I finally took our leave. Bobbie Sue didn't need us hanging around in her way. As we walked out the front door, two of Bobbie Sue's neighbors walked up bearing casseroles.

"What do you think about Pierce?" whispered Nina.

"Seems like an opportunity for him to zoom back into their lives and replace Tate," I said.

"I think so, too. People have killed for less."

As we headed home, we cut through the alley that ran behind Tate's restaurant. I recognized the crime scene unit van from the Alexandria police department parked near the open back door. People wearing disposable full-body coveralls came and went.

"Well, well," said Nina. "Looks like Bobbie Sue was dead-on."

"Wolf is no dummy. I'm sure he recognized the problems with that crime scene long before Bobbie Sue," I said.

We slowed our pace.

"Do you see Wolf?" she asked.

I shook my head. "I don't see his car, either."

"Ready to head over to Marsha's?"

"That's probably where Wolf is. How about we go home, take care of our pups, and hop in the shower first?"

We continued on our way home and agreed to meet in an hour.

Right on time, Nina met me on the sidewalk. Suitably presentable, we headed for Marsha's place.

She lived in a narrow, pale yellow townhouse with a burgundy door. A lush wreath of giant silk roses hung on it.

Nina knocked and Marsha swung the door open. The rims of her eyes were red from crying.

There wasn't much of a foyer to speak of. We were ushered into her parlor. Moss-green damask wallpaper covered the walls. Lush swag curtains in the same shade were trimmed in gold fringe and tassels. On both sides of a mostly obscured window, the drapes were long enough to puddle on the floor.

A white ceiling and heavy molding broke the overwhelming green a little bit, as did the mahogany Victorian furniture upholstered in a cream-colored velvet. It was very formal. The kind of room that made me want to sit up straight.

"Wow," said Nina. "You're really into Victorian décor."

"It's my passion. Victorian style is so romantic. I come into this room and feel like it's embracing me."

I could understand that. The sole window was so heavily draped that almost no daylight entered the room, which gave it a cocoon feeling. "It's lovely," I said. "Thank you for taking the time to talk with us. You must be devastated."

She stared at the embroidered white handkerchief clutched in her hand and sniffled. Her chest heaved as she took a deep breath. "Honestly, I don't know how I'll manage without Tate. He wasn't just my boss. He was my best friend. We had been together for so many years."

Best friend? That concerned me. I wondered if their relationship had gone farther than that. "Bobbie Sue asked us to speak with you because you were with Tate every day. She thought you would be in the best position to know if someone had a beef with him."

She stared at me for a long moment. "I find that pathetic. Seems like a wife would know about that. The police detective who was here asked me the same thing. When I wanted to know what was going on, he said he was following up. Just making sure it was an accident." She gazed at me with the austere look of a schoolmarm. "Do they think someone murdered him?"

"We would like to believe it was an accident. But we don't think that was the case," I said.

She looked around, probably without seeing anything. It was as though she was having trouble accepting the situation and couldn't focus. "At least Bobbie Sue had the sense to send you to me. I'm surprised she admitted that I knew him better than anyone. Even better than her."

"He was your work-husband," said Nina.

Marsha's jaw clenched. Nina had clearly hit a sensitive area. I wondered how we could broach the subject of her relationship with Tate. I didn't want her to clam up. Hopefully, she would reveal the true nature of her relationship with Tate, but we needed her to be comfortable enough with us to speak freely. "Did Tate often go to the basement to retrieve wine or champagne?"

"He was a very generous person. If a couple was celebrating an anniversary, he would bring them a bottle of champagne on the house. He also popped a bottle of champagne when employees celebrated their birthdays. It wasn't a daily or even weekly occurrence, but he was big on celebrating the events in people's lives. Engagements, new babies, that sort of thing."

"Then it wasn't unusual for him to be in the cellar?" asked Nina.

"No." She looked at Nina like she had asked something odd. "It was *his* restaurant. I think some people didn't realize that he was actually a professional chef. He was constantly in the kitchen, even though he didn't do much of the cooking anymore. Tate was very much a hands-on owner. He was so full of life. It's inconceivable that he's gone."

"When did you last see him?" I asked.

"I think it was about seven, maybe a little past. He was going to see Jo dance in *A Midsummer Night's Dream*."

Nina shot a look at me. "He told you that?"

"Yes."

"Did he return to the restaurant afterward?" I asked.

"Not that I know of. That was the last time I saw him."

I leaned toward her. "I know this is difficult, but was anyone angry with him? An employee or a vendor, perhaps?"

She sucked in a deep breath. "He fired a fair number of people over the years. Always for cause, of course. It's difficult to run a restaurant if the servers and kitchen staff don't come to work. I have never understood why people think it's okay to blow off their shifts. It makes it so much more difficult on everyone else because they have to pick up the slack. Trading shifts or letting us know they can't work for a day or two for some reason, well, it's not fun but we can deal with it. But the ones who just don't show are always a problem. If they pull that act again without good reason—" She smiled sadly. "Tate used to tell his employees that a good reason was being in the hospital with all their fingers broken so they couldn't use the phone."

"He sounds like a tough boss. Had he fired anyone recently?" asked Nina.

"We have a pretty good crew at the moment. Sometimes the bartenders are aware of undercurrents. I can ask around."

"What about girlfriends?" blurted Nina.

I froze, worried about Marsha's reaction.

She shook her head. "I would have known about that." Marsha stared at a little side table. "There is only one person who would have liked to eliminate Tate. Competition between restaurants can be fierce. If anyone had a hand in Tate's death, it would be the manager of The Laughing Hound. A British guy named Bernie Frei."

Chapter 9

Dear Sophie,
My wife insists on using cutting boards made of
wood. I think they're dangerous because they can't
be sanitized. She says we would all be dead if that
were the case. What do you think?
                    Bacteria-phobe in Chopersville, Pennsylvania

Dear Bacteria-phobe,
I agree with your wife. Wash your cutting board with
warm water and soap, then dry. However, if it makes
you more comfortable, buy plastic cutting boards.
You can even get them in different colors for different
foods so there's no chance of cross-contamination.
                                                Sophie

Nina shrieked when Marsha mentioned Bernie's name. I
was equally appalled but restrained myself. Bernie was
one of our dearest friends. There was no way he could be a
murderer!

Marsha recoiled. "I gather you know him." Her voice was
flat and droll.

Before Nina could protest, which I was fairly certain she would do, I asked, "Why would Bernie want to kill Tate?"

"They had a not-so-friendly rivalry going. It was an embarrassment to Bernie. He made no secret of that. I can't tell you how many times he threatened Tate."

I held my hand up, palm out to stop Nina from defending Bernie. "What sort of threats?"

"'I'll get you, Tate.' 'You'll pay for that.' Except Bernie usually used British expressions that sounded cute. People found them funny, but they were serious." Marsha looked smug.

I tried reading her. She seemed almost pleased with herself.

"You seemed shocked," she said to Nina. "You must not know him as well as I do."

I held up my hand again. Maybe it would be better if Marsha didn't know exactly how close we were with Bernie. "Has he threatened *you*?"

"I find him intimidating."

Nina gasped.

I wasn't sure how long I could keep her from blurting something impolite. I was equally outraged. "Thank you for that information, Marsha. If you think of anything else we should know, please give me a call."

She followed us to her front door, but I could have sworn she was smirking when she said goodbye.

Nina blew up on the sidewalk. "Bernie would never kill anyone! The nerve of that woman. What was she thinking? I wanted to punch her right in the nose. Why didn't you defend him?"

"Because we might need her. I know Bernie didn't murder anyone. It was an odd accusation, but I was getting a weird vibe from her. Didn't you feel it?"

"She was in love with Tate. Couldn't you see that? Did you notice the photo of the two of them? An employee doesn't pose with her hand on her boss's chest like that. That was an adoring and proprietary posture."

I had to agree. "I wonder just how close they were. Maybe some of the employees know. Do you think she has a problem with Bernie, or his name was the first to come to mind?"

Nina stopped walking and turned toward me. "I think she planned to place blame on Bernie. Ohhh, I do not like that woman. I wouldn't be one bit surprised if she schemed to kill Tate because he wouldn't leave Bobbie Sue. After all these years working by his side every day, her love probably turned to anger. You know they say there's a fine line between love and hate. It wasn't a coincidence that Bernie was the first person that came to her mind. She's trying to cast suspicion on him to deflect it from herself."

That was entirely possible. "I know an easy way to find out."

We turned at the corner and headed for The Laughing Hound. When we walked inside, there was no host waiting to seat patrons. Shane Hasler, an African American bartender with a slim athletic build and admirable biceps, rushed toward us. "Sophie, am I glad to see you! This way. Quick!"

"What's wrong? What happened?" I asked.

"They're arresting Bernie!"

He led us through the kitchen and out the back to the alley, where Wolf was putting a handcuffed Bernie into a squad car.

Nina and I dashed toward them. "Wolf!" I cried. "What's going on?"

Wolf was as much a friend as Bernie. A seasoned detective, he saw through most ridiculous claims. But now he turned to me with the poker face that I found so annoying, and said, "I'm sorry, Sophie."

"Sorry?" Nina squealed. "That's the best you can do?"

"Bernie!" I shouted. "I'll call Alex. Don't say anything!"

The police vehicle took off, leaving Bernie's employees and

friends in shock. Everyone, except Wolf, watched in horrified silence as the police car turned onto the street.

Wolf started to walk toward his car.

"Wait a minute," I said, catching up to him. "What happened?"

Nina was right behind me. "Surely you didn't believe that Marsha woman?"

"Look, I know how you feel about Bernie, so I'm not going to tell you to stay out of police business. You wouldn't do it anyway." He lowered his voice. "I might as well tell you. There's blood on Bernie's car."

"Blood?" Tate's body on the cement floor of the cellar flashed in my mind. There had been surprisingly little blood. But there was the droplet I thought I'd seen just inside the back door. "Someone moved Tate to the restaurant cellar."

"Sophie!" Nina screeched. "You know it wasn't Bernie."

I looked into Wolf's brown eyes. "She's right. It couldn't have been Bernie."

"We'll know that soon enough," said Wolf.

"If you haven't confirmed that it's Tate's blood, then why is Bernie in handcuffs?" demanded Nina.

"Because that's protocol. Would you want to drive a car with a suspected killer sitting behind you without handcuffs?"

"No!" Nina frowned. "But this is *Bernie*!"

"Look, I like Bernie, too," Wolf said soothingly. "But we have a witness who says he threatened the victim and there's blood on his car. Call Alex like you were going to, and—"

"—and hope it's ketchup on the car?" Nina asked, sarcasm creeping in.

Wolf didn't respond. He simply stepped into his vehicle and drove away. Shocked employees still lingered outside. I heard one of them ask, "Should we close the restaurant?"

I felt certain there must be an assistant manager who took over when Bernie was off. "Absolutely not!" I said. "The restaurant stays open. We have to do that for Bernie. Let's all get back to work." I hurried over to Shane. "Who is the assistant manager?"

"There are two." Shane wrinkled his nose. "Eva Rosales is working today."

"You don't like her?" Nina asked.

"You might say she has a different management style than I'm used to."

I smiled at his delicate explanation. The three of us followed the others inside.

A woman about five feet tall, like me, with a round face and high cheekbones demanded, "Who are you and why are you in my kitchen?"

I liked her immediately. Bernie needed a no-nonsense assistant taking a firm hand in his absence. "Sophie Winston and Nina Reid Norwood. We're friends of Bernie's."

Her dark hair was pulled back neatly in a bun at the nape of her neck. She lifted her chin. "Nice to meet you. Now get out of my kitchen. You, too, Shane. Back to work."

Nina and Shane rushed for the door.

I paused to hand her my card. "Thank you for taking control while Bernie isn't around. If you need me for anything, please don't hesitate to call."

She glanced at my card with a confused expression. "Why would I need you?"

I smiled at her. "I don't expect you will. But just in case . . ."

She nodded but her gaze went right past me. "Donald, I thought I told you to use the blue cutting boards when cutting raw meat."

She hustled toward him, and I headed for the door.

"You gave her your card?" Nina laughed. "She's going to throw it out."

I turned around to see if that was what Eva was doing. She stopped, her back to me, and looked at my card. Then she jammed it in her pocket.

At that moment, my primary concern was getting Alex over to the police station to spring Bernie before he landed in a cell. I walked through the restaurant pressing Alex's office number on my phone.

His assistant put me through to him just as Nina and I stepped out on the sidewalk. I explained the situation.

"I'm on my way," was all he said.

It was all I needed to hear.

"Do you think they've impounded Bernie's car yet?" asked Nina.

Moving as a unit, we turned left in the direction of Bernie's house. I called my ex-husband, Mars. If anyone knew what was going on, it would be him. His phone rolled over to voicemail and I left a message.

I'd had the pleasure of helping decorate a room in the mansion before Bernie moved in. The wonderful old place had high ceilings and huge rooms. We passed the house and turned the corner to the detached garage in the back where Mars and Bernie parked their cars.

Our favorite local police officer, Wong, was sitting on a bench studying the back of Bernie's house. African American, she had kept her wrong-by-a-mile husband's last name when they divorced. Her uniform fit snugly. Like me, she had never met a cupcake she didn't like. Her hair was shaped in a tapered cut, shorter in back and chin length in front. "Wolf said you two would show up."

"He left you here to guard the car from us?" I asked. "He knows we wouldn't tamper with evidence."

She grinned and raised her eyebrows. "Guess he doesn't trust you."

"Where's the blood?" Nina asked.

"Driver's side. There may be some inside but don't touch the vehicle. Fingerprints."

My heart plummeted. Blood on the outside of the car could be explained, but blood inside the car was serious. No wonder they had carted Bernie off to the police station. "Did you see inside the car?"

"No. I'm not allowed to touch it, either. I heard Tate must have bled profusely. I'm still hoping that smear on the door will turn out to be something else. Or at least not Tate's blood."

I joined Nina at the driver's door. The blood stain could not be missed on Bernie's alpine-white BMW. It was more of a swipe than anything else. It looked to me as if bloody fabric had brushed along the car door. It contained no fingerprints or anything helpful in identifying the culprit.

"I don't suppose you would open the back for us?" asked Nina.

"You suppose correctly." Wong shook her head. "Bernie is a great guy. I can't imagine him killing anyone. But he has that kink in his nose. Makes me wonder if he has a violent past."

I wanted to protest, to defend Bernie. But we all knew about the kink that was a result of a broken nose. Bernie's colorful tales about it varied. They were usually quite funny, but I had always assumed his nose had been broken in a brawl with someone.

"It wasn't Bernie," said Nina. "We all know that. The killer will turn out to be someone else. We just have to figure out who it was."

Wong nodded. "If there's anything *legal* I can do to help you two, just let me know."

Her offer lifted my spirits a little bit. No one who knew Bernie was going to believe he was a murderer.

"How long before they spring him?" I asked.

"Hours, maybe days. This is a really serious charge," said Wong. "It's a good thing so many people know and like him. If it were almost anyone else, they'd be looking hard for a reason to hold him. Even if they had to charge him with something else to keep him in the slammer."

Chapter 10

Dear Sophie,
I'm making a triple chocolate cheesecake for my daughter's slumber party. I don't want to use cookies in the base, can I make it with honey graham crackers and cocoa powder?
Busy Mom in Graham, Arizona

Dear Busy Mom,
You absolutely can! It's a great way to get in more chocolate flavor without making the base too sweet.
Sophie

I was appalled, even though I knew the police sometimes came up with a lesser charge to keep someone in jail while they investigated a murder. If it were only Marsha's claim that Bernie had threatened Tate, then he might be out quickly. Or perhaps they would only question him and not detain him. But the blood on Bernie's car was an issue. I peered at it again, wishing I could declare it to be strawberry jam or some other harmless substance. But it sure looked like blood.

"It will take a while to get the test results back on the car," said Wong. "He'll have to post a whopper of a bond, though, especially since he could flee the country and head back to England."

I thought about my own bank account balance, which no one would describe as a whopper. Maybe between Mars and me, we could manage it.

A loud truck rumbled along the road and squealed to a halt. A man and woman emerged and acknowledged Wong.

Nina and I moved out of the way so they could load Bernie's car on the truck and take it to the impound lot. We walked toward our homes.

Nina stopped at her house to collect Muppet. The midday sun was getting uncomfortably hot. We rushed back to my house and air-conditioning. Muppet and Daisy romped in the backyard for a minute before returning to the house. I poured cold water into their bowl and put the kettle on for a large pitcher of iced tea. And then I phoned Mars again.

Thankfully, he was already at the police station and confirmed Alex's presence. "We're still early in this process," said Mars. "They're questioning Bernie right now. Alex is with him. He gave me the name of a bail bondsman. I'm setting that up so we can get Bernie out of here ASAP."

"Do you need money?"

"We've got that covered. What we need is for you to find the real killer."

A tall order, but I was relieved that they had enough money to bail Bernie out. I put Mars on speaker. "Nina is here with me. Tell us what you know."

Mars sighed. "I'm clueless. The first I heard of it was when Shane phoned me from the restaurant and said Bernie was being arrested for murder."

"Mars, where did the blood on Bernie's car come from?" asked Nina.

"Blood?" Mars uttered it in a whisper. "This is the first I've heard of it."

"I was hoping you could explain it. Maybe Bernie cut himself in the garage?" I asked with a smidgen of hope.

"Not that I know of." He paused and his voice changed. "Bernie and I don't drive a lot. He usually walks to the restaurant. I haven't been in the garage in days."

"What are you saying?" asked Nina.

"I'm not sure. We keep the trash cans in the garage, but we're not out there puttering on the cars or woodworking. You're the same way. When is the last time you were in your garage?"

It hadn't been that long for me. "I drove to see my parents last week. But I know what you mean. I can easily go for a week without driving if I don't have an event or a convention in town. But that doesn't change the fact that there's blood on Bernie's car door."

Nina and I could hear voices in the background. Mars said quickly that he had to go, and the call was disconnected.

"Swell," Nina grumbled. "We've got nothing but Marsha."

I poured boiling water over teabags in a large heat-safe glass pitcher. "We have one other potential lead—Worried in Old Town. If there was really something illegal going on at Blackwell's Tavern, then that would open a whole new arena of possible suspects. It could let Bernie off the hook entirely if we can establish some kind of criminal activity."

"How are we going to find her? Are you planning to wave that envelope at people on King Street and hope someone recognizes the stationery?"

I chuckled at the thought. "As fun as that might be, I took the note to Wolf. He needs to know that something fishy might be going on. If nothing else, it will plant doubt in his mind about Bernie. And in my column, we're running a request that she contact me. How about dinner tonight when Bernie is sprung? I need to get some groceries anyway."

"Dinner! That sounds great. While you shop, I'll see what

the scuttlebutt is about Tate in general and about Marsha specifically." Nina took off with Muppet.

Dragging my shopping cart along, I gladly suffered the heat on my way to the store, relieved that I didn't need my car to get there. I didn't know what time, or heaven forbid, even what day Bernie might be sprung, but I had him in mind while I shopped. It wasn't easy planning his favorite dinner, because he could eat whatever fancy dish he wanted every day at The Laughing Hound. I decided that he would prefer to be outdoors after sitting in an interrogation room, so I chose pork tenderloin and giant shrimp that we could cook on the grill. I added red peppers, yellow squash, mushrooms, and asparagus for veggie kabobs, potatoes that could steam in foil on the grill, and a loaf of Italian bread. I loaded up on cream cheese, with Bobbie Sue's cake contest in the back of my head, added blueberries, blackberries, and strawberries, and I was done.

The cashier with graying hair in need of a trim wore a name tag that said JENNY. She looked at me with sad eyes. "I heard about Bernie. If there's anything I can do . . ."

"Thank you." I loaded my bags into my cart, then asked, "Did you see Bernie anywhere last night?"

She squinted at me. "That would help him, wouldn't it?"

"It might." It all depended on when and where she saw him.

"I'll ask around."

I thanked her and left the store. Bernie had friends everywhere.

I went home and unloaded the groceries, thinking all the while about Bernie. I honestly didn't know where to start. The only real lead was Marsha, and for some reason, I didn't feel like she was being honest with us. I whipped up easy cream cheese and blueberry parfaits as dessert, then tackled a triple chocolate cheesecake with a chocolate crust, a chocolate cream cheese middle, and a chocolate mousse for the top. I slid the entire cake into the refrigerator to firm, wishing it would be ready by the time Mars and Bernie were home, but knowing it needed to settle in the fridge overnight.

If Bernie didn't want to come to my house for dinner, that would be fine. I could understand. But in that case, I would bring dinner to the two of them. If nothing else, they would have something to nosh on when they felt like it.

I had no sooner finished the cheesecake than my old friend Humphrey Brown called. "I heard," he said. "What can I do to help?"

I invited him to join us for dinner and phoned my next-door neighbor Francie. She was a hoot, and very sharp. She had lived in Old Town for decades and knew the older crowd who had resided here most of their lives. An avid bird-watcher and gardener, Francie's face reflected her time in the sun. She didn't bother with makeup. I wasn't sure anything could hide her deep wrinkles, but it didn't matter. Francie wore them with pride.

As it turned out, Bernie was released early enough to grab a nap and a shower. I had set the table outside, and marinated the pork and the veggies ahead of time. Nothing was left to be done, except light the grill and cook our food.

Nina came early and whipped up Very Berry Coolers just in time for Humphrey and Francie to arrive.

Francie's golden retriever, Duke, romped off to play with Daisy and Muppet, who didn't appear to realize that she was much smaller. Nevertheless, she held her own with the big dogs.

Humphrey had gone to school with Natasha and me. Apparently, he had a crush on me back then, which I hadn't known about until I was an adult. He was the palest person I had ever met, with a wan physique that rivaled Barney Fife. I always suspected a strong wind could topple him. Poor

Humphrey had a difficult time meeting women. It probably didn't help that he was a mortician at a local funeral home.

While the meat sizzled on the grill, we nibbled on cherry tomato bruschetta and grilled shrimp.

When we sat down to eat and I sliced the pork tenderloin, Bernie said in his very calm, cool British accent, "I want you all to know that I did not murder Tate."

Chapter 11

Dear Natasha,
My husband loses his keys constantly. I'm tired of
searching for them. It slows us down in the morning
and has become a sore topic. I'm at the point where I
want to hang them on a string around his neck. Help!
Exasperated Wife in Key Biscayne, Florida

Dear Exasperated Wife,
Find a drawer near the door and train him to place
his keys in it the minute he enters the house. As for
what he does with them when he's away from home,
well, that's not your problem.

Natasha

"In fact," said Bernie, "I happen to have liked Tate."
Everyone stopped. No knives or forks clinked. No
glasses were raised. We all stared at Bernie, his hair mussed
as usual, his expression sad.

"Of course you didn't kill him," I said. "We're going to
figure out who did."

In a voice so small it was little more than a whisper, he said, "Thank you, Sophie."

I reached across the table and grasped his hand in mine.

"We've got your back, Bernie," said Mars.

Our friends chimed in with their assurances. Francie snorted. "They could have picked a more suitable killer to pin it on."

I released Bernie's hand and sipped my cocktail.

"What I don't understand is—why me? Why would someone target me?"

"How well do you know Marsha Bathurst?" I asked.

Nina stopped eating and watched Bernie as he responded.

Bernie winced and rubbed his forehead. "Tate's assistant manager?"

"That's the one," I said.

"I went out with her once."

"Oh no!" said Nina. "What happened?"

"I just wasn't interested. She had this weird idea that I must be interested in the Victorian era because I'm British. She blathered on and on about it. It was one of those dinner dates where you feel squeamish and wish it weren't rude to look at your watch."

"Why would she hate you?" I asked.

"She kept calling and would drop by the restaurant. I made excuses to avoid another mind-numbing evening with her. What's a guy supposed to do?" Bernie frowned at us. "Are you saying she murdered Tate and tried to pin it on me?"

"No," I said. Then I changed my mind. "Possibly. There's something going on with her. She claimed you and Tate had a vicious rivalry going on."

Bernie's knife clattered as it fell to his plate. "It was a friendly thing. Both restaurants sponsored local sports teams. We provided T-shirts imprinted with our logos and then cheered them on. Tate and I would make bets. The loser's money always went to a deserving charity in Old Town. I hardly call that vicious."

"You never threatened him?" Nina added butter to her steaming potato.

"Only in jest. I'd tell him he was off his trolley and he'd ask me if we were still serving roadkill."

Nina's eyes met mine. Marsha clearly meant to throw blame on Bernie. And she had done a splendid job of it. She was the main reason the police questioned him. Could she have anything to do with the blood on his car?

Mars pierced a piece of asparagus. "Was Marsha having an affair with Tate?"

Bernie shrugged. "How would I know?"

"Rumors?" suggested Humphrey. "Aren't restaurants fonts of such rumors?"

"There may be some truth to rumors arising in restaurants. After all, we see a lot of people, and catch some of their private moments, but I never heard about an affair between the two of them," said Bernie. "If anything, I'd have said Tate was devoted to Bobbie Sue."

"Marsha had a definite reaction today when Nina called Tate her *work husband*," I said. "Maybe he refused her affections. Unrequited love? She labored at his restaurant every day, secretly pining for him, and she finally couldn't stand it anymore?"

"Who would know?" asked Nina.

"Possibly some of his employees," said Francie.

"Does anyone know one of them well enough to approach them?" asked Mars.

"Let's send Shane over when they reopen. He's a good guy. He may be able to elicit some information." Bernie seemed to relax, as though that plan, albeit tiny, might solve his problems.

When we finished dinner, Nina offered to fetch some Scotch. Mars and Francie were game, but Bernie and Humphrey declined.

"Would you mind if I made myself a cup of tea?" asked Bernie. "I know it sounds like something a granddad would ask for, but I feel like I need to keep my wits about me. Someone has it in for me and I don't know why."

I assured him I would be happy to make us both a cuppa. Minutes later, with help from Bernie and Humphrey, we carried mugs of steaming tea, the blueberry parfaits, and a pad and pen, to the outdoor table.

"Just what I needed," said Bernie as I handed around parfaits.

I handed Mars the pen and notepad.

Mars took a bite of the parfait. "Mmm. Definitely summery. What am I expected to do with the notepad?"

"I thought we could make a timeline. You're the one who likes to write down facts. Let's figure out where Bernie was last night and who might have noticed him. He's surrounded by people at the restaurant most of the time, so that's a great alibi."

"Have you heard yet what time Tate was killed?" asked Mars.

Humphrey nodded. "I understand rigor mortis had set in. Preliminarily they're thinking between ten-ish the night before and one or two in the morning. I also heard that he must have lain faceup after he died. Sometime later, someone flipped him."

"Why would anyone do that?" asked Francie.

No one had an answer.

"At least we have a window of time," I said. "Marsha claims Tate left the restaurant around seven thirty in the evening to go to the play. So where was he between then and the time he died?"

Mars spewed his Scotch. "They're going to suspect me!"

I handed him paper napkins to wipe up the mess.

"Were you out running around last night?" asked Nina.

"I'm the only other person who had access to Bernie's car keys. And I have no alibi after midnight."

"Maybe we should make a timeline for you as well then," said Bernie in a surprisingly calm tone.

Mars finished his parfait and divided another between Nina and himself. I didn't say a word, but it made me smile. The creamy parfaits were a hit!

"Then let's get back to where you were. What time did you walk over to the play?" I asked.

"About a quarter past seven. It was already underway," said Bernie.

"Did you speak with anyone?" Nina asked.

"That would have been impolite. The production was underway. I was over on the left side, near a tree."

"You didn't sit down?" I gazed into his eyes.

"It was a full house. Standing room only."

"Did you see anyone you knew?" I pushed him a little because it might be the only way we could prove where he really was that night.

"I was watching the stage, not the audience," he protested.

"It ended about eight thirty. Where did you go then?"

"Back to the restaurant."

"Presumably you spoke with people there, so that should be easy to confirm," I said.

Bernie nodded. "I spent some time in the bar because we were going to shut down dining around eleven but expected a crowd of people after the midnight race."

"And what time did you leave again?"

"A few of our servers and bartenders ran in the race, so I walked over to the starting point with them a little after eleven. You can confirm with Shane, Sean, Eliza, and Lanky. His real name is Lambert, but everyone calls him Lanky."

"And then?"

"I walked over to the finish line and waited for them."

"Was anyone with you?"

"Not *with* me. The crowd dispersed when the race started. I guess people went to different points along the route to cheer them on. I just ambled along, enjoying the lights and the atmosphere."

"Bernie," I asked, "didn't you see *anyone* you knew?"

"Not really. I think a lot of people had gone home by then. The streets were getting quiet. It was nearly midnight, Sophie. There was a big celebration as they ran to the finish line. Somebody sprayed champagne all over everyone and awards were presented. I walked back to the restaurant with my crew and bought them all drinks on the house at the bar. We closed up at one in the morning. *That* was when I realized my keys were gone. I went up to my office to grab them and they weren't there. I had to ask one of the assistant managers, Eva, to lock up. I don't think the police believed that."

"It would be an easy lie. Where do you keep your car keys?" I asked.

"On a brown leather key fob embossed with my initials."

"We have a bowl in the kitchen near the back door that we use. We place them in there when we come home," explained Mars. "I knew Bernie was at work. All I had to do was take the spare key."

"I see what you're getting at, Mars," said Bernie. "If the substance on my car turns out to be Tate's blood, then you could be a suspect because you had easy access to my car."

Nina frowned. "That's bad news all around. I've heard of thieves driving along streets with universal remotes to see which garage doors will open. But even if the killer planned ahead and found he could access your garage, he wouldn't have known where to find the keys to your car. That sort of narrows it down to the two of you, doesn't it?"

"Bernie, when you leave the restaurant, do you take the keys with you?" I asked.

"Not usually. Not if know I'm going back to the office."
Mars began to look panicked.

"Mars, did you even know Tate?" I asked him.

"Only casually. I ate in the restaurant from time to time. Less often once Bernie opened The Laughing Hound." He shrugged. "Seemed like a nice enough guy."

"Is there a camera on your office?" I asked Bernie.

"Good grief, no!"

"Then it would have been easy to take the keys from your office. That means it was someone in the restaurant," I mused.

Mars perked up. "Then anyone could have taken them. Absolutely anyone."

Chapter 12

Dear Sophie,
I must be the worst mom in the world. After work, I pick up the kids, all at different schools, and by the time we get home it's seven. Who has time to cook? I know about the kits you can order, but (feeling a little embarrassed here) I really want dinner ready when I come home. Is there a way to afford that?
  Exhausted and Starving in Hungry Horse, Montana

Dear Exhausted and Starving,
There are chefs and cooks who deliver to local homes daily. If you cannot find one in your area, get together with two or three other families and find a cook who can make meals for all of you.

Sophie

I was relieved by that revelation, too. "Did you mention that to Alex?" I asked.

"It didn't even come up," said Bernie. "The cops wanted to know about my relationship with Tate. They even asked if I was secretly seeing Bobbie Sue! Over and over again."

Nina eyed Bernie. "Is there any reason they would think you were having an affair with Bobbie Sue?"

Bernie burst out laughing. "No. I hardly know the woman. Do you suppose that real killers change their stories and that's why they ask the same questions repeatedly? Maybe they can't keep them straight? In any case, I was telling the truth, so it wasn't difficult to be accurate. In fact, I think my consistency may have aggravated some of the police. It wasn't what they wanted to hear."

Francie tsked. "I hate that. It probably means she's having an affair with someone else."

"It sounds like there aren't many gaps when you would have had the opportunity to kill someone," I observed.

Bernie shrugged. "There's the time I was at the play, then the thirty minutes or so while the race was on, and then walking home after work."

That was his weak spot, I thought. Time-wise he could easily have murdered Tate after the restaurant closed.

"Where were *you*, Mars?" asked Nina.

"In case that's some kind of snide way of asking whether I am the one having an affair with Bobbie Sue, allow me to put any such fears to rest. I like her cheesecake but that's about as far as my relationship with her goes. I happen to have an airtight alibi. I watched the fireworks from a party at a snazzy house that overlooks the river."

"What time did you get home?" I asked.

"About half an hour before Bernie."

I didn't like that. Not at all. The next thing I knew, the police would say Mars helped Bernie.

Even though he'd caught a nap earlier, Bernie looked beat. I thought we had better wind things up. "Okay, then. Our job is to get out there and find people who saw Bernie last night. If we can do that, then the only window of opportunity would be after one in the morning."

Humphrey piped up. "I'll see if I can get anything more from the medical examiner's office. That might help as well."

Before Mars and Bernie left, I showed them my copy of the letter from Worried in Old Town. "If we could figure out who sent it, we might have a lead on what was going on at Blackwell's Tavern."

The two of them nodded but neither seemed hopeful.

On Saturday morning, I was up early. Daisy was pleased to go outside in the cool morning air, but Mochie yawned and waited patiently beside his food bowl.

Although I felt quite certain that friends and neighbors had probably brought Bobbie Sue loads of casseroles by now, I happened to know that the most overlooked meal for the bereaved was breakfast. And I suspected the last thing Bobbie Sue wanted to do right now was cook breakfast for heaven knew how many people.

I put on the kettle to make coffee and fed Mochie and Daisy. Then I prepared a cupcake pan with cupcake papers. I stirred together flour, sugar, eggs, cinnamon, and melted butter and poured in plump, sweet blueberries. Using a large cooking spoon, I ladled the batter into the muffin cups. When they were baking, I grabbed a fresh bowl and whisked eggs. Eying the refrigerator, I found spinach and sweet red peppers to chop. I considered adding mushrooms, but kids weren't always fond of them, so I left them out. When the blueberry muffins came out of the oven, I slid in the savory egg muffins. Then I dipped each of the warm blueberry muffins into melted butter and a small bowl of sugar. The sun shone in through the window and gleamed on the sparkling sugar on top of the muffins. I set them aside to cool and poured myself a cup of French press coffee.

As tempted as I was to eat a muffin, they were needed at Bobbie Sue's house. When the blueberry muffins had cooled, I packed them in a disposable aluminum pan. It wasn't as pretty as a dish, but Bobbie Sue would have enough problems remembering which dish belonged to which person. I tied a dark blue ribbon around each pan to dress them up a little bit without being festive.

Dressed in a white sheath covered with blue and purple flowers, and simple white sandals, I locked the house and walked over to Bobbie's Sue's place. I knocked on the door gently in case the kids were still asleep.

Bobbie Sue's ex-husband, Pierce, answered the door. I tried to hide my surprise and held out the muffins. "I brought breakfast!"

Pierce wiped his face with one hand like he wasn't fully functioning yet. "Great." His voice was husky, as though he hadn't spoken yet this morning. He motioned me in with a tired wave of his hand.

I headed straight to the kitchen.

Jo trailed into the kitchen from the stairs. She wore a pink and white gingham sundress with ruffles at the shoulders. "Mom says she'll be downstairs as soon as she's presentable, which could take a while because she didn't get *any* sleep last night. And she said to tell Uncle Pierce that he is not allowed to make coffee because he nearly burned the house down yesterday."

Pierce blushed. "That is a wild exaggeration." He turned to me. "Someone figured it out yesterday afternoon, but I don't know who."

I opened the two muffin packages. "I'd be happy to make the coffee for you."

"Are those for us?" asked Jo.

"They are. Are you hungry?"

Her hand darted to the sugary blueberry muffins. "Thank you." She peeled back the paper and took a bite.

"What do you drink for breakfast?" I asked.

"Could I have some orange juice?"

"Absolutely." I hoped Bobbie Sue still had some. I didn't

have to look far. I could see it through the glass door of the refrigerator. I took it out and poured her a glass.

I turned my attention to the monster coffee machine. "Let's see. I think the left side makes coffee." I picked up the bag of coffee beans just as someone rapped the door knocker.

Jo paid no attention. She was busy picking blueberries out of her muffin and eating them one at a time. Pierce left the kitchen. I heard the front door open, and then a man's voice, not Pierce's. "You're here early, or . . . ?"

Pierce didn't take the bait. "Come on in. Some lady brought food."

Coach followed him into the kitchen just as we heard Spence upstairs, yelling, "Mom! I can't find my backpack. It's got all my stuff in it."

Pierce and Coach started for the back stairs in the kitchen. Pierce said calmly to Coach, "I can handle this, thanks."

Coach stopped in his tracks and watched Pierce disappear upstairs.

I turned my focus back to the monster coffee machine. The aroma of freshly brewed coffee began to fill the air.

"Hey!" said Coach. "That smells like success to me. If there's one thing Bobbie Sue will need, it's her coffee."

"Sounds like you know her pretty well," I said.

"We go way back. Before Jo was born. We were neighbors in an apartment complex. I used to help the kids with impromptu soccer games."

A landline telephone rang. Coach picked it up and took a message for Bobbie Sue.

"Coffee?" I asked him.

"That would be great."

I found a small serving tray with pewter handles shaped like branches. A matching stoneware creamer and a sugar bowl with a pewter lid were also in the cabinet. The lid of the sugar bowl was curiously shaped like a branch with berries.

There was already sugar in it. I filled the creamer with the half and half I found in the fridge and placed the entire set on the serving counter. A quick peek in a drawer yielded napkins, both paper and cloth. I nabbed one white cloth napkin and a bundle of paper napkins. I unfolded the cloth napkin so it was halved and positioned it next to the cream and sugar, then loaded it with a row of spoons. Sleek white mugs with tapered bases stood lined up in a perfect row in the cupboard. I arranged them beside the spoons on a pewter tray and set the paper napkins with a gray branch theme next to them.

A stack of casseroles had caught my eye in the refrigerator. I took a quick peek in case any of them were breakfast casseroles, but they looked to be chicken, mac and cheese, something with penne that I couldn't identify, and something topped with mashed potatoes.

No dishes cluttered the sink waiting to be washed. I didn't see anything else I could do to be helpful.

Bobbie Sue and Pierce came down the stairs. She would always be beautiful, but her makeup didn't disguise her exhaustion. She looked haggard.

"Sophie! You're just wonderful to have come by." She eyed the coffee and poured herself some. "Pierce? Don't tell me you mastered the coffee monster?"

"Happily, I didn't even have to touch the thing. Sophie did it." He pointed at me.

"I guess I really should learn," muttered Bobbie Sue. She stroked her daughter's hair.

The door knocker sounded again just as Bobbie Sue was swilling coffee. "Would you get that for me, Pierce? I have got to get some caffeine in my system before I deal with anyone."

I refilled her cup and handed it to her. "Do you have a carafe I should fill?"

She stared at the gleaming monster. "No. I'll make it Coach's job to fill the mugs. If he insists on being here, he might as well be useful. It will keep him out of my hair."

I rounded the counter. "I suspect a lot of people will be coming through today. If you need a hand with anything, just give me a call." I knew she wouldn't but felt I should make the offer. One never knew.

Spencer ambled down the stairs in torn jeans. From the locations of the tears, I surmised that they were the expensive torn kind, not like mine where the fabric grew thin from wear. Besides, he was at the age where he was shooting up. I seriously doubted that jeans fit him long enough to wear thin. He had Pierce's height and build and while a bit more growing would probably happen, he already looked more like a young man than a gangly teen.

Three people rushed in from the foyer. The two women had their arms outstretched and aimed at Bobbie Sue. I took that as my cue to make an exit and slipped out the front door.

It was still early in the morning, a lovely time to walk. I wished I had brought Daisy along. When I approached my block, things weren't quite so serene.

Natasha's half sister, Charlene, stormed out of their house, followed by Charlene's mother, Griselda. I could hear her mom saying, "Honey, we'll work this out."

Charlene resembled Natasha quite a bit. She wasn't as thin nor as tall, but she had the same beautiful black hair and facial structure.

They stopped almost in front of me. I couldn't help hearing their conversation.

"How am I supposed to cook with no food?"

"A trip to the store will solve that. You'll be back up and cooking—"

"Where? Where am I supposed to cook? Do you think I can just conjure up a kitchen? What am I going to do?"

"You just calm down now. There's a solution to every problem."

I felt obligated to stop. I couldn't exactly walk by them as though I hadn't seen them. "Is there anything I can do to help?"

Charlene puffed up her cheeks and blew air out of her mouth. "Not unless you know of a commercial kitchen for rent."

"What happened?"

Her mother, Griselda, said, "Our refrigerator went on the fritz during the night. Almost everything is spoiled. And on top of that, someone left a pot holder in one of the ovens and it caught fire!"

I could just imagine what Natasha had to say about that.

Charlene spoke in a dead tone. "I have no food, no place to cook, and two dozen families expecting meals today."

Chapter 13

Dear Natasha,
My sister cooks and bakes all the time. Every meal.
Every day. But she refuses to clean up the kitchen. I
am not her maid. It drives me crazy that she expects
me to clean her mess. How can I convince her to
clean up after herself?
            Tearing Out My Hair in Sister Bay, Wisconsin

Dear Tearing Out My Hair,
Stop cleaning up. She won't like it when she wants to
cook and all the pots and pans are dirty. She'll have
to wash them herself then.

                                                Natasha

"What about the kitchen in the garage apartment?" I
asked.

"Natasha rented it to some cute young guy," said Charlene. "He's quiet and pays the rent, I'll say that for him."

"You would be welcome to use my kitchen, but I have a
dog and a cat, which probably violates all kinds of rules."

But then an idea popped into my head. "Come inside and let me make a phone call."

They followed me into my house.

"I would love to cook here," said Charlene. "Although I will admit that Natasha's stainless countertops make cleanup and sanitizing easy."

I walked over to the wall phone, called Mars and explained the situation. "Is your B and B available by any chance?"

Charlene gazed at me hopefully, her eyes wide.

I gave her a thumbs-up and hung up the phone. "He's at home, waiting for you with the key. It's not a huge place, but it might tide you over until you can find somewhere else to cook."

"You know," said Griselda, "this might be a blessing in disguise. It's time you got a real commercial kitchen. You can't possibly expand if you limit yourself to what you can do in our house."

Charlene didn't respond. But she didn't say no, either. Sometimes a suggestion plants a seed, and I had a feeling that was what had just happened before my eyes.

With my car still in the shop, I couldn't help transport Charlene's cooking equipment. I apologized for that, but Charlene quickly said, "You found me a place to cook. And that was the biggest problem. Besides, my assistant can load it all up in the van and bring it over."

They left to pick up the key from Mars, and I checked for an email from Worried in Old Town. She hadn't responded yet.

An hour later, I was surprised when Bobbie Sue showed up at my kitchen door. Dressed head to toe in black, she was clearly in mourning. But mostly, the spark in her eyes was gone. I invited her in and offered her a cup of coffee.

"Yes, *please*. Everything is such a muddle. I sneaked out of the house before more well-meaning friends could drop by. I am so thankful for everyone's kindness, but I feel like no one will give me a minute to myself to be brokenhearted."

"I expect that will come after the memorial service," I said softly. We sat at the banquette in my kitchen. "Could I make you some breakfast?"

"Heavens, no! There is so much to eat in our house that the refrigerator is about to explode." She took a long swig of coffee. "This is perfect. I need to pay you. How much do I owe you?"

"That's what you're worried about? It could have waited, Bobbie Sue. I certainly would have understood." She had paid half of the price for her party in advance. I told her how much remained.

She wrote a check and handed it to me. "And how much for investigating Tate's murder?"

"No charge for that."

She stared at me unhappily and licked her lips. "No, no. You don't understand. It's over. You don't have to search for his killer any longer. They've arrested someone."

I shuddered at the word *arrested*.

"I appreciate all the time you put into it. Just tell me how much I owe you and we'll be squared away."

"Nothing. I don't charge for that."

Bobbie Sue bit her upper lip. "I presume you know that they caught the man. He's been released, but we know who he is so there's no need to pursue this any longer."

I wondered if she knew Bernie and I were friends. It didn't sound like it. Should I tell her? Should I let her know that I thought they had the wrong guy? She had so many things to do and to worry about. Maybe it would be kinder to take that concern off her back by letting her believe that it was Bernie.

I smiled at her. "When is the service?" I asked, changing the subject.

"Ugh. They're not turning Tate over to me yet. It's absolutely awful. I can't even bury him. Everyone has been calling and asking that question. So we're having a memorial service tomorrow at one o'clock. They can do that without . . . without Tate being present. Tate's brothers are arriving this afternoon." She twisted her pen nervously. "Please let me pay you. I asked you to find Tate's killer. I would feel so much better if I could just wrap up that one thing."

For the third time I tried to explain. "I never charge when someone asks me for help with a murder. I'm not a private investigator or any kind of professional. It would be wrong to do that. You owe me nothing."

"Then you will stop?" She let out a little laugh. "Of course, you will. They have their man. Though I can't imagine what his problem was with Tate. I've been to his restaurant. It's very nice and the food was wonderful, but I fail to see why he would want to murder Tate. I suppose the police will figure that out and let me know."

Bobbie Sue drained her coffee mug and stood up. "Thank you for your help. I hope I'll see you at the service tomorrow, Sophie."

I closed the door behind Bobbie Sue and watched her walk away. She took a deep breath and exhaled almost like she was glad to put one thing behind her. She walked quickly at first but when she reached the sidewalk, she slowed dramatically. That was how grief affected us. It came in waves.

In a way *I* felt relieved. It wasn't as though I had a conflict of interest pursuing Tate's killer. I knew it couldn't have been Bernie. Finding the truth would be the best scenario for both Bobbie Sue and Bernie. But now I didn't feel obligated to answer to Bobbie Sue. My sole concern was getting Bernie off the hook.

As far as I knew, Tate had been a well-respected businessman. But being in business came with a price. I knew that from personal experience. Not all clients and customers were happy. Unfortunately, Blackwell's Tavern would be closed for a few days, so I couldn't wander over to chat with employees and find out the real scoop. But maybe that was just as well. With a little luck, maybe Marsha hadn't had a chance to tell them all to keep mum. I just needed to find someone who knew them.

But where to start? I couldn't trouble Bobbie Sue for information. It would be inconsiderate and downright horrible to barge in and ask for Tate's records. Besides, the police had probably taken his computer by now. I figured Nina and I had pretty much burned our bridges with Marsha. If I had the nerve to show up at her door, she would most likely slam it in my face.

Maybe it would be worth taking a walk to the restaurant and dropping in on the neighboring stores. It was still early in the day, though. Stores wouldn't be open yet. I poured myself another cup of coffee and spent a couple of hours in my little home office, working on my advice column.

At ten, wearing a simple periwinkle dress and comfortable sandals, I took a stroll over to Blackwell's Tavern. Candles and bouquets of flowers lay at the front door around a framed photograph of Tate. It didn't seem like the kind of thing Bobbie Sue would have set up and I wondered who had created the impromptu tribute.

As I looked at it, a number of people paused and commented to one another. Mostly they said what a great guy Tate was. But a lone woman in her early twenties sniffled and stood alone. She hung a homemade lace ribbon angel on the side of the photo frame.

"That's beautiful," I said to her. "You must have known Tate very well to make such a lovely angel for him."

She nodded, the muscles around her mouth quivering. "I worked for Mr. Bodoin. He was very good to me."

"You look a little shaky, could I buy you a latte? I'd love to hear more about him." I held out my hand. "I'm Sophie." I could tell she was hesitant by the way she sized me up. "There's a great place on the corner, we can sit outside in the shade."

She followed me and minutes later we sat under a tree with lattes.

"I'm Liddy Albertson, by the way," she said.

"You said you worked for Tate. Were you a server?"

"Yes, a terrible one! But he was so kind. I can't believe that someone murdered him."

I smiled at her. "Did you spill soup on customers?"

"Worse! I dropped a huge tray of steak specials. Filet mignons and Duchess potatoes flew across the floor." She touched her palm against her forehead. "All the juice from the meat . . . it looked like a massacre had taken place. Bless Mr. Bodoin, he didn't take it out of my pay. I was sure he would. Those were expensive meals. But he said not to worry because it happens to most servers sooner or later and that I was now officially an experienced server. Wasn't that sweet?"

I eyed her. She seemed so innocent. Could she possibly be Worried in Old Town? I tested her. "Is this a summer job for you?"

She gasped and murmured, "Oh no!" Her eyes widened and she fluffed her hair. "How do I look?"

"Fine."

"No tearstains on my face?" She wiped her fingers under her eyes.

"You look lovely." She did, and now that something had rattled her, color had returned to her cheeks.

Liddy raised her chin and smiled at me as though she were having the best time of her life. She laughed and said, "My college boyfriend, Austin Sinclair, is over there. I know he sees me. He begged me to move to Washington after graduation. He wants to be in politics and had a job lined up here, but I didn't so I moved home. Then I decided I could get a job waiting on tables here just as well as I could back home in

Virginia Beach, so I moved. But when I got here, he ditched me. It was as though he had become a different person. All these girls were hanging around him, and it turned out he was already seeing some girl named Sara. If I had known that, I never would have moved." The phony smiled vanished. "How can someone just dump you like that? What kind of guy does that? My roommate says men do things like that all the time. I don't want him to know that I don't have a fancy job. I'm still looking but I might move home to the beach instead. There's nothing keeping me here."

I nodded. "I'll play along if he comes over here."

"He won't. He knows he treated me like a worm. But I want *you* to know why I'm pretending to be happy when I'm really devastated by Tate's death."

"I understand. What was the atmosphere like in the restaurant?" I asked. "Was anyone upset with Tate?"

"I don't think so. Everyone gets along pretty well. Marsha is the one we're wary of."

"Oh?" I didn't say more because I didn't want to lead her line of thought.

"Yeah. The woman *never* smiles. We joke about her being a ghost. She's always watching and turns up behind you unexpectedly. It's spooky."

I was itching to come right out and ask if Marsha was having an affair with Tate. But I thought I'd better ease into it. "How was Marsha with Tate?"

Liddy's gaze flicked over my shoulder, past me. "He's watching us." She smiled brightly. "It's no secret that Marsha was completely in love with Tate. He pretended he didn't know, but you'd have to be a dolt not to realize it."

"Were they having an affair?"

Chapter 14

Dear Sophie,
I am delighted to be hosting a bridal shower luncheon for my niece. The menu is almost worked out, but dessert is causing strife in the family. The bride's mother (not a blood relative to me) insists that we must have a cake. But my niece cannot eat gluten. I have never baked a gluten-free cake in my life, and I'm overwhelmed by the choices. Any advice?
Dizzy Aunt in Bridesburg, Pennsylvania

Dear Dizzy Aunt,
Bake a cheesecake! Use cornstarch, which is naturally gluten-free, instead of flour. It will be creamy and delicious!
Sophie

The smile vanished and Liddy's eyes widened. Suddenly I had her full attention. "Gosh, I hope not. His wife is so nice." Her brow furrowed and she thought for a moment. "I don't think Mr. Bodoin was the type." She glanced around for her old boyfriend. "I should know, right? But . . . one night after we locked up, I was walking home in the same direction as Marsha. It's not like I was intentionally following her or anything, I just happened to be going the same way. She turned down an alley. I know people use them all the time as shortcuts, but just when I was walking by, I spotted her embraced in a very passionate kiss with someone."

"Was it Tate?"

She shook her head. "I don't know. It was dark outside. I really couldn't say. If I hadn't seen her turn into the alley, I wouldn't have known it was Marsha. And I didn't want her to catch me watching. That would have been *très* awkward!"

"Which alley was it?"

"Um, do you know where the turquoise garden bench is? You can see it through the gate and hear water trickling in a fountain?"

I knew exactly the place she meant and nodded.

"It's the next alley after that." Her brow wrinkled. "It never entered my mind that it could be Mr. Bodoin. Does he live around there?"

"Not even close to there."

Liddy appeared genuinely relieved. "I'm glad to hear that!"

"What about the people who work there? Was anyone angry with Mr. Bodoin?"

She took a deep breath. "I don't think so. I mean, there's the regular griping when somebody can't get off a day that they ask for. That kind of thing. But it's mostly aimed at Marsha because she's the one who sets up the work schedules."

I wasn't getting anywhere. "What about customers? Any that troubled you or seemed odd somehow?"

"They are so nice. And people in Old Town are generous tippers. There are one or two whom no one wants to serve, of course, because they don't tip. I have never understood that. It's common knowledge that servers don't get paid beans." Her body grew rigid. "He's coming over here!"

A moment later, an adorable young man arrived at our table. Medium height with light brown hair, he was a cross between bad boy and scruffy rascal. "Hi, Liddy. I haven't seen you around much."

"I've been busy."

"Me too. I'm working as an intern at Representative Saylor's office now."

My ex-husband, Mars, was a political consultant, so I knew a little bit about how things worked on Capitol Hill and suspected he had omitted the significant word *unpaid* in order to impress her.

"Still working at the restaurant?" he asked in a snooty tone.

Before Liddy could speak, I said quickly, "Now, Liddy, don't be shy. She just interviewed for a job with Mars Winston."

Mars's name had the desired effect.

The boyfriend's face grew pale. "No kidding? How'd you swing that?"

Liddy smiled and said lightly, "You just have to know the right people."

"So, how about dinner tonight?" he asked.

Liddy wrinkled her nose at him and shrugged. "I don't think so. Maybe I'll see you around."

I knew it was wrong to lie, but it was just a little fib to help Liddy get some of her self-confidence back. We waited until he was out of earshot and then both of us burst into laughter.

"Who is Mars Winston?" she asked.

"He used to be my husband. His name is fairly well-known in political circles. I thought it might put Mr. Snooty Nose in his place."

"I have to admit it felt kind of good turning him down. I

never realized he was such a jerk. Why would I get involved with him again after the way he treated me? No, thank you! Once was enough. But now I feel a little bit better about the whole thing."

I handed her my card. "Do you know where Antonio Hirsch lives? He was my server the other day and I'd like to talk with him. See if he noticed any problems at the restaurant."

"Oh sure. Antonio's a nice guy. He lives on South Henry Street, a couple of blocks down. It's a white house with a navy-blue door. You can't miss it. He shares it with a couple of other guys."

"Thanks. I appreciate your help, Liddy. If you think of anything that might be important or if you hear rumors, please give me a call." I handed her my card.

"This says event planner." She looked at me curiously.

"I plan events for a living. But I solve murders on the side."

"You're doing this for Bobbie Sue?"

"One of my good friends has been accused of murdering Tate. I know he didn't do it, but someone has gone to a lot of trouble to make it look like he did."

"Ohhh. That's terrible. I'll let you know if I hear anything. And thanks for the latte!"

I was considering what I might do for lunch when I received a text from Mars. **Meet me out front.**

I wasn't sure if he meant in front of my house or his. Not that it mattered since we lived on the same street. I hurried home and found Mars on the sidewalk in front of my house.

"Hi! Is Bernie okay?" I asked.

He mouthed something I didn't understand. With an exasperated expression, he held one hand near his ear as though he were holding a phone.

"Did you lose your phone?" I pulled mine out of my purse and handed it to him.

He turned it off.

"What's going on?" I asked.

"Phones hear things. Even when it seems like they're not turned on."

"I seriously doubt that I say anything of much interest to the kind of people who might listen."

"Walk with me."

"Okay, where are we going?"

"No place in particular. I need to talk to you away from prying ears."

"Eyes," I corrected.

"No, I meant ears."

"I wanted to talk to one of Tate's employees over on Henry Street. We could go there."

"Fine by me."

"How's Bernie?"

"Back at work like nothing is wrong."

I stopped walking. "You're kidding!"

"He said there wasn't anything he could do about it from home anyway, so he might as well go to work and see if he could figure out who stole his car keys."

We walked on. "If that person murdered Tate, they're not likely to confess to taking the keys," I pointed out.

"We have a new problem. This is why I didn't want our phones to be on. The cops will get around to it sooner or later, but there's no point in giving them a heads-up about it."

I winced. "What now?"

"There's a witness."

Chapter 15

Dear Sophie,
My neighbor spies on me all the time. She must think
I don't see her peering out between her drapes at all
hours. My life is none of her business. How do I tell
her to stop?

Annoyed in Watch Hill, Rhode Island

Dear Annoyed,
Bring her a gift of food. If you bake, you might make
a cake or some cookies and bring them over. Be kind.
Once she knows you, she might stop watching.
Maybe she needs someone to talk to.

Sophie

My breath caught in my chest. "Someone else saw Bernie threaten Tate?"

"Worse. Mrs. Grabowski lives in the house that backs up to the alley right behind our garage. She went out to *A Midsummer Night's Dream* but came home before the fireworks. According to her, she was in bed watching TV after the fireworks when she heard our garage door open. She got out of bed, peered out the window, and saw Bernie unlock the side door of the garage. He opened the garage door, started the car and drove away, leaving the garage door open."

I couldn't imagine worse news for Bernie unless Mrs. Grabowski had claimed to see him in the act of killing Tate. "Oh, Mars! Do you think he really went somewhere that night?" As soon as the words slipped out, I shouted, "No!" Lowering my voice, I said, "He has an alibi for that period of time. He was at The Laughing Hound. There has to be someone who can confirm that."

"Let's hope they back him up and that the cops don't think Mrs. Grabowski had the time wrong."

"Was the garage door open when you came home?" I asked.

"I have no idea. I didn't walk along that side of the property. I went in through the front door," said Mars.

We had crossed King Street and were getting close to Antonio's house. "Look for a white house with a navy-blue door." I was so distressed about Mars's news that I could barely focus. "Mrs. Grabowski is certain that it was Bernie? It was dark. How could she know for sure that it was him?"

"I had the same thought. Around nine tonight, I'm going outside to see just how much light is back there."

"Did you ask her if she saw him? Maybe you planted the notion in her head."

"Sophie! I'm not that stupid. She saw me looking at the garage doors when she was putting her trash out in the alley. She said, 'You boys were sure out late last night. Did I miss a big party?'"

"So I asked her if she saw us come in."

"And then she told me what she did last night and that she was in bed when Bernie drove out. Is this the house we're looking for?"

I gazed up and down the street. "It's the only one that fits the description." I banged the door knocker that was shaped like a sailboat.

A handsome young man with dark hair and engaging brown eyes opened the door.

"Hi, I'm Sophie Winston, and this is Mars. We're looking for Antonio Hirsch?"

His eyes swept over us. He wasn't very tall, but I bet women chased him all the time because he was darling. "How can I help you?"

My mouth dropped open. He definitely was not the server I'd had at Blackwell's Tavern. That Antonio Hirsch was older, taller, and had a slightly receding hairline. "You're Antonio Hirsch?"

"Yes."

By now Mars was staring at me like I had lost my mind.

"You are not the Antonio Hirsch who served my party at Blackwell's Tavern on Tuesday morning."

He smiled. "That would be correct because Tuesday was my day off."

"Are there two Antonio Hirsches?" I asked doubtfully.

"What's this about? Did you lose something?" he asked.

"We wanted to talk with you about Mr. Bodoin and whether anyone might have wanted to do him harm."

He nodded. "Come on in."

We walked into a combination living and dining room that looked more like a man cave. Weights and workout equipment occupied a space where a crystal chandelier hung from the ceiling.

Mars whistled at the television. "Wow! Nice setup!"

It was huge, and two only slightly smaller TVs hung over top of it. Speakers were mounted on the walls and a sprawling leather sofa in the shape of an enormous C took up way too much space.

"Excuse me," he said. He yelled up the stairs, "Jonah! Could you come down here?"

Jonah loped noisily down the stairs. He stopped abruptly at the sight of us. Pointing at me, he said, "I know you from somewhere."

"And I know you as Antonio Hirsch," I said. He was definitely the man who had served us at Blackwell's Tavern on Tuesday.

The real Antonio glared at him.

Jonah sighed. "Man, I couldn't find my name tag and you weren't working, so I borrowed yours. No biggie. You know how Marsha hates it when we don't wear a name tag."

Antonio crossed his arms over his chest. He looked at Mars and me. "This is what I put up with."

"We're looking into Mr. Bodoin's murder," I said quickly, "and I hoped you might be able to shed some light on what was going on at Blackwell's Tavern."

Antonio relaxed visibly and gestured to the sofa, "Have a seat. How can we help you?"

"Was anyone upset with Mr. Bodoin?"

Antonio shook his head. "Not that I know of. He was a great guy. We've been wondering why anyone would have killed him."

I looked over at Jonah, who said, "I agree. There might be some people who would like to see Marsha dead. But Bodoin was great. We have a little restaurant league competition each season. Softball, basketball, bowling. He always came to our games and kidded around with us."

"Was Bernie Frei at those games?" asked Mars.

"Oh sure," Antonio said cheerily. "Another great fellow."

"Did you ever hear Bernie threaten Bodoin?" I asked.

"Threaten?" asked Jonah. "They were friends, joking around with each other."

"They usually made a bet, with the loser donating money

to some local charity," said Antonio. "Is it true that they arrested Bernie?"

"Unfortunately," said Mars. "That's why we're here. Bernie is a friend of ours. We're trying to figure out who else might have had it in for Tate Bodoin."

Antonio and Jonah looked at each other blankly.

"Any chance he was having an affair?" asked Mars.

"Not that I know about," said Antonio.

Jonah shrugged.

"Is there a young woman working at Blackwell's Tavern who is in college or high school and has a summer job there?" I asked, thinking of the letter I had found in my purse.

Jonah frowned. "Blackwell's is open seven days a week from lunch until midnight. There's a pretty big crew of servers, but that doesn't ring any bells for me."

"Me either," said Antonio. With a sly smile, he added, "I usually notice the ladies." He blushed. "My sisters get mad at me when I say things like that. Don't get me wrong. I totally respect women. What I mean is that I probably would have noticed her."

I suspected he would have. It was a disappointing meeting, though. I had hoped they might have pointed a finger at someone who had a beef with Tate Bodoin.

We thanked them, gave them my card, and left.

"That was a major bust," I said to Mars as we walked home.

"Are you kidding? They confirmed something really important."

"That the woman who wrote the letter doesn't work at Blackwell's Tavern?"

"That, too. But more importantly, Marsha was lying about Bernie threatening Tate. Bernie already told us that he didn't, and those two guys were clearly involved in the sports rivalry between the two restaurants. They never heard threats, just good fun."

I stopped in my tracks. "You're right. Marsha is the one who pointed the police in Bernie's direction to begin with. Do you think she could be the one who smeared blood on his car door?"

Mars groaned. "I'd like to know where *she* was that night after the restaurant closed."

We resumed walking. "It's not like we can ask her. I think Nina and I upset her. Besides, I don't think I would trust what she said. No, we have to go around her somehow."

"There's no point spinning our wheels that way," said Mars. "She'll only say that she went straight home to bed, which is something that none of us can prove unless she had company, which I doubt."

We arrived at my house at the same time as Humphrey stepped out of his car. He jogged toward us.

"I bring news," he said.

I unlocked the door and Daisy, refreshed from her nap, sprang out and danced around the three of us in greeting. We walked into the kitchen, where Mochie stretched and yawned as though we had wakened him from his nap.

"Iced tea?" I asked.

Mars and Humphrey chimed, "Please!" while patting Daisy and Mochie.

When I brought the tall icy glasses to the table, Mars held out his hand to Humphrey. "Do you have your phone on you?" he asked.

Humphrey handed over his mobile phone and Mars promptly turned it off, asking, "Sophie, have you bought anything that can listen to our conversation? A smart appliance or gadget?"

"Not yet," I said. "What's going on? Why do you think someone is listening?"

"We can't be too careful. Bernie is in a precarious situa-tion. The last thing we need is someone hearing our discussions and using them against him. Frankly, it might be wiser to chat out in your yard."

Bernie and I exchanged a look. It was getting very warm outside.

"I don't have any smart gadgets, Mars," I protested.

"All right. Speak softly."

We sat down at the banquette in my kitchen and Humphrey said, "According to my source, the medical examiner has shifted the time of Tate's murder to be between nine in the evening and one in the morning. But I don't know why."

"That matches what we thought," said Mars.

"His last meal was crab, shrimp, and flounder, white wine, spinach puree, rice, cheese, and"—he looked me in the eyes—"chocolate mousse."

"Wow, that guy ate well," said Mars.

"I would have to check, but crab, shrimp, and flounder together don't sound like anything on the menu at Blackwell's Tavern," I said. "I suppose he could have eaten a crab appetizer, a shrimp appetizer, and then had flounder as a main course, but I think he ate dinner somewhere else. That would be consistent with Marsha's claim that he left Blackwell's and didn't return."

"They have all those seafood items except for flounder at The Laughing Hound, and I don't think the crab and shrimp are together in one dish," said Mars. "I know their menu very well."

"Good job, Humphrey. Thanks!"

Humphrey smiled at us. "If you happen to see me dining out with a tall redhead, I'd rather you didn't mention it. I had to cajole the information out of my source by bribing her with a nice dinner."

"A girlfriend, Humphrey?" asked Mars.

"I wouldn't go quite that far yet. And she would never get my mother's approval." Humphrey smiled at us.

"Oh, come on, Humphrey," I said. "No woman will ever be good enough for you as far as she's concerned."

He considered for a moment. "Maybe Kate Middleton, but she'd just squeak by."

Mars tapped his fingers on the table. "What about the mousse?"

"Lots of places serve that," I said. "What are you getting at?"

"What if he returned home and ate mousse as a midnight snack?"

"Are you suggesting that Bobbie Sue murdered him?" I asked.

Chapter 16

Dear Natasha,
My aunt is coming to visit and asked if I know of a
restaurant that serves fish paupiette. What on earth is
that? She can't just eat a nice grouper?
                    Perplexed Niece in Fisher Island, Florida

Dear Perplexed Niece,
A paupiette is basically a roulade. A piece of meat or
fish is wrapped around other meat or fish and then
cooked. While grouper is delicious, imagine it wrapped
around shrimp!

                                            Natasha

Mars tilted his head. "Don't the police usually try to eliminate the spouse first? There's a reason for that."

"She said she'd been up all night," I mused. "And she called me instead of the police when she couldn't find Tate."

Mars and Humphrey raised their eyebrows.

"No, I think that's unlikely," I protested. My voice grew softer as I said, "She was here just this morning to pay me, relieved that the police had arrested Bernie."

"Sophie, listen to yourself. If Bobbie Sue murdered her own husband, then she would be thrilled that the police thought it was someone else. She might even be the one who framed him. She's at the top of my list," said Mars. "At least for now. We don't have any other suspects, except for Marsha."

I sat back in my chair. "I don't know, Mars. I like Bobbie Sue. And she talks about her husband so tenderly. I think she truly loved him. Besides, almost no one is going to have an alibi from midnight to one in the morning."

"Unless that person is married," said Humphrey.

"I'm not sure one can always believe the testimony of a sleeping spouse," Mars pointed out.

He was right, of course. "An awake spouse isn't always a reliable alibi, either," I said.

On that note, the two of them left, and I returned to work in my home office.

That evening, Nina and I set out to find the restaurant where Tate might have eaten his last meal, in the hope that it would lead us to someone who might have been with him that night. Nina took one side of King Street and I took the other. There were plenty of restaurants elsewhere in Old Town and beyond in Alexandria, but chances were good that he had remained local. We couldn't dismiss the possibility that Tate had gone to someone's home for dinner, either. But King Street was the most likely place he had eaten his last meal. If nothing else, we could eliminate it.

We examined menus and stepped inside restaurants to ask what the special was on Midsummer Night. By the time we reached the river, we'd had no luck at all.

"Everyone serves shrimp," said Nina. "I've given up asking about that. But almost no one has flounder. It's all salmon, salmon, salmon."

"Flounder is out of vogue," I said. "Salmon has been the trendy fish for years."

Nina pulled out her phone. "Bernie, hi! Listen, I'm looking for a place that serves flounder."

She pressed the speaker button and held out her phone so I could listen in. Bernie's voice came through loud and clear.

"Flounder? Good luck with that. You might find it at one of the restaurants near the river that specialize in seafood. How about Chilean sea bass? It's much more flavorful, but very pricy. I'm fairly certain that sea bass is sometimes on the menu at Auguste's over on Lee Street, near Queen. It's very exclusive, though. You have to make a reservation months in advance. If you go there, tell Auguste I sent you. That might help. One other thing. It's not marked. Look for the turquoise door with a lion on it."

Nina thanked him and ended the call. "Well, now we *have* to go there! Exclusive? It must be if I've never heard mention of it." She eyed my casual outfit. "Think we need to dress up?"

"If it's that exclusive, they won't let us in without a reservation. We don't have to eat there. We just need to see what's on the menu."

Nina grumbled a little but readily walked toward Queen Street with me. We found the turquoise door easily. The only sign of the restaurant was an Egyptian symbol of a lion on the door knocker. I had walked by dozens of times without realizing it was a restaurant.

Nina tried the door handle. It opened easily to a tasteful corridor with high ceilings and extravagant moldings. The hallway seemed dangerously long, and I began to have qualms about our little adventure, but just as I was thinking about turning back, we emerged into a small but elegantly appointed room. Classical music played softly, and the murmur of hushed voices was apparent, although no diners were visible.

A gentleman approached us. "Good evening. Do you have a reservation?"

"I'm afraid not," said Nina. "We just heard about your wonderful restaurant. Bernie Frei sent us."

I almost laughed when Nina said that. It seemed so sinister, like we were doing something illegal. Entering a speakeasy or an illicit gambling joint.

"You are very lucky. We had a cancellation this evening. Please follow me."

We trailed along behind him. The servers were all dressed alike in black trousers, white shirts, and black vests. They passed us carrying trays of food that smelled divine.

But none of the diners were visible. The restaurant had been cleverly divided into private alcoves. It was the perfect place for secret meetings.

He seated us at a small table and handed us menus along with a wine list.

"Wow," whispered Nina. "This is the place to come if you're having an affair! Almost no one would see who you were with."

I focused on my menu, which was a simple, good quality, eight by six-inch piece of white paper with five options on it.

Tomahawk Rib Eye for Two
Served with truffle mashed potatoes and roasted
asparagus.
Duck Confit
Served with French lentils in a red wine sauce, and
spinach puree.
Grilled Lobster Tails
Served with drawn butter, haricot verts, and our own
Asiago cheese biscuits.
Vegetarian Wild Mushroom Stroganoff
Served with Asiago cheese biscuits and Caesar salad.
Vegan Pasta e Fagioli with Roasted Vegetables
Served with fried plantains.

Nina flipped her menu around and looked at the blank backside. "That's it? I mean, it's some fancy stuff, but I'm used to more variety."

It was an interesting venture. I had been to restaurants with only two items on the menu that never changed. But they did them so well that they were extremely popular. "I'm game for duck confit."

Nina sighed. "Lobster tails for me. So much for flounder, shrimp, or crab. They don't even have any rice listed. Wherever Tate ate his last meal, it sure wasn't here."

The server came to take our order.

"This is such an interesting menu," I said. "How often does it change?"

"Daily. We source only the freshest and most exquisite ingredients for our guests."

That sounded like a line they were taught to say. Who spoke that way?

"Do you ever have flounder?" asked Nina.

"Not in the time that I have been here."

"Did you work on Midsummer Night?" I asked.

Our server now looked at me curiously. "Yes, I did. Is there a problem?"

Oh boy. I was going to have to come up with a reason for wanting to know what was on the menu that night—and fast! "Our friend dined here and recommended the fish entrée."

He smiled at me. "Ah, that was our Chilean Sea Bass Paupiette."

Nina frowned at him. "What's a paupiette?"

"The Chilean sea bass is wrapped around a filling of shrimp and crab. It is one of my favorites."

I took a chance. "Served with rice?"

"It was served with creamy risotto and spinach, madam."

Almost, I thought. Could the pathologist have confused Chilean sea bass with flounder? "Thank you," I said. "I believe one of my friends had dinner here that night. Tate Bodoin?"

"Word of mouth is our best advertisement." The server smiled and left.

"He obviously didn't recognize Tate's name," said Nina. "But I can see a medical examiner mistaking the kind of fish. It all looks alike."

Said like someone who didn't cook, although if I were in a contest and had to identify ten different kinds of fish, I wouldn't fare well. Plus, a medical examiner would be looking at cooked and eaten fish. It would likely have lost any distinctive appearance. I smiled at her and muttered, "Maybe you're right."

At that moment a petite man arrived. His sharp brown eyes took us in. "Ah, Sophie Winston and Nina Reid Norwood. I was told you would make your way here. Which is which?"

Nina blushed, obviously flattered. "You've heard of us? I'm Nina."

"Nina, my dear, your reputation precedes you."

Oh no! I knew what that reputation was.

He spoke with a slight accent that I couldn't quite place. "Then you must be the lovely Sophie. It is a pleasure to have you dining in my establishment."

He lowered his voice. "You are here because of Tate Bodoin. No?"

"To be honest," I said, "Mr.—" I drew a blank. Had he told us his name?

"Auguste Beausoleil." He bowed his head. "Please call me Auguste. I am very fond of American informality. May I?" He gestured toward an empty chair.

"Of course, Auguste." Beausoleil had to be a French name. Is that a French accent I detect?" I asked.

"You have a good ear, Sophie. My mother is Egyptian, and my father is French. My love of good food comes from both sides. How can I help you with the tragic death of Tate Bodoin?"

I was slightly taken aback by his eagerness to help. I couldn't tell whether he was a closet sleuth or had some ulterior interest in Tate's demise. "Are we correct that Tate ate dinner here on Midsummer Night?"

"He did. I have wondered if I should go to the police with this information."

Once again, I wasn't sure what to think. Why wouldn't he have volunteered that information to Wolf immediately upon hearing of Tate's murder? "Why didn't you do that?"

"You have surely noticed that my restaurant is the ultimate in discretion. We keep the secrets of our patrons. You understand that it is a delicate matter. Tate was a fine man, and I am broken by his death. When I opened my restaurant, I never imagined such a terrible thing could happen. It all seemed very clear to me. We would be most discreet, and our diners could rely on us for that. Washington, DC, is a political hotbed. There is a specific clientele who wish to dine together without making the morning news. Not only American politicians but also people from the embassies and those who visit from around the world to make deals. But now I have to think, what if our roles were reversed and someone had killed me? Would I not want my friends to seek the killer? To obtain justice for me? To help me in death? It is the final gesture of friendship. The police should know. But I will not reveal the information to his wife. It is not my place to do so. You understand."

I understood all right. His wife had spent most of the evening with me in a different restaurant.

"He was here with other people," said Nina.

"One other person, to be exact."

Chapter 17

Dear Natasha,
You are always exquisitely dressed on your show and in pictures. Alas, I must attend a memorial service. I have a suitable black dress, but now that little black dresses are worn everywhere, it looks very cocktail party instead of somber.

> *Sad, Not Jolly in Deadwood, South Dakota*

Dear Sad, Not Jolly,
The trick lies in your accessories. Wear light or medium brown shoes and belt, and carry a matching brown purse. No large stones in your jewelry or festive scarves. And, of course, the most important thing is a black hat with a veil.

> *Natasha*

"Who was he with?" I asked.

Auguste eyed us. "I don't know her name, but she was remarkably beautiful in the way an artist would paint a goddess. Just flawed enough to show her real beauty. She was tall, with a dark complexion, large intelligent eyes, a somewhat flat nose, and luscious lips. The kind made for kissing," he said dreamily.

My eyes met Nina's. This was not great news for Bobbie Sue.

"You have no idea who she is?" I asked.

"None. Tate paid the check, so I do not have her name, and of course, we do not ask such questions. This is our policy. Many important people, ones with the power to change our world, come here for privacy. We respect that." He sucked in air and sighed. "But had I known then that Tate would be dead the next morning, I might have made an inquiry. There is nothing I can do to change that now. Hindsight often begets regrets."

"She doesn't sound familiar to me. How about you, Nina?" I asked.

Our server arrived with our dinners, beautifully arranged on pristine white plates with a gold Egyptian lion figure at the top of each plate.

"This is the same lion that's on your door knocker," I observed.

He smiled. "The lion is a protector, a guard. It has been a personal favorite since I was a child. I bid you *bon appétit*, ladies."

"Just a moment, Auguste." I pulled a business card out of my purse and wrote Wolf's name and number on the back of it. I handed it to Auguste. "Wolf Fleishman is a police detective and a friend. You can trust him to be discreet. He needs to know about the woman Tate was with that night. And I was wondering, what time did they leave the restaurant?"

He shrugged. "I am not sure. I don't keep a record of such things."

A thought came to me. "You said Tate paid for their dinner. Did he use a credit card? Wouldn't the time be on the transaction?"

"Indeed, it would. I shall check on that now." Auguste clutched my card and bowed to us before leaving.

Nina took a bite of her truffle mashed potatoes and moaned. "This is amazing. No wonder he only has a few dishes on his menu."

My duck confit was outstanding. The meat practically melted in my mouth.

"I can't imagine who that woman was," said Nina. "I don't think we would forget anyone that striking."

I had to agree.

Auguste joined us when we had finished our Pear Helene, a heavenly poached pear on top of ice cream with a drizzle of chocolate sauce. It was the perfect light ending to our delicious dinner.

He took a seat and said in a soft voice, "We processed Tate's credit card at seven minutes past nine that night. I presume they departed shortly thereafter."

"I don't suppose they gave any indication of where they might have planned to go?" I asked.

Auguste's eyes became small slits as he thought. "I said goodnight to them and thanked them for coming." He shook his head. "I don't know where they went or what they had planned."

That night I phoned Wolf and got his voicemail. *Hi Wolf. It's Sophie. I have some information you need to know in regard to Tate. Give me a call when you have a minute.*

As we expected, the turnout for Tate's memorial service was enormous. The historic church in which it was held was packed. Even the balconies that ran the length of the nave on each side were full. It probably wasn't much comfort to Bobbie Sue, but Tate had clearly been a beloved man.

Nina, Mars, and I had taken seats in a rear pew where we could get a good look at everyone who came in. Wolf slid into the pew next to Mars.

I leaned over Mars's thighs and whispered, "Checking to see who comes?"

Wolf sighed. "Where's Bernie?"

"Under the circumstances," said Mars, "he thought it best to stay away. Bobbie Sue and the family deserve a proper service without the mayhem his presence might cause."

Wolf nodded.

I leaned over Mars again. "If you're so sure Bernie murdered Tate, then why are you here?"

The one thing that had always frustrated me about Wolf was his poker face. I guessed it to be enormously helpful in his line of work, but I hated that I couldn't read his emotions.

"Just doing my job," he said.

I sat back and tried to hide my grin. After all, it was a memorial service. I didn't want to appear happy or smug. But I took great comfort in the fact that Wolf had doubts about Bernie being the killer.

Francie waved at me as she pushed Estelle Fogelbaum's wheelchair. They stopped at the outside edge of a pew, where the wheelchair wouldn't be in the way. Each of them wore a small-brimmed hat, making me wonder what it was about funerals that brought out hats.

Bobbie Sue and her children processed in, followed by her ex-husband, the Coach, and two men whom I didn't know but who bore a striking resemblance to Tate. Perhaps the brothers Bobbie Sue had mentioned.

And then, just seconds before the service began, a woman entered the church like she owned the place. I would have known her anywhere. She wore a tailored black dress with a belt and three-quarter-length sleeves with the cuffs turned back. Two silver or white gold bracelets hung on one wrist. She had pulled her hair back into a chignon and wore a small black hat. The veil couldn't hide her large eyes and full lips. She was tall, too, over six feet I guessed.

Nina elbowed me.

Natasha, who was seated in front of us, turned to me and mouthed, "Who is that?"

I shrugged. I wanted to know, too, because she was undoubtedly the woman Tate had dinner with hours before his death.

I watched the woman take a seat and kept an eye on her throughout the service in case she planned to slip out early to avoid the family. But she stayed for the whole thing.

The family processed to the vestibule, where Bobbie Sue and the two men who looked like Tate stood in a receiving line. The double doors were open, and outside, I could see Bobbie Sue's ex-husband, Pierce, holding Jo's hand and leading her to a car. Spencer walked behind them, his head bowed.

I lingered in what I hoped was an unobtrusive way, waiting for the stunning woman to exit. Maybe Bobbie Sue knew her and would call her by name.

She walked up to Bobbie Sue, shook her hand, and said, "Your husband was a very fine man."

Bobbie Sue's eyes narrowed, giving away her concern. "How did you know Tate?"

The woman didn't appear put out. She responded calmly, "From the restaurant. I am so terribly sorry for your loss." And then she walked away.

That didn't tell me a thing, but Bobbie Sue's expression sure did. She did *not* know that woman. Bobbie Sue watched her leave, a perplexed look on her face.

Bobbie Sue couldn't dash after her, but I could. And Nina was right behind me. We caught up to her just as she approached a silver Honda and the automatic fob, probably located in the black Ralph Lauren satchel she carried, unlocked the door with a soft thwack.

"Hi!" I said breathlessly, holding out my hand. "I'm Sophie Winston and this is Nina Reid Norwood. It's so tragic about Tate."

She eyed me warily. "Yes, it is." She opened her car door. Trying to be chatty, and at a loss for something more clever to get her talking, I burbled, "The restaurant won't be the same without him."

Her large eyes narrowed with suspicion. "It certainly won't."

She was stepping into her car when Nina blurted, "I didn't catch your name?"

"I didn't tell you my name," she said coolly.

"We're looking into the circumstances of Tate's death," I said. "We know you were with him a few hours before he died."

Chapter 18

Dear Sophie,
I am planning a service for my grandfather. Everyone in the family wants it done differently. Memorial service or funeral or both? A wake or reception afterward? There are too many options! What is one supposed to do?
                    Devoted Granddaughter in Wake Forest, North
                                                       Carolina

Dear Devoted Granddaughter,
Families are spread apart these days, and not everyone can be present immediately after the death. People are choosing to do what works best for them, from lavish receptions to private services and interment. Some memorial services are put off for six months to a year, depending on when the family members can come.
                                                        Sophie

The woman nailed me with a stern stare. "I'd like to see your badges, please."

Nina screeched, "We don't have any badges!"

I couldn't believe my ears. I turned and shot her a look of disbelief.

The woman said, "I thought as much." She pulled her door closed and drove away.

"I cannot believe you said that."

"It's not like we could lie about it. What was I supposed to do? Tell her that by total coincidence we both left our badges at home? Badges!" Nina sputtered. "Who does she think she is?"

"Well, that was a big bomb," I said.

"We should ask Bernie who she is," said Nina. "He knows everyone."

"Sophie! Nina!" Bobbie Sue ran along the sidewalk toward us. In a hushed voice she hissed, "Who was that woman?"

Just as I feared. "You don't recognize her?"

"I'm pretty sure I'd remember someone like her. I looked through the guestbook, but I didn't find any names I didn't recognize." Her gaze moved back and forth between Nina and me. Her mouth tightened. "Was he . . . were they?"

"We don't know," I said quickly. I wondered if we should be the ones to break the news that he had spent his last night on earth with that gorgeous woman instead of his wife. It seemed too hurtful. How would Bobbie Sue feel if she knew he had skipped her party and their daughter's performance to be with this other woman whom no one knew?

Bobbie Sue's brows rose. "What did she say to you?"

"She wanted to see our badges! In all the years we've been doing this, I can't remember anyone else asking that," Nina whined.

"Why did you want to talk with her?" asked Bobbie Sue.

"Because she—"

Nina broke off quickly when I kicked her with the side of my foot. It wasn't hard, just enough to get her attention.

"Ow! Sophie!" she protested.

"Because she was seen with Tate," I said.

Bobbie Sue's eyebrows shot up. "I see. Doing what?"

Someone called Bobbie Sue's name. "I'm so tired," she said. "I can't think clearly. Thank heaven I hired a caterer. What a horrible day. The only bright side is that I can't bury Tate yet, so we can skip the graveyard part. I hope you're coming to the house."

She looked defeated. The woman who had been micromanaging everything had been drained.

"If you find out who she is, would you let me know?"

I nodded, unsure whether I would want to tell her. If Tate had been having an affair, would Bobbie Sue feel better or worse? In the end, I decided it wasn't my decision to make.

Bobbie Sue hurried off to a black limousine that waited for her.

"We should probably go over to her house to be helpful," said Nina.

"You just want to nose around and eavesdrop."

"Well, it's not like Bernie can go."

Nina had a point. I looked around for Mars, but everyone had cleared out. "Okay. Who knows what kind of information we might pick up."

Bobbie Sue's house hummed with people. They had spilled out onto the small front lawn, where they stood around in small groups, talking quietly. Inside wasn't any better. People clustered everywhere. A young woman with a tray of tiny tea sandwiches stopped in front of us. "There's a buffet in the dining room. Deviled ham sandwich?"

Nina picked one up and took a napkin. "Thank you. Where would I find drinks?"

"There's iced tea, water, white wine, and coffee in the dining room." She lowered her voice to a whisper. "But rumor has it that Mr. Bodoin's brother is serving harder stuff in the family room."

"Thank you, darlin'!" Nina abandoned me in search of the *harder stuff*, whatever that was. Probably bourbon or Scotch. I moseyed through the crowd and picked up a glass of iced tea in the dining room, trying to listen to the conversations going on around me.

I studied the room while I listened. Butter-yellow walls matched the background color of upholstered chairs around the table. The fabric was a blue toile print that looked mostly Grecian to me. The drapes matched the blue of the toile precisely. A collection of blue and white china ginger jars and urns decorated a long Hepplewhite-style sideboard. A butter-yellow tablecloth covered the table. Blue and white china vases ran down the middle, overflowing with yellow lilies, red roses, and purple gladioli. A sparkling chandelier added soft lighting.

Three women discussed the merits of the ham biscuits at various eateries in Old Town. Next to them, two gentlemen helped themselves to cheesy potato casserole, sausage and grits casserole, and fried chicken. They spoke quietly. I had to strain to hear them over the women, who hadn't budged from the platter of ham biscuits.

"I just don't see it," said the balding one with a pronounced Southern accent. "I know Bernie. He's not the sort of fellow who would do something like that. Besides, what was in it for him? He didn't stand to gain anything. No, I think they've got the wrong man."

The other one, who wore wire-rimmed glasses, replied, "I totally agree that Bernie is a nice guy. I have no beef with him. But there's more to life than money. Did it occur to you that Bernie did have something to gain through Tate's death?"

His gaze finally left the food and swung straight over to Bobbie Sue, who was fully visible chatting with someone in the foyer.

His friend followed his gaze. "Oh! You don't say? I never

imagined *that*, not even for a moment. Really? Bernie and Bobbie Sue?"

"Well, that's what they're saying. She's a looker, for sure. Wouldn't surprise me if she conned him into it and will claim there was nothing between them. Women have their ways of manipulating men."

I was horrified. Bernie didn't date much, that was certain. But a married woman? I didn't think so. His mother had replaced husbands more often than most people changed cars. Having suffered the repercussions of his mother's merry divorcée behavior, I didn't think he would engage in an affair with a married woman. Then again, anything could happen in life. Sometimes we revised our views. Had Bobbie Sue been the reason Bernie didn't date much?

Natasha strode toward me. Her black dress had little cap sleeves and clung to her figure. What I noticed most, though, was a chunky gold necklace, medium brown shoes, and matching purse. As usual, she made me feel shabby even though I'd thought my V-necked little black dress and black shoes looked quite fine at home when I had dressed.

"What a turnout," she said, picking up a glass of white wine. "But I don't see that woman."

"I haven't seen her, either."

"I wanted to thank you and Nina for your advice the other day. I have decided to put my energy into something new and modern. Something no one else with a big brand has launched yet. I'm starting a line of baked goods with CBD in them."

I was so stunned that I took a step back to steady myself. "CBD, like pot only it's from hemp?"

"Isn't that brilliant? It's the next big thing, and I will be the first to be on top of it."

"Aren't there CBD products out there already?" I asked.

"Not in high-concept cookies and cakes. Imagine eating a scone with CBD in it. Isn't that perfect? I will elevate CBD to tea-party-worthy delicacies."

I was speechless.

But Natasha wasn't. She smiled broadly. "And I met someone. I'm telling you, my luck changed the moment I left that horrid diner!"

"A man?" I asked.

"*The* man. The most perfect man you have ever seen."

I thought I might have heard that from her before.

"He makes Mars look like a country bumpkin."

"How did you meet Mr. Perfect?"

"I can tell you're saying that sarcastically, but you just wait until you meet him. He's tall, built like a runner, with thick, lush, black hair that has just a tinge of gleaming silver along the sideburns. Oh, Sophie! He's just dreamy. I was looking for a storefront for my business and he had one for rent and there was just an instant attraction. Did I tell you my brand name? What do you think of this? Natasha's CB-Delicious." She pronounced it *C B Deelicious*. "I think I might use a bee in my branding. Wouldn't that be adorable?"

"It would." I was happy for her. She had been so dejected and in the blink of an eye, everything had turned around.

Natasha gazed at Bobbie Sue. "I can't say I'm surprised about Bernie, though. I never did like him."

That wasn't news to me. Bernie didn't buy into Natasha's demands and wasn't keen on her haughty manner. The dislike was mutual.

"I knew he would come to no good. I just hope he doesn't drag Mars down with him." Natasha eyed the food on the table. "Good thing I'm not hungry." She gasped. "Oh . . . my . . . word! Do you see what I see?"

I had no idea what she was talking about.

"Jan Figueroa let her hair grow out gray. It's ghastly. Excuse me, Sophie, I need to go drop a hint or two."

"Natasha!" I protested. "You'll hurt her feelings."

"Nonsense. She needs to know. She clearly has no idea

how terrible it looks on her. If her friends don't tell her, who will?" Natasha scooted off in her haste to offend Jan.

I left the dining room and wandered into the kitchen, where I found myself smack in the middle of an argument. I tried to edge out of the room, but Jo grabbed my hand.

"Tell them to stop," she said with tears in her eyes.

My heart went out to her.

"Spencer would like to get away from all this and go for a run," said Coach. "I told him that was fine."

A flush had risen up Pierce's face. "Lower your voice, please. I do not want to upset Bobbie Sue, nor do I want to argue in front of all these people. In case you have forgotten, *I* have not died, and I am still Spencer's father." He looked his son in the eyes. "No one wants to be here. I certainly don't. But there are things in life that one must do and this is one of them. Tate was very good to you. The least you can do for him is stay here to show your respect. And if you can't bring yourself to do that, then at least behave and be here for your mother and your sister, who are very much alive and need you right now."

Well said, Pierce. I was glad it wasn't up to me. Jo still held my hand. I smiled at her and said, "Now that that's over, why don't you show me Oinky?"

She wiped her face and walked slowly through the kitchen to the family room. I followed her but glanced back. Spencer had capitulated and listened to his father.

Unfortunately, Oinky was in the room where hard liquor was being served, which meant it was crowded with men and women wearing dark suits. Most held lowball glasses, though a few carried brandy snifters. The mood was somber, with most people speaking in hushed tones. It probably wasn't the best place for Jo.

I was wrong. As soon as she entered the room, she became the center of attention. When I was her age, I would have grabbed Oinky and made a mad dash for the door. But Jo moved through the room like her mother would have, greeting each person by name. When she didn't know someone, she would ask their name and invariably respond with a very mature, "I have heard my father mention you." She was a little Bobbie Sue. She didn't need me or Oinky to distract her.

A woman I didn't know approached me. "Excuse me. Are you Sophie Winston?"

"Yes, I am." What had I done now?

"Aaaaah," she screeched. "They told me you would be here. Can I give you a hug?"

Before I could answer, she embraced me. When she let go, she said, "I never dreamed I would meet you. I tell everyone that you have the solutions to all of my problems. Why, when you wrote about hypoallergenic flowers, you changed my life. I planted roses and you wouldn't believe how gorgeous they are. It transformed the front of my house. Everyone raves about them."

She got my attention with *you have the solutions to all my problems*. Who was this woman? "I'm sorry, I don't believe I know your name."

She shrieked again. "Oh my gosh, you're so nice. I'm your biggest fan, Belinda Bodoin. I'm married to Tate's younger brother. Tate was a middle child, you know. There were three boys. That must have been wild for their mom."

I could see Natasha listening and sneaking up behind her.

"But they all grew up to be wonderful men, even though their parents struggled financially. Tate always cooked for us when we had family reunions—"

Natasha wedged beside me and interrupted. "Hi. I'm Natasha."

Belinda nodded at her. "Nice to meet you. Tate was our anchor. Always the voice of reason. Such a calm and even-tempered man. We all loved him so much. I can't imagine how Bobbie Sue and the children will manage without him.

And I cannot believe that anyone would want to murder him. They tell me that you investigate murders. I hope you're doing that for us. Whoever did this must be caught."

"We'll do our best," said Natasha.

I turned and shot her my best look of disbelief.

"Do you need any help?" asked Belinda. "My husband and I live over in Maryland but it's not that far away."

Natasha brightly asked, "Do you read my column?"

Belinda blinked rapidly. "I'm sorry. Who are you again?"

"Natasha."

"Natasha who?"

Oh boy. We were headed for an encounter of the ugly kind.

"Belinda, would you please excuse us? I believe we're needed in the kitchen. It was so lovely meeting you."

I grasped Natasha's bony arm and tugged her into the kitchen.

She sputtered, "I must find out where that woman lives. Do you suppose they don't carry my column in the local paper there?"

"I'm sure that's it."

"I'll have to get the name of her newspaper." She started to return to the den, so I said, a little too loud, "Oh look! The mayor is here!"

Natasha did an immediate one-hundred-and-eighty-degree turn and disappeared in the crowd. I hadn't seen the mayor, but while she searched for him, maybe she would forget about Belinda.

Through the window, I spied Spencer in the backyard, sitting on a bench, his head sagging forward. I stepped outside and skirted a few other people who gathered in small groups.

"May I?" I pointed to the bench.

Spencer glanced at me. "Yeah, sure."

"I understand you're a terrific runner."

"I'm okay."

"Are you thinking about college yet?"

"A little. I'd like to go to William and Mary. That's where my dad went."

Dad was a complicated word in his life. I wondered if he meant Tate or Pierce.

"I wish I had told him that," he said. "I wish he had known how much he meant to me."

Aha. Tate was the graduate of William & Mary. I spoke softly. "I'm sure he knew."

Spencer swallowed hard. "I doubt it. We had a big blowout the day before he died."

"Spencer!" called Bobbie Sue. She hurried toward us, deftly avoiding the people who tried to snag her for a chat. "How are you doing, sweetheart?"

He looked up at his mother with a *you have to be kidding me* expression.

"It will be over soon. In an hour or so, most of these people will go home and we'll get back to normal."

Spencer stared at his mother. "Nothing will ever be normal again."

Chapter 19

Dear Natasha,
My husband bought cookies made with CBD and al-
lowed our children to eat them! CBD! He thinks I'm
making a big stink over nothing. Can you eat CBD?
A divorce is riding on your answer.
                    Furious Mom in Pot Spring, Maryland

Dear Furious Mom,
Baking with CBD is the latest craze! Relax. CBD is
derived from hemp and is non-psychoactive.
                                        Natasha

Bobbie Sue pressed her hands against the sides of her face. "Oh, Spencer. Please don't say that. Indulge me and allow me to believe that it will."

She held out her hand to him. "Do me a huge favor and come with me to say hello to Cal Simmons." Bobbie Sue bent toward us. "He always says something highly suggestive and inappropriate to me, but I'm willing to bet he won't do it in front of my son."

Spencer reluctantly got to his feet and walked away with his mother.

I returned to the house and flagged down Nina. "Ready to go?"

She nodded. "The fried chicken was superb. But they could have done a better job with the desserts. Serving Bobbie Sue's cheesecakes would have been a good idea."

We walked to the foyer and just as we reached the front door, I noticed Marsha watching us. She gave me a look so cold that I actually shivered.

I wondered why. She barely knew me. Was it because of my association with Bernie? Or was something else going on with her?

Nina chattered as we strolled toward the center of town. We entered The Laughing Hound and stopped short. It was packed. A line of people waited to be seated. Nina and I slipped past them and into the dining room. It was too early for dinner, yet every table was occupied. Bernie walked around, stopping to chat with people. I could hear them expressing their support for him.

Bernie spotted us and discreetly motioned toward his office with his head. The restaurant occupied a building that had once been a grand townhouse. Bernie had arranged dining areas in various locations, making them more private and special. The conservatory with windows all around and the outdoor patio were my personal favorites. As we walked up the stairs, I noted how easy it would be for anyone to enter the restaurant and take the stairs up to Bernie's office without being noticed. Even if that person happened to be seen, there were special rooms on the second floor for business luncheons, not to mention additional restrooms. No one would give a second thought to anyone climbing the stairs.

At the top, I stopped for a moment. It was quiet. The soft murmur from the dining room below seemed far away. Not a soul was around. I heard peals of laughter coming from one of the private rooms on the same floor as Bernie's office.

"What's wrong with you?" asked Nina.

"I was just thinking how easy it would have been for the killer to come up here and steal Bernie's keys."

Nina swirled around. "No kidding!" She hurried to Bernie's office.

I followed at a good clip. The door was open.

Nina slipped behind the desk and pulled out the two top drawers. She rummaged in them. "No keys!"

Bernie's voice came from the doorway. "Aha! Caught you!"

Nina held up her palms in mock dismay. "Where are you keeping your keys?"

"I now place them in the safe. It saddens me to do that. There was something special about tossing them into the desk drawer. Such an ordinary thing. But I've lost that sense of security."

"It took only one person to do that." I reached out and gave him a little one-armed sideways hug. "I'm sorry, Bernie."

He wrapped an arm around my shoulders. "I'll get over it. Did you come for lunch?" His arm dropped off my shoulder as he turned to face me.

Nina groaned. "I don't say this often, but I'm stuffed. We just came from Bobbie Sue's house. Tate's memorial service was today."

Bernie nodded. "I heard about that. Wish I could have gone."

"A very attractive woman showed up," I said, "but no one knows who she is, not even Bobbie Sue. Very tall, probably over six feet. Dark complexioned, with big eyes and full lips. Quite striking."

Bernie's brow wrinkled. "Doesn't ring any bells with me."

"Rats!" Nina scowled at him. "I thought you knew *everyone*."

Bernie chuckled at her. "I probably don't remember half the people I have met over the years."

"No matter, we just thought we'd check with you."

Nina nodded. "Keep an eye out for her. Okay?"

Bernie cocked his head. "Did I miss something? You think she's a suspect in Tate's murder just because she showed up at the service for him? I want to find the person who killed Tate more than anyone. But suspecting that woman just because you and Bobbie Sue don't know her seems unfair."

I chose my words carefully. "She was seen with him the night he died. We think she may know something that could lead us to his murderer."

Nina added, "There's also the possibility that she and Tate were having an affair."

Bernie frowned.

"Well, you know how that goes," Nina added. "Jealousy rears its ugly head when a romantic partner decides not to leave his spouse."

Bernie appeared pained. I reached for his hand and squeezed it. "The restaurant is packed. It looks like you're getting a lot of support."

"That's true. I never expected an outpouring of friendship like this. It seems as though everyone has a theory."

"Really?" I snatched my hand back and grabbed a pen and notepad off his desk. "Like what?"

"Nothing to get excited over. Mostly they think Marsha killed Tate. Apparently, she didn't hide her devotion to him. It would have been easy for her to take a bottle of champagne, lure him somewhere, and then bash him over the head with it."

"Do you know if she was dating someone else?" I asked. "I have a witness who saw her smooching with some guy in an alley."

Bernie's eyebrows arched. "No kidding? Like everyone

else, I thought she was busy mooning over Tate. I can ask around."

"Who else have they mentioned?" asked Nina.

Bernie shifted uncomfortably. "A lot of them think it was Bobbie Sue. Tate was a little older than her, and people let their imaginations run wild. They suggest that she's getting back together with her first husband, she found a new lover, or that she doesn't need Tate's money anymore now that she's expanding her cheesecake empire. There's no truth to any of it. As Mars would say, it's all speculation."

"Bernie," I said softly, "have you thought of anyone who might want to frame you? Someone who wants you out of the way? Someone who could be angry with you? Even if it's for some unintentional slight? Did you give someone a bad reference? Fire someone?"

"Sophie, I try to be fair to everyone. I've worked most of the jobs people have in this restaurant. I know what it's like to count my pennies and wonder if I'll make enough to pay the rent. There are undoubtedly people in this world who don't like me for one reason or another." He grinned when he said, "And I have thrown countless drunks out of this place. But I don't know what I have done to anyone to make them so angry that they would frame me for murder."

Bernie's face had flushed red. "I feel so helpless. How can I fight a faceless enemy?"

It was a good question. I wished I had answers. Nina and I assured him we were doing our best and headed home.

In spite of Bernie's issues, I was enjoying the long summer days. Walking Daisy around sunset was a treat. The warm air felt comforting on my bare arms, one of the true joys of summertime. As we walked, I thought about Marsha, who seemed to have a grudge of some kind against Bernie. What if she was seeing someone who was jealous of Tate? She wouldn't have been the first person to talk too much and far too adoringly about someone at work. Liddy, whom I had no reason to doubt, had mentioned seeing Marsha near the turquoise bench, so I steered Daisy in that direction. The sun would be setting soon but I could still get a feel for that alley.

We found the bench easily. A brick fence ran along the side of the house. The bench was barely visible through an ornate iron gate, surrounded by pink geraniums in clay pots. I paused for a moment to enjoy the vignette before entering the alley. It was wide enough for a garbage truck and worked well as a shortcut for those familiar with the area. Otherwise, it served mostly as easy entry to garages and a convenient spot for trash collection. I paused before the entrance, noting that there weren't any streetlights so it would be dark when the sun had set. But if Marsha and friend had been kissing fairly close to where I stood, they would have been visible. Enough to be identifiable at any rate.

We ambled along. The homes that backed up to it on both sides were impressive. Stunning gates opened onto the alley, most of them were solid wood so that the gardens behind them were obscured. My own gate was like that. Everyone wanted privacy and I didn't blame them.

I sighed. I had hoped for a clue about the person Marsha had been with that night. Maybe Francie or Nina knew someone who lived in this neighborhood and could fill us in.

Leafy tree limbs peeked over some of the brick garden walls and an occasional urn full of daisies or impatiens brightened the alley. Daisy tugged me to the right. I stopped to let her sniff something of interest. When I coaxed her to walk on, she stood her ground and continued sniffing.

I looked over her shoulders to see what was there. Probably garbage that fell out of the truck, I thought. Or maybe a piece of food that some bird had scavenged and dropped. Daylight had turned to dusk, making it harder to see small details. I asked Siri to turn on the light in my phone and flashed it on the area that interested Daisy.

A fat shard of broken glass gleamed as the light caught it. But that wasn't what fascinated Daisy. Just beyond it, near a gate, something had smeared. Her tongue darted out and I stopped her just in time. It looked like—no, it couldn't be. I dabbed it with the tip of my forefinger. The little brownish chunk was creamy. I smelled it. No question about it, among dark dried drips of something were bits of chocolate cheesecake. They vanished under the gate.

I shone my light at the crack under the gate. The spots could be anything, I thought. A cola that had spilled. The remnants of a bottle of wine that had tipped over. But cheesecake? Had someone dropped a chocolate cheesecake? Moving slowly, I lifted the latch on the gate. It made only the tiniest sound as metal scraped metal.

The owners of the house probably wouldn't like me peering into their yard. I opened the gate only enough to see the house. The windows were black as pitch. If anyone was home, they were asleep or sitting in the dark. I focused my light on the ground. A similar dark stain had smeared on the brick patio that stretched to the gate. Ants had formed an orderly line to consume the bits of cheesecake. It appeared to be on the ground near bushes as well, where more tiny bits of glass glimmered under my light.

My heart beat faster. As much as I wanted to believe that someone had dropped chocolate cheesecake and spilled red wine, I knew the red parts were blood.

Chapter 20

Dear Sophie,
Is it true that people can hear you through your phone and watch you through the camera?
I Have Secrets in Hideout, Utah

Dear I Have Secrets,
This isn't really in my area of expertise, but I'm told that people can listen to you through the microphone in your phone and that it is possible to spy on a person through the camera in their phone. You can turn the microphone off, which would be advisable if you want to keep those secrets!
Sophie

If Tate had been murdered there, someone had bothered to clean up, but hadn't done a great job of it. I phoned Wolf.

"This better be good. It's my first night off in days."

"Have you figured out where Tate was killed?"

Wolf groaned. With reluctance in his tone, he said, "No. Where are you?"

I explained how to locate the alley.

"Let me be clear. You're trespassing if you go inside that gate."

"I don't think anyone is home."

"It's still trespass."

"Wolf! I didn't actually enter the yard. I'm worried that it could be a crime scene. There are shards of glass. Cheesecake and something that could be dried blood is smeared on the bricks." I supposed it could be dried cherry topping, too, but I wondered if it would dry as dark. And wouldn't it be more gooey?

He was silent for so long that I was on the verge of asking if he was still there. "Ten minutes. Get out of there and close the gate." The call disconnected.

I had no problem following his instructions. I closed the gate as quietly as I had opened it. I studied the location of the house. Unless my count was wrong—after all, it was fully dark now—the house was the fourth one down from the cross street. Daisy and I retraced our steps, walked by the house with the turquoise bench, and found the street on which the houses fronted. Counting as we walked, I thought the house in question was a three-story Federal style red brick house with dormer windows on the third floor. I didn't have a purse with me so I made a note of the address on my phone.

As I watched, a light turned on in the house somewhere on the first floor. Minutes later, one turned on upstairs on the second floor. Someone was home after all. It was a good thing I wasn't snooping in the backyard.

Daisy and I walked along the sidewalk to the next cross street block and entered the alley from the other end. We arrived at the gate just as a car pulled in. Between the dark and the headlights, I couldn't make out the model of the car. It drove toward us and parked. When the headlights switched off, it seemed all the darker in the alley.

"Hi Sophie. Which gate is it?"

I was relieved to hear Wolf's voice. I caught up to him as my eyes adjusted to the lack of light. It had been a long time since I had seen him in jeans and a golf shirt. He carried a flashlight that looked big enough to be used as a weapon.

"Let's see what you found, Soph." Wolf reached out to scratch behind Daisy's ears.

I led him over to the first chunk of glass Daisy had sniffed. He examined it without touching it. "The rest is inside the gate?"

"There's a little bit of cheesecake right there under the gate and more inside. While we were waiting for you, we walked around front and a couple of lights came on in the house, so I guess someone came home."

Wolf rubbed his chin.

"What's the problem?"

"I need to get their consent to enter. You're sure you saw something that looked like blood?"

"Wolf! It could be something else, but it sure looked like dried blood." I opened the gate.

"Sophie!" But in spite of his protest, he shone his flashlight inside the fence. "I think you might be right. Thanks, Sophie. Go on home and I'll take care of this." He patted Daisy. "Good sleuthing, Daisy!"

He never said that to me!

"Did you get the address?" he asked.

I read the address to him. "We'll hang around for a little bit if you don't mind."

"Listen, Soph, I don't know who lives here. When I knock on the door, the person inside may bolt out of that garage and barrel down the alley to get away." Wolf pulled out his phone and asked for backup and information on the homeowner. He started to walk toward the cross street, but he stopped and looked back. "He could come out shooting, Sophie. You have to leave. You never know how someone will react."

Daisy and I tagged along a good distance behind. Meanwhile, I phoned my own best source of information—Nina. I described the house and gave her the street address. She promised to call back as soon as she had information.

I knew Wolf was right. Daisy and I should leave, and yet we hung around and watched Wolf from the other side of the street. We were three houses down, peering out from behind a good-sized tree. I wanted to see what happened and felt safe enough from that vantage point.

He waited for two squad cars to arrive. After filling the officers in, Wolf walked up to the door and banged the knocker. The same two lights were on that I had seen before. No changes there.

No one answered the door. He tried again.

My phone vibrated. I answered it in a whisper. "Nina?"

"Yes. It's the Eklunds' house. They're in Sweden."

"Are you certain? I see lights on in the house."

"They're probably on timers. They wanted the children to experience a Swedish midsummer celebration."

"They must have come home," I said.

"I'm on my way." Nina disconnected the call.

In the shadows of the streetlights, a man approached me on the sidewalk. "Sophie! Good to see you. Hey, do you know what's going on out here?"

It was none other than Auguste Beausoleil, the owner of the restaurant where Nina and I had dined. "Hi, Auguste. Your night off?"

"Yes, it is. My wife got worried when the police cars arrived. Do you know what's going on here?"

I wasn't sure how much I should reveal. "Do you live on this street?"

He pointed down the street. "We live across from the Eklunds."

"Do you know them?"

"Of course. The Eklunds are very nice. They have two active teenagers. Their son is friends with my boy. Is something wrong? They're away. Should I phone them? My son has been feeding their cats every day."

"You're certain they're not home?"

"Yes. Absolutely. Elsa's parents live in Sweden. They took the children to visit."

"But I saw lights go on. Is someone housesitting?"

He smiled. "If there were, my son wouldn't be taking care of their cats. The lights are on timers. Obviously, they work. They fooled you."

I took Auguste across the street and introduced him to Wolf. Auguste repeated what he had told me.

Wolf grinned at him. "You wouldn't happen to have a phone number for the Eklunds?"

Half an hour later, the Eklunds had been awakened in Sweden and informed that the Alexandria police wanted to go into their backyard. Not only did they give their permission but they asked Auguste to unlock the house with the key given to his son so the police could ensure that no one was hiding inside.

Auguste promptly fetched the key. Wolf insisted we remain outside. While we waited, poor Daisy was so bored that she lay down. The police returned in minutes, claiming the house was secure. Auguste made a call to let the Eklunds know everything was fine so far.

When Wolf hopped into one of the squad cars, we hurried around to the alley. By the time Auguste, Daisy, and I arrived, the gate was open and strong lights shone on the brick patio. Nina ran up, panting. "What's happening?"

I filled her in.

Wolf called for crime scene specialists to come and take samples of the material that looked like blood. We overheard one of the officers say, "It almost looks like someone was dragged along here."

There was another wait. But shortly after the CSIs arrived, we heard a shout.

They were still working when Auguste, Nina, and I gave up. The police would be toiling into the wee hours of the morning. Poor Daisy was bushed. The initial excitement had worn off and it was nearly midnight, so I was beat, too.

In the morning I let Daisy out, turned on the news, and scanned the newspaper. There was no mention of the discovery at the Eklunds'. I guessed that made sense. The media probably hadn't heard about it. But I was curious. I tried to imagine what had gone on. Had Tate's killer invited him to meet there? It almost seemed that way. Who had brought cheesecake and why?

I heard Muppet barking before I saw Nina at my kitchen door in an oversized T-shirt and shorts. No sooner had I opened the door than Mars and Bernie sprinted across the street in similar garb. I didn't feel quite so bad about being in my bathrobe, because the guys hadn't shaved, and Nina wore no makeup. Mars held a package of bacon.

"Is that a bribe?" I teased.

"I didn't know if you had any."

Bernie waved his hand. "Forget the bacon. What happened last night?"

"Ah," murmured Nina, "the Old Town grapevine must be sizzling this morning."

Mars turned on the stove. "Eggs or pancakes?"

Nina sounded like she was ordering in a restaurant. "Cheese and mushroom omelets with toast and strawberry butter."

I put the kettle on for tea and coffee and retrieved all the necessary ingredients from the refrigerator. I washed the mushrooms and started slicing them while Bernie cracked eggs into a bowl.

"Is it true that they found the spot where Tate was murdered?" he asked.

He seemed calm and matter-of-fact. But he must have been churning with worry inside or he and Mars wouldn't have rushed over first thing this morning.

Nina measured coffee into the French press and explained about the Eklunds being in Sweden. Mars set the table with Villeroy & Boch's Spring Awakening breakfast plates, my newest acquisition. They were round but had scalloped edges with a sunny yellow band around them from which sprang delicate daffodils and tulips. He set the matching mugs on the island for Nina to fill.

Bernie whisked and flipped omelets, while I filled them with sautéed mushrooms and Havarti cheese. Our chatter came to a halt as we settled at the table with our food.

"Mmm. Delicious," Nina declared.

"It's the garlic powder," said Bernie. "It's subtle, but that hint of flavor makes the difference." He looked at me. "Did I understand correctly that you found cheesecake?"

"The police lab will have to confirm it, but it felt like cheesecake and smelled like it, too."

"Cheesecake has a scent?" asked Mars.

"A little bit," said Nina. "Mostly from the vanilla, I think."

"What am I missing here?" asked Mars. "Which one brought the cheesecake? Tate or his killer?"

"Do you suppose," said Bernie, "that his murder had something to do with cheesecake? An argument about stealing Bobbie's Sue's recipe maybe?"

Mars blinked at him. "And one of them brought a piece to prove it?" He began to laugh, and it was contagious. In a moment, all four of us were laughing about the notion of a murder over a piece of cheesecake.

Nina wiped laughter tears off her eyes. "I will grant you that it sounds improbable and stupid. However, maybe we're on to something. Champagne and cheesecake? That sounds like something friends would do."

"Or lovers," said Bernie.

Chapter 21

Dear Sophie,
My mom wrote to a person called Natasha, who said it was okay for us to eat CBD cookies. But I heard on the news that some places have been raided because of CBD. Mom is still really upset with our dad. What do you think?
Confused Kid in Hempfield Township, Pennsylvania

Dear Confused Kid,
You are not the only one who is confused. At the moment, some states, but not all, permit baking with CBD. What you might have heard about is that CBD has not yet been approved as a food additive by the federal government. Some companies are using CBD in ways that violate federal law. Suggest that mom bake other cookies and maybe they won't argue about it.
Sophie

The idea of lovers sobered us up.

"There's no way to know, but it would stand to reason

that Tate brought the cheesecake," I said. "He had easy access to it at home and at the restaurant."

"Wait a minute," said Mars. "I'm sure they didn't plan to meet in someone else's backyard. I can't imagine saying, 'I'll bring the champagne. Let's meet in the Eklunds' backyard because they're out of town.' Who does that?"

"Someone who's married and doesn't want to be seen." Nina slathered her toast with strawberry butter and bit into it.

"Aw, come on," Mars protested. "Fifteen-year-olds think someone being out of town is an opportunity to get away with something, not mature adults. If they wanted privacy, there are dozens of Airbnb's they could have rented for the night."

"The tall woman he was with!" I gasped. "I don't know why I assumed they went their separate ways after dinner."

"What woman?" asked Mars.

I glanced at Bernie. "You didn't tell him?"

"Not yet. I haven't had a chance."

I started to fill in Mars about Auguste and his restaurant, but he interrupted me.

"I've been there with clients several times. Auguste seems like a decent fellow. Are you saying you think they had an amazing dinner and then they took a bottle of champagne and some cheesecake and had a tête-à-tête in the Eklunds' backyard? I don't think so. That doesn't make any sense for adults."

Nina choked on her coffee. "She was tall enough to conk him over the head with a bottle, that's for sure."

Mars was on a roll. "And then she moved Tate's body to his restaurant? Why? Why not leave the body where it was? If they knew the Eklunds weren't home, it would have been wiser to have left Tate in their backyard. It could have been a week or more before anyone noticed the body. Did she think she would fool the police into believing it was an accident in the basement of the restaurant?"

"That sounds more like Marsha," Bernie said. "And she would have had a key to the restaurant."

"If Tate had his keys on him, then anyone would have had access to the restaurant," I pointed out.

Nina's eyes grew large and round. "What if Marsha took a dinner break? What if someone at Auguste's, or a friend who saw them go there, phoned her and told her Tate was having dinner with another woman? Marsha could have left the restaurant. Her office is upstairs, no one would have noticed she was gone. She waited for Tate and his girlfriend to leave Auguste's. He and the girlfriend went in different directions. Marsha followed Tate, confronted him, and bashed him over the head with the champagne bottle."

It wasn't entirely out of the question. "There could very well be a gap of an hour or so that Marsha wasn't missed," I said.

Mars groaned. "And then she went to steal Bernie's key and use his car?"

I grew cold as I considered the amount of planning that the murderer must have gone through. I shook my head. "This wasn't a crime that happened in the heat of the moment. The killer had figured out where Bernie's car was parked and where he kept his car keys. Someone bothered to plan this well in advance."

"It could still have been Marsha," Nina said. "One of the cops last night said that it looked like something had been dragged. I bet she hid the body in the Eklunds' backyard, went back to work, and moved him with Bernie's car after she had closed the restaurant."

"That is entirely possible," I said. "She would have known that the camera wasn't working at the back door of the restaurant."

"First of all," said Mars, "she wouldn't have been able to carry him into the restaurant or down the stairs. Unless she's Wonder Woman, I can't see her doing that. Tate wasn't very tall, but he was a bit portly. If she dragged him from the car into the restaurant, there would be a trail of blood. Secondly, she would have been splattered with blood. There's no way the person who killed Tate didn't have blood all over his clothes."

"She could have had help. An accomplice," suggested Nina.

"Then why take Bernie's car?" asked Mars.

"You're beginning to make Marsha sound like a mob boss, ordering someone else to murder him while she looks on," I said.

Bernie sat quietly. He stared out the bay window.

Nina snapped her fingers at him. "Earth to Bernie!"

When he turned his focus back to us, he smiled sadly. "I love you guys. Don't know what I would do without you." He checked his watch. "Better get going."

Bernie took off, but Mars stayed behind to help with the dishes.

"I'm worried about him," said Mars, while washing dishes. "He's more troubled by this than he lets on. Both of us were raised when boys were supposed to buck up and have a stiff upper lip."

Nina dried dishes while I put away leftovers. "Do you know how he really got that kink in his nose? Does . . . does he have a police record?"

Mars stopped washing. "He was just a kid. I can't recall which husband it was, four or five, maybe. Apparently one of his mom's worst choices. Bernie woke up one night and heard things crashing. He slipped out of his room and found his new stepfather beating up his mom. She was on the floor and the guy was throttling her. Bernie jumped on the man's back, which gave his mom the opportunity to roll away, grab a phone, and call the police. That husband must have been a brute, because he shook off Bernie and punched him in the face, breaking his nose."

I almost dropped the bowl I was holding. "I can't believe he never told us that. How awful!"

"Poor Bernie," said Nina. "He lived in castles and manor houses growing up. It all sounds so enchanting, like a fairy tale. But in reality, he had a rough childhood, didn't he?"

Mars finished and dried his hands. "His mother is quite the character. He loves her dearly, but there was a great deal of upheaval in his life before he came here. Several doctors have told him they could probably fix his nose with plastic surgery, but he's not interested. I keep joking with him about attracting more women with a straighter nose, but he just laughs at me. I think the kink in his nose is like a badge of courage to him. Not that he likes it, but he's come to terms with it, like a war wound that is part of him and doesn't let him forget." Mars dried his hands and headed for the door. "I'm off to work, too. Hey, don't let on that I told you the real story. Bernie would be very upset with me."

Mars left and Nina soon followed.

After a shower, I dressed for the warm weather in a crisp sleeveless blouse and knee-length twill skirt. A cup of coffee in hand, I settled at the desk in my home office and worked for a few hours, scheduling events and sending out contracts.

Every time my computer dinged to let me know an email had arrived, I gave a start and glanced to see if it was from Worried in Old Town. So far, she had not responded.

But I had a text from Humphrey. **Sorry to be the one to share bad tidings, Sophie. Per the office of the medical examiner, the blood on Bernie's car matches Tate's.** He added a frowny face.

I supposed that news wasn't really unexpected, but it was still a blow. It seemed like a new bit of evidence arrived every day that chipped away at Bernie's defense. Distracted from my work, I went to the kitchen to make myself a cup of tea. While the kettle heated, I stood in front of my kitchen sink and gazed out the window.

It was such an easy case to make now. Scientifically, Tate was linked to Bernie's car. Did they check for other DNA or fingerprints on the car? Mine should have been there. What about Daisy's fur? She surely left a hair or two in the back.

The kettle whistled, breaking me out of my thoughts. I poured the steaming liquid over a tea bag and watched the water turn color.

I mixed in sugar and milk. There was no point in fretting about what the police had or had not done. The person who had taken Bernie's car had thought this through. He or she knew the car would be searched if someone saw it behind the restaurant or got the license plate or passed a camera in transit. We weren't dealing with a goofball. The killer had planned everything very carefully. And it was all working out to his advantage. So far, anyway.

I reminded myself that there was no perfect crime. Something always went wrong. I just had to find it.

I sipped my tea. Marsha, Marsha, Marsha. She was all we had. Everything kept coming back to her. We had figured out how she could have done it. She even had a reason. She wouldn't be the first person to have murdered someone out of jealousy or promises of a life together that weren't kept.

Daisy jumped up and ran to the door. A second later, I heard a gentle rap.

Francie waved at me.

I opened the door for her. She walked in with her golden retriever, Duke.

"I'm on my way to see Estelle Fogelbaum. I thought you might like to walk Daisy and come with me."

"It's not too hot for the dogs?" I was worried about the dogs, but even more worried about Francie.

"It's lovely outdoors, not bad at all."

I grabbed my purse and dressed Daisy in her halter. I locked the door behind us, and we were off. "I saw you pushing her wheelchair at Tate's service."

Francie nodded. "She can't get around like she used to."

"That must be hard on her."

"She's making the best of it. She always was a bit of a homebody anyway. Back when our husbands were alive, we used to go dancing together. Those were the days! Nobody took a phone with them everywhere. When you went somewhere, you were there, not thinking about other things. And the band music was so grand. Did you know that Estelle was an ornithologist?"

"I had no idea." I knew Estelle, but not well. She had attended a number of wildlife and animal rescue events that I had arranged.

Francie stopped at a door with a woodpecker door knocker. But instead of knocking, she rang a regular doorbell three times in a row. "That's my signal, so she'll know it's me." A lock clicked and Francie pushed the door open.

The foyer wasn't very big, but I soon realized why. Francie led me along a corridor, turned left, and opened a white door. We stepped into an elevator. Daisy and Duke went along, surprisingly calm about it.

We emerged on the third floor into one huge room. On the opposite end was a giant balcony visible through a glass wall that curved back until it met the ceiling.

Estelle rolled her wheelchair toward us. "Who is this with Duke?"

Daisy ran to her as though some instinct told her Estelle was a dog lover. Daisy's tail swished and she laid her head on Estelle's lap.

We walked past a yellow tabby with half an ear and a battle-scarred face. He opened one eye but didn't run from the dogs.

"This is Daisy," I said. I gazed outside. She had an amazing collection of bird feeders. I wondered how she kept it clean.

"I miss having a dog!" Estelle patted Daisy and Duke at the same time. "It's just not practical for me anymore because they have to be taken out."

"Cats are lovely, too," I said.

"Hah! I always thought cats would scare away the birds, but old Tiger doesn't care one whit about them. Nina Reid Norwood brought him to me. That rascal! She knew I couldn't turn down a beat-up old alley cat."

"He's living in the lap of luxury today," said Francie, smiling at him.

"He's a delightful companion for me. Almost as immobile and grumpy as me. We understand each other."

I wandered over to the window. "This is amazing. It's like you're in Paris with a view of the rooftops."

"There isn't a season when it's not marvelous," she said. As she rolled close, one of the doors automatically opened for her.

The three of us walked out onto the balcony, and with a start I realized that I was looking down at the alley where Tate had been killed.

Chapter 22

Dear Natasha,
My mother-in-law loves watching birds. Everyone gives her bird feeders because they make her happy. Can I tell you what her deck looks like? I have to sweep hulls and birdseed every single time I go to see her. It's disgusting. How can she keep it clean?
       Not a Bird Lover in Ravenswood, West Virginia

Dear Not a Bird Lover,
This is a two-step process. It must be undertaken gradually so she will not notice. First, eliminate a bird feeder each time you visit. Simply remove it when she's not looking. The second step is to move the remaining two birdfeeders away from the house and into the yard where the debris won't be a nuisance.

                                                    Natasha

I swirled around to Estelle. "Can you see the alley in the dark?"

"Only if there are headlights."

"Did you see anything on Midsummer Night?"

"The night Tate was murdered," she muttered. "Honey, I wish I had. My son and daughter-in-law took me to dinner, and to see the play. Then we watched the fireworks from the park. After I came home, I didn't even venture up here. I went to bed on the second floor. My bedroom looks out over the street on the other side, so I didn't hear anything, either. I saw when all the police cars arrived yesterday, though. That was interesting to watch."

My balloon of hope deflated. "I bet it was."

"I'm simply devastated by Tate's death. He was a wonderful man. I will truly miss him."

"It sounds like you knew Tate quite well."

"We went way back. Even before he met Bobbie Sue. Before he was a successful restaurateur. Back when he was married to his first wife. Now, that woman was a shrew. Nothing was good enough for her. She pushed and pushed. Bigger house, fancier car, more clothes. She was pretty, I'll give her that. I never told Tate, but I was relieved when she left him for another man. He was better off without her. Tate deserved someone who would appreciate him. My husband and I were delighted when he told us about Bobbie Sue." She stopped speaking for a moment. "I can't believe someone murdered him. And almost at my back door."

"Can you believe her view?" asked Francie.

Estelle smiled like an elf with a secret. "I see things from here. People don't know I'm watching." She nodded her head.

"Why, Estelle," I teased, "don't tell me you spy on people?"

She grinned and nodded her head at binoculars. "Those are so I can watch the birds." Estelle threw her head back and laughed.

I had no idea she was such a rascal.

"What do you know about the Eklunds?" I asked.

"They're a very nice family. Their kids are older now, high

school age. They're remarkably well-behaved, especially in contrast to the Wheeler family two doors down. Those children are noisy! Mrs. Eklund likes to have a glass of wine outside in the yard after work in the summer. Her husband usually joins her."

"Wow. You're quite a font of knowledge."

"It's not like I'm snooping, you know. I can't help what I happen to see from here."

If that aided her in keeping a clear conscience, I wasn't about to disabuse her of that notion.

"You know Tate's son, Spencer?" she asked. "He's quite fond of the Eklund girl. They're away at the moment, but I've caught the two of them engaged in more than one smooch."

I stared at the Eklunds' backyard. Spencer. He said he'd had a blowout—was that what he had called it?—the day before Tate was murdered. He hadn't even really crossed into my lineup of suspects. If he was dating the Eklunds' daughter, then Spencer knew the Eklunds were away. He was large enough to attack his stepfather. What had they argued about? I hadn't considered where he was that night. Bobbie Sue said he would be running in the 5K race. Had he? Where was he before that?

I was so deep in thought that I hadn't noticed Francie and Estelle bickering quietly about something.

"Tell her! You like Bernie, don't you?" asked Francie.

"Oh, Francie, it makes no difference whatsoever. And I adore Bernie. No matter what I order, he always brings me a little bit of bangers and mash because he knows how much I love them. They take me back to the days when I lived in England. He has good ones, too. Not everyone has good bangers."

I took a deep breath, still reeling about the possibility that Spencer had murdered his stepfather.

Francie nudged Estelle.

"Oh, for goodness' sake." Estelle looked up at me. "I don't really like to gossip. Most of what I see stays right here. They're like my own private reality shows. I don't need TV to amuse me. There must be hundreds of fascinating stories going on at any time, right here in Old Town. It's the nature of humans, isn't it?"

"Estelle," grumbled Francie, "we officially forgive you for gossiping. Now tell her already!"

Estelle pointed across the alley. "See the house next to the Eklunds'? The one on the right?"

I nodded my head to encourage her.

"That's the Milburns' house. He's a pilot and she's an environmental protection specialist for the Federal Aviation Administration, so the two of them are away a lot. They fixed up the basement apartment and rented it to Eli Dawson. You know him?"

I racked my brain to place the name. I met so many people through my event planning business. Not to mention the people to whom I was never introduced but saw in passing at charitable events. We smiled or nodded a greeting, but I had no idea who they were. "I don't think so."

"He probably runs in different circles than you do. Your friend Bernie probably knows him. Eli moved here from Houston about thirty years back when he was a young buck. He's worked as a bartender at Blackwell's Tavern for about five years now. The Milburns give him a discount on his rent in exchange for Eli keeping an eye on their place when they're gone."

As soon as she said Blackwell's Tavern, my ears perked up. One of Tate's employees lived next to the spot where he had been killed? "What do you know about this Eli?"

Estelle smiled at me. "Well, you might be interested in knowing that he's two-timing Marsha Bathurst!"

Now she had my full attention. I hardly knew where to start. "You know Marsha?"

"Oh sure. I met her when we took a class on making Victorian-style Christmas ornaments. You should try it. I put up two trees, one out here for birds, and another inside that's one hundred percent Victorian."

"It's gorgeous," said Francie.

I nodded, unable to focus on Victorian décor when all I wanted to think about was Eli and Marsha. "What does Eli look like? Could Tate have been mistaken for Eli?"

"I wouldn't think so. Tate wasn't a very big man. Eli is husky. Not portly, you understand, more broad-shouldered than Tate."

"Who's he two-timing her with?" asked Francie with a tinge too much glee in her voice.

"Have you met Bernie's new assistant manager at The Laughing Hound?" asked Estelle.

I drew in a sharp breath. "Eva Rosales?"

"That's the one. Younger and much prettier than Marsha, if you ask me."

Staring most impolitely at Estelle, I asked, "How do you know all this?"

"I eat out quite a bit and I favor The Laughing Hound and Blackwell's. I cooked in my younger years, but it doesn't hold much interest for me anymore. And, of course, I have the best seat in the house for *that* soap opera." She gestured toward the alley. "I'm an early bird. Sometimes I'm up here with a cup of java before the sun rises. I see who's coming and going." She smiled gleefully. "But they don't see me. Funny thing, really. They never ever look up. I suppose they're so intent on where they're going and not getting caught that they never consider who might be watching up above. They only look around to see who is at street level. I feel like a bird, watching life happen from the safety of a high branch."

"Do you suppose the two women know about each other?" asked Francie.

"I have no way of knowing *that*," said Estelle. "But all it takes is a phone or a lipstick left behind and Eli's love life will implode."

"Estelle, do you have a theory on who might have murdered Tate?" I asked.

She shook her head. "It wasn't his time. He had so much to live for. Tate knew his way along this alley quite well. He always came to my back door instead of the front. He joked that it was so he wouldn't run into my other suitors at the front door!" Estelle smiled sadly at the memory. "He used to bring me cheesecake. Just every now and then as a treat. I hope they catch his killer and nail him." She shook her forefinger at me. "And you better make sure Bernie gets exonerated."

I kneeled by her wheelchair and asked softly, "Who would want to frame Bernie?"

"Now there's a good question. Marsha comes to mind."

"Do you have any idea why Marsha would dislike Bernie so much?" I asked, even though I knew what Bernie claimed. Maybe there was another reason, too.

She broke into a smile. "Oh, honey, that one is easy. Bernie is the upstart who came along and gave Tate a run for his money. There were other restaurants, but nothing like Bernie's place."

I thanked her, said goodbye to both of them, and walked Daisy toward the stairs near the elevator.

As I started down the steps, I heard Estelle say, "I'm going to miss that man. He worked so hard to make something of himself and now to end like this. At the hands of another. It's a tragedy."

When we reached the main floor, we stepped into a Victorian room. It felt huge, probably due to the creamy walls and high ceiling. The chairs were modern in shape and covered in a pale blue velvet with just a touch of green in it, an ocean shade. Fringes hung around the bottoms for a bit of Victorian style. The square coffee table was covered in tufted cream that matched the walls. A large chandelier hung in the middle of the room, which dressed it up even more.

I pressed a button by the back door. It buzzed, unlocking the door, and the two of us left. A concrete walkway led to a large patio in Estelle's backyard. It had been beautifully arranged with wheelchair-accessible raised garden beds. The concrete path wound around them in circles. Estelle had adorned the backyard with bird feeders of all kinds and too many garden ornaments, but I bet every one of them brought her joy. No wonder Tate liked coming through the back way.

She probably had a security system. I gazed around for a camera and spotted one. It was aimed at the back door of the house, which was appropriate, but it wouldn't have picked up what happened out in the alley.

Daisy and I exited through the gate and I took care to latch it behind me. We crossed the alley and looked at the spot where I had seen glass shards. They were gone. It had been thoroughly cleaned. Turning, I looked up at Estelle's balcony. Three flights up, she and Francie were small figures waving at me. No wonder no one noticed Estelle when they walked through the alley. I waved back.

So, this was where Liddy, the waitress, had seen Marsha kissing someone. Given the location, it was most likely Eli she had been embracing. Not Tate.

Had Marsha and Eli taken different routes from Blackwell's Tavern after work and met in the alley? We started to walk home.

Why so secretive? Both of them were single. Was it Eli who needed to hide his relationship with Marsha because of Eva?

Or was it because Marsha was still in love with Tate and didn't want him to know that she was seeing Eli?"

I was still thinking about them when I rounded a corner and passed by the alley in back of The Laughing Hound. I glanced toward the back deck. In shock, I came to a complete halt. Bernie had lied to me.

Chapter 23

Dear Sophie,
I'm working with a limited budget and trying to make my bedroom look Victorian. What items do you think would have the most impact? I can't afford a four-poster bed.

    In Love with Victoriana in London, Ohio

Dear In Love with Victoriana,
Go for a palette of shades instead of contrasting colors. Paint always brings the most immediate results for the money. Use a calm shade on the walls. It doesn't have to be dark. An eye-catching chandelier doesn't have to bust your budget. Prowl secondhand shops and be ready to gild an old one with gold paint. Check clearance sales and eBay for lush curtains. Remember to mount them at ceiling height, not right above the window. And with your last dollars buy a few velvet pillows for your bed.

        Sophie

On the other side of the Dumpster, where they couldn't be seen by anyone who stepped out of the back door of The Laughing Hound but where they were in full view by me, Bernie was deep in conversation with the tall woman who'd had dinner with Tate the night he died. The very one who showed up at his memorial service but none of us had known who she was.

Daisy pulled toward Bernie, eager to see our friend. I tightened my grip on her leash.

Bernie knew Daisy well. She would give our presence away. Fortunately, they were so engaged in their discussion that I thought they hadn't seen me. I instinctively backed up, out of their line of view, coaxing Daisy along because Bernie would recognize her immediately. My heart pounded and I could feel the flush of shock rushing into my cheeks. I had trusted Bernie. Of all the people in the world that I knew I could rely on, he was in the top ten, along with most of my family, Nina, and Mars. How could this be? I felt like he had punched me in the gut.

Hugging the rough brick wall of the building behind me, I felt like a spy as I slowly rotated and leaned my head out just enough to peer into the alley behind the restaurant again. They were still there, looking serious and unhappy. I squinted. Could I read their lips? Hear what they were saying? No. Nothing.

The woman abruptly got into her car and drove toward me! I whirled around, seeking a refuge where I wouldn't be seen. If we ran across the street in any direction, she would surely notice us. We doubled back and entered the first door we came to. I pushed it open with my back while watching the street.

The glass door closed. Looking out, I fumbled in my purse for sunglasses and slid them on without taking my eyes off the street. Her car turned left, away from us.

"No dogs! Get, get, get!" an angry voice shouted.

I whirled around to find Natasha behind me. She literally pushed me out the door onto the sidewalk. I half expected her to say, *And take your little dog with you.* But she surprised me. "Good grief. What *are* you wearing?"

I looked down at my blouse and twill skirt. There was nothing wrong with them. No spills I hadn't noticed.

"Honestly, Sophie. Anyone could drive by and see me with you. How embarrassing."

I was still reeling from Bernie's betrayal. Natasha's words weren't clicking with me.

"Sophie," she said in a chiding tone. "A skirt and a blouse do not an outfit make. I'm telling you this as your best friend. You look like you're going to take a bunch of kids hiking in the outback. Just because you're short and tubby doesn't mean you can't dress well."

That came through my Bernie fog loud and clear.

"And just because you are tall and beautiful does not give you the right to be unkind."

"Now don't be offended. You are my very best friend and I'm just trying to help you by being truthful. Who else would tell you?"

I turned and gazed at the door she'd shoved me out of. "What is this place?"

"It's going to be my new CBDelicious store. Well, if I get it. Someone else is interested, too. Isn't it darling? There's a huge commercial kitchen in the back." She gasped. "You could work for me. You could leave your sad little job and come to work for *me*! You would have to bake according to my recipes, of course. None of your plain-Jane boring cookies. But you could do that, couldn't you?"

I stared at her big brown eyes. She was smart. I knew that. So how was it that she could not understand that I had built a business of my own?

"We would have so much fun. Of course, you couldn't bring *that* with you." She pointed to Daisy.

Was there any point at all in explaining? Probably not. Natasha's biggest problem was that she thought she was smarter than anyone else. Coupled with her inability to see anything that didn't impact her directly, it resulted in a skewed vision of the world.

I simply said, "No, thanks," and marched off, but I heard her shout, "I'll see you later. Put on something decent."

Natasha was the least of my worries. I had bigger problems. For the very first time, I wondered if Bernie could have actually murdered Tate. I desperately wanted to rid myself of that notion. How could I think such a thing? Bernie was kind and thoughtful and had saved his own mother! That wasn't someone who murdered. But why had he lied about knowing the tall woman?

I trudged on, reasoning with myself. Bernie could never harm anyone unless it was in self-defense. Oh no! That was worse! I shuddered as possibilities ran through my mind. Were he and Tate both seeing the same woman? Was it a horrible triangle that had ended in death? Had he and Tate fought over the tall woman with the big eyes?

I *had* to be wrong about that. Maybe he had a good reason for not admitting he knew who she was. I grasped for anything, desperate for a satisfactory explanation. He wanted to spare Bobbie Sue the pain of knowing her husband was having an affair? Or had the tall woman murdered Tate, and Bernie was misguidedly trying to make sure Nina and I didn't follow up and discover that she had killed him?

Good heavens! Was Bernie willing to go to prison for her?

I barged into my kitchen. Not even attention from sweet Mochie could calm me. He cuddled in my arms, the top of his head against my chin.

I clutched him, listening to his soothing purrs as long as he tolerated it, but in a matter of moments he had recovered from my absence and was more interested in seeking a spot in the sun for lounging. I set him down and contemplated my options. I could confront Bernie. Maybe that was the best route. He wouldn't be able to lie to me then. Not to my face when it was clear that I knew the truth. Or I could tell Mars what I had seen. Would he be able to get the truth from Bernie?

I needed to think this through. A peek in the refrigerator reminded me that I had bought loads of blackberries and had better use them before they went bad. With all the talk about cheesecake, I thought I would try a new recipe. One that didn't have to be baked. A truly summery no-bake blackberry cheesecake.

I washed the blackberries and patted them dry, thinking about Eli. The proximity of his apartment to the spot where Tate had been murdered seemed almost too good to be coincidental. Was he jealous of Tate because of Marsha? That didn't seem likely since he was also involved with Eva. Who would know more about Eli and his relationship to Tate?

By the time I slid the blackberry cheesecake into the refrigerator to set, I knew what I had to do. An accidental glimpse in a mirror reminded me of Natasha's rude comment about my attire. I didn't see anything wrong with it. It was too hot to add a jacket, but I added coral earrings, a chunky coral bracelet, and fun coral thong sandals. Wearing my trusty oversized sunglasses, I was set to go.

I walked down to The Laughing Hound, considering what kind of excuse I would make up if Bernie saw me there. A late lunch would be a decent cover for my true intentions. And it wouldn't really be a lie, either, which was more than I could say for him and the tall woman.

The restaurant was blissfully cool. I had arrived in the slow hours between lunch and dinner. I waved at the hostess and made a beeline for the bar. It was my lucky day. Shane was working. Exactly the man I wanted to see. I took a seat at the far end of the bar.

Shane arrived promptly. "Hi, Sophie! What can I get for you?"

"How about an iced tea and turkey on rye with lots of lettuce and a little mayo?"

While he placed my order, I gazed around at the nearly empty bar. I couldn't have timed it better.

Shane set an iced tea on the bar in front of me.

"Is Bernie around?" I asked casually.

"Maybe. Should I check his office?"

"No! That's okay. I don't want to disturb him. Actually, I came to see you."

Shane cocked his head. "Need a bartender for an event?"

"Not today, but I'll keep you in mind. I thought you might be able to help me with something."

He grinned and flexed a bicep. "You, my mom, and my sisters. All the ladies need a hand moving furniture. Am I right?"

"Um, not this time. I need a spy."

He leaned against the bar. "Now *that* sounds intriguing."

"Do you know Eli Dawson?"

His eyebrows shot up. "Sure."

"Tell me about him."

"There's not much to tell. He's a nice guy. He used to work here. Excuse me, let me get your order." He walked to the other end of the bar and returned with a sandwich that made my mouth water. Sliced turkey was piled high, on top of that crisp lettuce peeked out between the slices of bread, and a red drizzle gave away the presence of cranberries.

"Who is Eli dating?" I bit into my sandwich.

He smiled broadly. "Ahh. You're going to have some competition."

"Not for me!"

"Oh. Well, he's caused a little buzz around here." He lowered his voice. "We were pretty certain that he was dating Marsha Bathurst, the manager over at Blackwell's Tavern, but rumor now has it that he's seeing our very own Eva Rosales, which, if you ask me, would be my personal choice between the two."

"I thought you didn't like Eva."

"It's not that I dislike her. She's a tough boss. I've got a sister like that. She's so tiny you could put her in a teacup, but she bosses all of us around. You don't say no to *her*."

I smiled and took another bite of my sandwich.

"But now if it came to looks, I'd date Eva over Marsha any day. So what do you want with Eli?"

"Tate was killed right outside of Eli's apartment."

He shrugged. "So?"

"I thought Marsha had a thing for Tate."

Shane stared at me. "Oh man! I see where you're going with this. Okay, listen. Blackwell's is supposed to be opening back up tonight. I pulled the early shift today, so I'll go down there and hang around the bar and chat up Eli a little after I get off work. How's that sound?"

"Terrific." I dabbed my mouth with a napkin. "One other thing. I noticed a very tall woman here recently. Well dressed, large eyes—"

"I know who you mean." He grinned. "She's hard to miss."

"Who is she?"

"I don't have a clue. She's only been here a couple of times. Never alone. She usually looks like she's having a business meeting. You know what I mean—she wears suits like she's going to the office, not sexy to impress a date."

"Was she here this morning?"

"If she was, I didn't see her."

I had finished my sandwich and was sorry to see that I had devoured every last delicious crumb. Would I ever learn to eat half of something? Probably not.

I paid my tab, thanked Shane, and was walking home feeling perplexed when I happened to spy Spencer sitting on a garden bench. His legs stretched out in front of him, and his head leaned back like he was looking at the sky. I tiptoed into the garden. He heard me anyway and turned his head to look at me.

"Mind if I join you?"

"Sure."

"You know this is someone's private garden?"

"It's okay. It's my best friend's house. They're at the Outer Banks. I'm supposed to check on the house while they're away."

"That's nice of you."

"Everybody is gone. I wish I were, too."

"It will get better."

Spencer stared at the house. "Nothing will ever be the same again."

He was right about that.

And then he said, "I can't undo anything I did."

Chapter 24

Dear Sophie,
I love baking cheesecakes. They're so much less work
than layer cakes. But they always crack! What am I
doing wrong?
                Pass the Cream Cheese, Please! in Cheeseville,
                                                    Wisconsin

Dear Pass the Cream Cheese, Please!,
There are a number of reasons. The first is over-
baking. You may be leaving it in the oven too long.
Or you could be cooling it too fast. Try leaving it in
the oven after you turn off the heat. Or you could
be baking at a temperature that is too high. Try ad-
justing these things one at a time and see what works
for you.

                                                    Sophie

For just a few seconds, I stopped breathing. Had Spencer
killed his dad? Was he about to confess? I gazed at him
surreptitiously. He wore large running shoes. His feet probably hadn't stopped growing yet. I knew he towered over me,

probably over Tate, too. He would have been strong enough to move Tate. He was intimately familiar with the restaurant. And he knew the Eklunds weren't home. I wondered if Spencer was on Wolf's suspect list.

Speaking softly, I asked, "What would you like to undo?"

"Everything. I wish I hadn't been a jerk. I wish I had been kinder and spent more time with him. I wish my last words to him hadn't been so ugly."

I assumed he meant the argument they had. "What did you argue about?"

He snorted. "Advanced placement classes for next year. He was pushing me to do them, but I didn't want to." Spencer sighed. "He was right. I knew he was right all along. I just didn't want to have to work that hard."

I silently let out a long breath of relief. I hoped that was all and he hadn't been angry enough to bash a bottle of champagne over his father's head. Even if he hadn't, I feared Tate's death would force Spencer to grow up very fast. It was a painful way to mature. He deserved a couple more years of thinking like an aggravated kid. But those years were taken from him when the bottle hit Tate over the head.

"Pierce is driving me crazy. He acts like he thinks *he's* my father. Like he can just step in and take over. But I remember. Why do people always think kids are too stupid to understand what's going on? Maybe I don't remember the day he left, but I will never forget growing up without him. Tate was more of a dad to me than Pierce ever could be. Hanging around now won't make up for the years when I needed him. I had a great dad and a coach. I didn't need Pierce."

"I'm really sorry about the pain you had as a child. But I'm glad Tate came along and filled that void."

"I've been talking to him. Is that weird? Like, have I gone mental or something?"

"I think it's very normal and that a lot of people talk to those they've lost."

"Are you just saying that to make me feel better?"

"No. I'm being honest."

"That's a relief. None of my friends have had a parent die yet. Much less be murdered."

"You worked for your dad, right?"

He nodded. "The restaurant is opening back up today, but Mom doesn't want me working there anymore."

"Why not?"

"Dunno." He frowned. "I swear it's like they never let me out of their sight since Tate was killed. They're probably freaking out right now."

"Can you blame them?"

"I don't know if Mom would survive losing me or Jo."

"That's probably why she's keeping tabs on you."

"They're going to send me away."

"Are you serious?"

Spencer took a deep breath. "I overheard Mom and Pierce talking about it."

Had that been discussed between Tate and Bobbie Sue after the big argument over advanced placement classes? It might have already been in the works. I tried to soften the blow. "Maybe they think it will be easier on you if you're in a new environment instead of feeling Tate's absence every day. In a few years you'll be off to college anyway."

"How do I know that the guy who murdered my dad isn't going to knock off my mom, too?"

His question stunned me. It had never even crossed my mind that anyone would also want to murder Bobbie Sue. "Why would you think that?"

Spencer shrugged. "I figure Dad must have ticked off somebody big-time. Maybe a business deal went bad or something? If that's what happened, my mom was probably involved, too."

I tried to press him. "Do you know of anything like that? Anyone who was angry with your parents?"

He seemed to think about it. "No. But they didn't tell Jo and me everything. Especially about the businesses."

He stood up, towering over me. "How long does it take to get over someone's death?"

"You never get over it. You learn to live with it."

He turned abruptly and ran, which I gathered he did quite often. It was his way of dealing with pain and sorrow.

Later that afternoon, Mars drove me to the dealership to pick up my car. On the way home, I stopped at a couple of big box stores to replenish supplies and visited a grocery store as well before heading home. It was dusk when I pulled into my detached garage. A covered outdoor dining area and walkway connected it to the French doors in the living room.

I carried in a load of bulky items and set them on the kitchen floor so I could pet Mochie and Daisy. When the welcome home had subsided, I returned to the car for groceries, accompanied by Daisy. It was dark by then. I switched on the outdoor light over the French doors but it didn't extend far into the yard. Carrying more bags than I should have, I left the garage and was walking toward the house when someone grabbed me from behind.

Chapter 25

Dear Sophie,
How early in the day do I need to bake a cheesecake
so it will be ready to serve at dinner?
        Having a Dinner Party in Las Vegas, Nevada

Dear Having a Dinner Party,
The day before. Cheesecake takes its time settling to
become smooth and creamy. If you slice it too soon,
you may find the texture isn't smooth enough. Al-
ways bake it the day before you intend to serve it.
        Sophie

Daisy snarled and I screamed, dropping my groceries. He held me tightly against his body with his left arm and pressed something cold against my throat. The scent of menthol permeated the air.

A voice whispered into my ear, "You won't be as lucky next time. Let it go. Do you hear me? Let Tate's murder go, or I'll be back."

"Sophie?" I heard Francie's voice next door. "Is everything okay?"

Her voice must have startled him. I felt his arm loosen. In that second, I turned as far as I could and reached for his face, but only succeeded in scratching his left upper arm like an angry cat.

He threw me to the ground. Daisy barked like a crazy dog. I could hear the gate creak open on Francie's side.

"Get him, Duke! Get him!" yelled Francie.

I groaned and twisted in an effort to see my attacker. He was nothing but a dark silhouette in the night as he ran out my gate. It slammed behind him. The two dogs continued to bark.

I could hear Francie giving my address to someone, the police I presumed. She hurried toward me, wielding a baseball bat in one hand and holding her phone in the other. "The police are on the way. You okay, Sophie?"

"I think so. It's a good thing you shouted when you did. Did you get a good look at him?"

"Nah. He was wearing one of those pull-on masks. Balaclavas, I believe they're called. Need a hand getting up?"

If she had been younger, I would have accepted her offer. But there was no point in me pulling her down to the ground with me. "I'm fine." It wasn't true. My hands trembled uncontrollably.

Daisy and Duke left the gate, still emitting an occasional yelp like they were cautioning the attacker not to return. They ran to me and licked my face as though they thought they needed to revive me.

I stood up and very nearly fell, thanks to my knees buckling. It wasn't because I was injured, it was from the shock of being attacked.

"Should I take you to the emergency room?" asked Francie.

"Good heavens, no! I'll be fine. A little bruised, I imagine, but you came along just in time."

"What did he want?"

"For me to stop looking into Tate's murder."

Francie gasped. "Then it wasn't Bernie!"

I gazed at my elderly neighbor in the faint light from the house. "Did you really think Bernie murdered Tate?"

"Don't be silly. Of course not! What I meant was that it proves Bernie didn't kill anyone. Whoever attacked you doesn't want you figuring out who really did it." She raised her forefinger and shook it at me. "I bet it was your attacker who murdered Tate."

Just then we heard crunching.

Francie grabbed my arm. "What's that?"

I turned on the light in my phone and pointed it at the gate. No one was there.

"Where are Duke and Daisy?" I asked.

I flashed the light around my backyard. It wasn't a great flashlight, but it was just enough for us to make out a dark mound in the grass.

Francie clutched my arm as we made our way closer.

Duke and Daisy had swiped a box of graham crackers from the groceries that fell to the ground when I was attacked. They had managed to rip open the box and merrily chomped on their snack.

The relief I felt went a long way toward settling my nerves. I grabbed their plunder so they wouldn't get tummy aches and we all returned to the house. To be on the safe side, I turned on all the outdoor lights.

"He won't be back tonight," murmured Francie.

"Probably not. But it makes me feel a whole lot better to have all the lights on."

She patted my shoulder.

Francie and I collected the other groceries and carried them into my kitchen. I was relieved to find that the eggs were not in the bags that fell when the guy grabbed me.

I rushed to put the groceries away and pulled out the triple chocolate cheesecake I had baked. Just as I started the kettle for a strong, bracing cup of tea, I saw a police car arrive, along with Wolf's unmarked vehicle.

Francie smirked at me. "You're such a lightweight. Nina would be drinking Scotch."

She was absolutely right. I felt better laughing about it.

"The police are here," I said.

Francie smiled at me. "Fix your hair."

"It's not a date," I protested.

"Must you fight everything, Sophie? Just fix your hair."

Francie's hair usually looked like straw. I would be surprised if she did anything more than run a comb through it. But I took her advice and dashed upstairs to the bathroom.

She was right. Not only was my hair a mess, it had grass in it. As I ran a brush through it, I was horrified to see a bruise developing on my throat. One painfully straight red line, where the attacker had held something against it. A knife maybe?

I shuddered and located the rubbing alcohol. I poured some on a soft cotton swab and pressed it gently against the red line. The intense sting let me know that he had broken the skin.

"Sophie! Wolf is here!"

I walked down the stairs and made every effort to smile and at least *act* like I wasn't too concerned.

"Thanks for coming so quickly, Wolf. Triple chocolate cheesecake and a cup of coffee or tea?"

"It's almost too pretty to cut," said Francie.

I had to agree. I had piped whipped cream stars around the top. Francie settled at the banquette in my kitchen.

Wolf did not smile. His eyes studied me, his gaze lingering on my throat. Wong was with him. She glanced at me, but the cheesecake got her attention.

"Where were you attacked?" asked Wolf.

"In the backyard."

"You're sure he's not in the house?"

Francie emitted a little shriek. "Lordie, I hope not!"

"Wong, you take the house," said Wolf. "I'll check out the backyard and meet the others in the alley." He looked from Francie to me. "You two wait here."

I busied myself in the kitchen, wondering how many people *the others* might be and if I should prepare tea for them, too. But then I reasoned that they were most likely needed on the streets for other emergencies so I fixed tea for Wolf and Wong, hoping she could stay. The way she had eyed the cheesecake, there was little doubt in my mind that she would not leave without eating a piece.

"Oh, for heaven's sake, Sophie! Will you sit down? You're flitting around the kitchen like a lost hummer bee."

I stopped in my tracks and realized that I had been trying to push it out of my mind. To minimize what had happened. Someone had threatened me. He had held a knife against my throat, and I had the mark to prove it. A shudder ran through me, top to bottom. I plopped down in a chair at the table, my entire being cold as ice.

"It never occurred to me that he could be in the house," said Francie.

"He's not in here," I assured her. "Even if he ran all the way around to the front, nothing was unlocked. He would have had to sneak in through the back. Besides, don't you think Daisy or Duke would have noticed someone else in the house?"

She patted her baseball bat. "All the same, I'm sleeping with my trusty Louisville Slugger tonight."

"Why would he come back to attack you?"

"I *saw* the man. He doesn't know that I couldn't see much, but he knows where I live. Are you going to call Mars?" she asked. "He would come and stay with us."

I could be obtuse sometimes, but that little slip *us* made it very clear to me that Francie was afraid to be alone. "How about you come over and stay with me? Daisy and Duke can have a pajama party, and the two of us can watch an old movie." Probably not Hitchcock, I thought. "Maybe something with Doris Day and Rock Hudson?"

I tried to gather myself enough to make things seem normal to Francie. I brought the mugs of tea to the table and set a small tray in the middle. It contained a sugar bowl, a creamer of milk, and a bowl of lemon slices. I handed Francie napkins, forks, and spoons, and I set four stacked Vietri Incanto Baroque stoneware plates on the table. I had bought them recently at a yard sale because I had fallen in love with the simplicity of the white dishes with architectural curves around the edges that almost made them look squarish.

"You're just offering that to be nice."

I sat down and met her eyes. "We both had a shock tonight. I know I'd rather not be alone."

"Aww, I'm too old. I wouldn't be any help if he came back."

"You have a baseball bat," I teased.

Wong returned to the kitchen. "I've searched from the basement up to the attic. I don't see anybody."

"Can you stay for a piece of cheesecake?" I handed her a mug of tea.

"You're not getting rid of me until I get a taste. Triple chocolate? Yum!"

Wolf opened the kitchen door. "No sign of anything or anyone in your backyard or the alley." He sat down at the banquette. "Tell me what happened. Start with what time it occurred."

Francie handed him his tea while I sliced the cheesecake and served it.

"It was just after nine o'clock," said Francie. "I know that for sure because I let Duke out at nine every night. I had just opened the door when I heard Sophie scream."

Wolf's eyes narrowed and he looked at Francie.

"*You* called the police?"

"I did," said Francie. "I'm not big or strong, but I can dial my phone and call for help."

"Did you get a good look at this person?"

"It was dark out, but it looked to me like he was dressed in black. Black pants, a black short-sleeved shirt of some kind, maybe like a T-shirt, and a black balaclava. You know, the ski mask that covers everything but the eyes and mouth."

Wolf turned his attention to me. "What happened?"

"I was bringing in groceries when someone grabbed me from behind. I only saw him from the back when he fled out the gate."

"Both of you are saying *him*. You're certain it was a man?"

"The person was strong. He gripped me around my chest and held me tight. I'm not sure I could have wrested loose. The one thing I noticed was that he reeked of menthol. I didn't see him coming or know he was there before he grabbed me. I did, however, scratch his upper left arm pretty well."

"Did he say anything? What about his voice?"

"He whispered. I couldn't swear to it, but I think it was a man. Maybe some women are able to lower their voices and sound like a man when they whisper?"

"What did he say?"

"That I wouldn't be as lucky the next time and that I should stop investigating Tate's murder."

Chapter 26

Dear Natasha,
Can you please tell me how to cut a cheesecake? The
ends often look goofy or break when I cut slices.
            Cheesecake Mama in Knife River, Minnesota

Dear Cheesecake Mama,
There are two recommended methods. Dip the knife
in hot water and wipe it dry before each cut. Start the
cut in the middle and pull toward the outside. The
other method is to "saw" across the cheesecake with
one-strand fishing wire.
                                                    Sophie

Francie proudly announced, "Which proves that Bernie didn't murder Tate. Otherwise, that guy wouldn't be worried about what Sophie might turn up. It means he's nervous."

Wolf showed no reaction to Francie's theory. "What's that mark on your throat?"

"He held something metallic against it. I assume it was a

knife. It wasn't really bleeding but I cleaned it with rubbing alcohol and it stung, so I guess he broke the skin a little bit."

Wolf put down his fork. "I don't like this at all."

"I think it's delicious," said Wong. "For someone who didn't like it, you sure inhaled it."

Wolf gave her a look. "The cheesecake is delicious. I don't like the situation—that Sophie was attacked. You've obviously gotten under someone's skin, Soph. What did you do that agitated someone?"

"Nothing! Not today anyway. Francie took me over to Estelle Fogelbaum's house. I stopped by The Laughing Hound for lunch and had a nice chat with Shane. And on my way home, I talked with Spencer, but I don't think anyone saw us. We were in a backyard that was fairly private. Then Mars took me to pick up my car."

"Where was your car?" asked Wolf.

"At the dealership being repaired. A part gave out and had to be replaced."

I took a bite of the sinful cheesecake.

"No one got angry with you or said anything odd?"

"Natasha did. She fussed at me because I backed into a store with Daisy, and Natasha didn't like the way I was dressed."

Wolf and Wong snickered.

"Oh! There is one person. She was at Tate's service. A tall woman. Attractive, with full lips, big eyes, and a rich, dark complexion. Very well dressed. Nobody knows who she is."

Wong looked at Wolf curiously.

Wolf sipped his tea before responding. "I know her. I have spoken to her personally and she had nothing to do with Tate's murder."

"She was *with* Tate just before he was murdered!" I persisted.

"I am aware of that. Your friend, Auguste, not only phoned

me and told me what he knew, but he also invited me to dine at his restaurant gratis."

"Are you allowed to accept free meals?" asked Nina.

Wolf grinned. "One of the few perks of the job. Restaurants often like to see us. A police presence can help keep crooks at bay, so a free meal or a cup of coffee while we're on duty is acceptable."

"So who is she?" I asked.

"She's been thoroughly vetted and excluded from the list of suspects."

I couldn't believe that he dodged my question. What was it about this woman? I glared at him. He wasn't going to tell me, and I wondered why. "Was she having an affair with Tate?"

Wong was on her second piece of cheesecake. Her eyes widened and she looked to Wolf, waiting for his response.

He tilted his head and said, "I don't think so."

"Now see," I said, "if you weren't being so cagey about her identity, I would have taken you at your word that you don't *think* she was having an affair with Tate. But you kind of blew it. You're not sure, are you?"

"Well, Miss Marple," he said snidely, "I'm afraid Tate isn't around to ask, so I have to make my own determination about that."

A firm rap on the kitchen door caused us all to jump. Shane peered in the window.

I got up and let him in. "Perfect timing. You know Wolf, Wong, and Francie Vanderhoosen, don't you?"

He grinned at Francie and nodded to Wolf and Wong. "Is this a bad time?"

"Not if you'd like a piece of cheesecake."

He held both of his palms up. "Looks great. I'd love a piece." He slid into the banquette.

I pulled out another plate and cut a slice for him. "Tea?"

"Not my usual, but beer doesn't go with cheesecake."

"Shane went over to the bar at Blackwell's Tavern tonight," I explained, handing him the cheesecake and a mug of tea.

"To spy?" Wong got excited. "I should have done that!"

"Don't you think Marsha would have recognized you?" I asked.

"It's not like I'm never going to eat there again," said Wong. "What did you find out, Shane?"

"Can I speak freely? You won't go arrest him?" asked Shane.

Wolf's expression was deadpan, but Wong's eyebrows raised with interest.

Wolf responded, "You know I can't guarantee anything like that. It all depends on what he said or did."

Shane sat back and scowled at him. "Well, you didn't hear it from me. Okay? Eli has got a gig going. He's under-ringing drinks and pocketing the difference."

"Under-ringing? What's that?" I asked.

"Say a drink costs thirteen dollars regular and six dollars at happy hour. He'll sell a drink for thirteen dollars, ring it up as a happy hour drink at six dollars, and the seven-dollar difference goes into his pocket."

"Woah," said Wong. "He could make hundreds of dollars every night."

Shane nodded. "You bet. He's cheating the owner."

"How could you tell?" asked Wolf.

Shane shrugged. "I tend bar. Listen, I don't cheat Bernie, but I've been around long enough to know what a bartender is doing on the sly. I saw him pocketing money. There must be two dozen ways to cheat, but he's lining his pockets all right."

"I should tell Bobbie Sue," I said.

"There's more." Shane grinned, flashing perfect white teeth. "I told him I'd heard he was seeing Eva Rosales—"

"Who's that?" asked Wolf.

"One of the assistant managers at The Laughing Hound," said Shane. "Very pretty but runs the place like she's a drill sergeant. When I mentioned her, Eli nearly came over the bar at me. He begged me to quash any talk about the two of them because he'd lose his job at Blackwell's Tavern if Marsha heard about it."

"Because he's sleeping with their competitor?" asked Wong.

"No, because he's also dating Marsha, his manager, on the sly."

Wong looked at Wolf. "I thought Marsha had a thing for Tate."

Wolf slid a hand over his nose and mouth. "So did I."

"And my friend Estelle Fogelbaum can confirm that he's two-timing them," Francie exclaimed proudly. "I'll take you to see her tomorrow."

"You really should go," I said. "She has the most amazing view of the crime scene." Lest he get the wrong idea, I quickly added, "But she wasn't watching when Tate was killed."

"Shane, at what time were you observing Eli at Blackwell's Tavern?" asked Wolf.

"I got there at eight, left about eleven, and came straight here."

"Then Eli has an alibi for his whereabouts tonight when Sophie was attacked," mused Wolf.

Shane frowned and his brow furrowed. "You were attacked?"

"Yes," I said. "But the real question is where was Eli the night Tate was murdered?"

"Sophie," said Wolf, "I'd like you to come down to the station so we can get a decent photo of the mark on your throat."

Francie froze. "And leave me alone?"

"Maybe Nina can come over," I said.

"We'll be keeping an eye on you, Francie," said Wolf.

Nevertheless, I phoned Nina. When she arrived with Mars in tow and a big bowl of popcorn, I followed Wolf in my car to the police station to have my throat photographed.

It was surprisingly quiet there.

In a low voice, Wolf said, "I want you to give this a lot of thought, Sophie. I know how close you are to Bernie. But someone had to be desperate to attack you tonight. There are things going on that I can't reveal to you. I'm sure you can understand that. Soph, I don't want you to get hurt."

"Is Bernie still your prime suspect?" I asked.

Wolf closed his eyes for a long moment. When he opened them, he sighed. "You're the one who found the broken glass and the cheesecake. The killer tried to clean up that scene. He just didn't do a thorough job. But he did take the larger shards of glass and the crushed clamshell with cheesecake in it."

I swallowed hard. "You're saying he must have taken them because those things weren't in the alley or the Eklunds' backyard?"

"That's right. They were in the back of Bernie's car."

Chapter 27

Dear Sophie,
What is a Japanese Cheesecake? My cousin has been
raving about it, but I can't find it in stores.
                    Itching to Try It in Wonder Hills, Ohio

Dear Itching to Try It,
You may have to bake it yourself. The recipe is
known in Japan as Cotton Cake or Jiggle Cake. It's
much lighter than an American cheesecake. Imagine
a cross between a chiffon cake and a cheesecake.
                                        Sophie

I swayed at the thought and Wolf caught me. He gripped my
forearms until I was steady. I was so sure it wasn't Bernie!

"No," I insisted. "It wasn't him. Someone took his car.
The killer used his car." I hesitated for only a second before
daring to ask, "Did you find Bernie's fingerprints on the
clamshell?"

"It wasn't in good condition. The only fingerprints we
found were Bobbie Sue's and Spencer's."

"You see?" I pressed, even though I knew good and well
that anyone clever enough to use Bernie's car without getting
caught probably knew to wear gloves.

Wolf groaned. "I don't know who attacked you tonight,
but I have a really bad feeling that it was a thug, the likes of
which you have never dreamed."

I backed away from him. "What do you mean?" I couldn't imagine what he was talking about.

"We're going to put your house under surveillance. It's that serious, Sophie. You know how to reach me. If anything at all unusual happens, I want you to call me immediately."

I nodded, appropriately chastened. "You're scaring me, Wolf."

"Good!"

He asked a uniformed officer to walk me out to my car and follow me home. It was past midnight, and I was glad for the escort. I drove home and wished that my garage were attached to my house. I would have to walk through the yard again, like I had earlier that night. All the outdoor lights were still on. From the window in the door of the garage, I could see Mars waving at me. I felt more comfortable leaving the safety of the garage. Daisy and Duke rushed at me, and right behind them, Mars strolled toward me.

"You, okay?" he asked.

"I'm fine. Sorry to keep you up so late."

"No problem."

"Mars"—I reached out to nab his arm—"do you remember me telling you about the tall woman?"

"The one we all noticed at the service?" he asked.

"That one. I saw Bernie talking with her. They looked serious, not like they had just met as casual acquaintances."

Mars wasn't like Wolf. I could read his expressions very well. He was as dismayed as I was. "And one other thing. The police found the larger shards of glass and the container that had held cheesecake in Bernie's car."

Mars rubbed his forehead. "But whoever stole it could have tossed it the car."

"That's exactly what I said. Here's the thing, Mars. I have to be getting close to the truth. I must have talked to someone or discovered some detail that has made the killer nervous. It means we're on the right track, I just don't know what it is that upset him." I added, "Or her. Or them."

"Good point." He looked up at the sky where stars sparkled in the clear night. "Seems so peaceful right now. How can this be happening?" He reached out and hugged me to him. He whispered, "I'm so thankful that you're okay."

He let go of me and stood back. "There's an unmarked police car in front of your house, so you should be okay tonight. Francie has gone up to bed. I'm going to take Bernie home. Maybe I can get him to tell me about the woman."

I nodded and we went inside.

"Francie wants French toast made with challah and served with maple syrup, strawberry butter, and fresh strawberries."

I had just walked into my kitchen. I blinked at Nina and Francie, already perky and energetic. I poured myself a cup of coffee that one of them must have made. "Then you're very lucky that I bought challah and strawberries yesterday."

"How are you feeling, Sophie?" asked Francie.

"I'm fine. Just tired. It was a late night."

"Bernie was so sweet last night. Jittery, if you ask me, but so thoughtful," said Francie. "There's no way he murdered anyone. He just doesn't have it in him."

I retrieved eggs from the fridge and whisked them with a sprinkle of cinnamon. While the griddle heated, I sliced challah and dunked it in the eggs. That done, I washed the plump, ripe strawberries. After slicing them, I sprinkled them with sugar.

In a matter of minutes, we sat down to eat, the fresh strawberries glistening atop the challah.

Francie glanced out the bay window. "Isn't it incredible how different things look in the sunshine? It feels like last night never happened."

I felt the mark on my throat. A very tiny ridge had formed.

I'd had worse cat scratches. Not from my sweet Mochie, of course, and not on my neck.

Francie asked me questions about my trip to the police station the night before. I told them about it and emphasized Wolf's concern.

"You're not really going to give up on Bernie, are you?" asked Nina.

The two of them looked at me with worried faces.

"I don't think we can. No one else is looking out for him. And Bernie himself seems to be too nonchalant about it."

Francie shook her head. "That's an act. He's trying hard not to let on how upset he is. I watched him last night. He's not his usual self. He gives it a good try, but he's reserved and a little withdrawn. Didn't you think so, Nina?"

"Definitely. Of course, he was upset about you being attacked. We all were. I was thinking about this in bed last night. Could Marsha have sent someone over to attack you? I bet she and Eli have some unsavory connections."

I sipped my coffee. "Why now? I didn't see her yesterday. Didn't have anything to do with her except for sending Shane over to Blackwell's Tavern. But he didn't go over there until shortly before I was attacked."

"While you were out last night, we decided to team up with you. Take turns being your buddy, like at camp!" Nina said cheerily.

"I'm sure that's not necessary." It was nice of them, but no one needed to babysit me. "I don't have any plans that will get me into trouble today. I'm going to walk Daisy before it gets too hot, then I need to verify that everything is in place for Marjorie Hollingsworth-Smythe's big Fourth of July bash I'm handling next week."

Nina mimicked a snore. "I'll walk with you. Muppet might be tiny, but she still has to be walked. You can do your boring job by yourself, though."

That suited me just fine. "Francie, will you be okay at home by yourself?"

"I won't be there long. I have a birdwatcher meeting this morning."

We were all set then, and I was relieved. After we washed up the dishes, Nina and Francie went home. I dashed upstairs to change into a white skort, a pink blouse, and walking shoes. I didn't bother with makeup and pulled my hair back into a ponytail to keep it off my face. I slid on my sunglasses, dressed Daisy in her halter, jammed my phone in a pocket, and we were off.

Nina and Muppet met us on the sidewalk. Slightly brisk, the air was refreshing, though I knew from experience that heat and humidity would follow shortly. Other runners and dog walkers must have had the same idea.

Nina and I strolled along, talking about Marsha, Eli, and Eva.

"Love triangles are always dangerous," said Nina. "But I don't see how Tate fits in there, unless Eli was jealous of him." She gasped. "When I was in college, I dated a guy named Rob. We broke up and moved on. Six months later, I ran into him at a bar. He told me he was seeing someone named Gracie. I was just being friendly and said I'd like to meet her. Well, you should have seen him. His face actually turned a dark red. I thought I'd caught him in a lie, that this Gracie didn't exist. He told me that wasn't a good idea because she hated me. Needless to say, I asked why on earth this woman would hate me when she'd never met me. Turned out he was making up lies about me to make her jealous. Can you believe that? What a worm! So maybe Marsha was lying to Eli about Tate to make him jealous!"

It was a long-winded way of getting there, but it was an interesting theory. It was entirely possible, but as Mars would have pointed out had he been there, it was nothing more than empty speculation.

About that time, a man who was running toward us slowed down. He walked a few steps and drew my attention because of the way he bumped into the trunk of a tree. He wore a baseball cap, sunglasses, and running attire.

"Did you see that?" I asked Nina.

"See what?"

"That man. There's something wrong with him."

"Should we cross the street?" she asked.

He began to stagger, as if each step he took was a monumental effort. Because of his difficulty walking, he lurched toward the street.

"He's going to be hit by a car!" I picked up my pace and ran toward him as he fell off the curb and lay facedown in the street.

I stepped out into the street to be sure no one hit him. Thankful that I had brought my phone, I called 911 and told them someone needed medical help. At least that was what I thought.

Nina took over on the street, waving cars away.

I knelt beside the man. "Hello? Are you okay? We've called the ambulance."

"Need . . . help." His voice was raspy and weak.

"You'll be all right," I said, not at all confident about that. His face was pale, his breathing shallow. It dawned on me that maybe he had a chronic illness. "Do you have meds on you? Is there anything the EMT should know?"

He struggled to roll over on his back but couldn't. His knees jerked as though he was in extreme pain.

I gazed at his knees. They were covered with blisters, like they had been burned. The insides of his hands bore the same sort of blisters, bulging and horrific. Had he fallen forward onto something hot? A grill? That would account for the burn blisters on his hands but not his knees.

And then I realized with a start that he reeked of menthol.

The scent took me back to the night before. There wasn't a chance that this was the man who had attacked me. Was there? He had been running toward us. Did he intend to assault Nina and me on the street? Was he running toward my house?

I reminded myself that dozens, if not hundreds of products smelled of menthol. Still, I drew back, away from him, even though I seriously didn't think he could manage to reach out to me.

The sound of sirens approaching came as a huge relief. Who was the man? I couldn't make out much of his face. I probably should have removed his sunglasses. They had to be stabbing him. This man was in dire need of help, yet I didn't want to touch him or be too close to him.

The ambulance stopped in the middle of the street. Wong and an EMT walked over and looked at him.

"Do you know who this is?" asked the EMT.

"I'm not sure. I don't think so. Did you see his hands and knees?"

The EMT frowned. "Sir? What's your name?"

The man mumbled something completely incoherent.

"Can you sit up?"

The man tried to move his hands, but it was a feeble gesture.

"Okay. We're going to load you on a stretcher. All right?"

Wong and I stepped out of the way.

Working together, three EMTs managed to roll him onto a stretcher. In the process, his hat and sunglasses fell off and I knew exactly who he was.

Chapter 28

Dear Natasha,
I love your TV show! You have inspired me to orga-
nize and redecorate my house. Per your instructions,
I have neatly stashed everything, but I find it annoy-
ing to have to browse through my stationery to jot a
quick note to someone. How does one handle that?
            Love Writing in Paper Mill Village, Vermont

Dear Love Writing,
You need a paper caddy. Don't stuff it full of receipts
and notes. It should show off your beautiful sta-
tionery, making it easy to find and write a quick note.
                                    Natasha

"Pierce," I said.
    "He's Pierce Carver, Bobbie Sue Bodoin's ex-husband."
It was then that I noticed blisters on his face, near his eyes,
and on one elbow. What had happened to him?
    In minutes, Pierce was in the ambulance and the siren
started as it slowly pulled away leaving Wong, Nina, and me
on the sidewalk.

"He smelled of menthol," I said.

Wong nodded. "I noticed that. Do you think he's the one who attacked you?"

"I don't know. What do you suppose happened to him?" I asked.

"I've never seen anything quite like that. I'd guess he got into some kind of poison," said Wong.

Nina gasped. "He was planning to poison someone! What do you bet he killed Tate?"

Wong's radio squawked at her. She gave us a wave and hurried away. Nina and I walked home somberly. Back in my office, I tried my best to focus on my work, but I kept seeing Pierce in his misery, blistered with his knees pulled up, cramping on the road.

I pulled out the recipe for Japanese Cheesecake that I had been itching to try. The hottest new dessert, it was supposed to be super light and wonderfully delicious. No wonder it was light. It contained much less cream cheese than American cheesecakes. I whisked egg whites to fold into the batter, another reason it would be light. I could hardly wait to try it. After it had baked, I slid it into the refrigerator.

The cake had distracted me for a while but at noon I drove to the hospital. The first person I saw was Jo. She walked out of the cafeteria carefully carrying a tray.

"Hi! Can I help you with that?"

"Hi, Sophie. No, thanks, I've got it. Did you come to see Pierce?"

"I did. How's he doing?"

"Not good. Mommy is really worried about him. We've been here all morning. I have a ballet dress rehearsal this afternoon. I hope we can go home soon."

She led me down a long corridor and into a waiting room where Spencer looked out of a floor-to-ceiling window.

"Spencer!" called Jo. "I brought food."

He turned around and saw me. "Hi." Spencer picked up a soda, pulled back the tab, and guzzled it.

I sniffed the air. "Do you smell like menthol?"

"They all do," said Jo, with a mouthful of French fry. "It stinks!"

Spencer made a face at her. "It's for runners. For muscle pain."

"Pierce uses it, too?"

"The old guys, like Pierce, use it for their joints."

It didn't mean he was my attacker. Did it? "What did you guys do last night?" I asked cheerily.

Jo poked her fingers in the French fry box. "Mommy and I watched a movie about a girl who was a princess but didn't know it."

"That sounds like fun." I looked to Spencer.

He shrugged. "Hung out with some friends."

"Mommy said he could because he was supposed to go on vacation today," said Jo.

I looked to Spencer for clarification.

He shrugged. "Pierce and I were supposed to leave this afternoon on a fishing trip. I guess that's off."

"Yes, I would think so. If you'll excuse me, I'll peek in on him."

"Second door on the left," said Spencer.

"Don't eat my fries!" Jo yelped as I was walking out.

"You should have gotten more," her brother groused.

Bobbie Sue sat in a chair beside Pierce's bed, her head bowed forward.

Pierce breathed regularly and appeared to be sleeping.

I tried to tiptoe in, but Bobbie Sue heard me and lifted her head.

"Sophie!" she said softly. "How nice of you to come."

"Nina and I were worried about him. Pierce collapsed right in front of us."

"You're kidding."

"He was running and slowed down and then started staggering and fell into the street."

She raised a hand to her mouth in horror. "Did he say anything?"

"He asked for help. Did you see the blisters?"

"No. They didn't let us see him until they brought him up here."

I checked out his hands. They were wrapped in white gauze. A sheet covered him so I couldn't see his knees. "I guess that's why his hands are bandaged."

"Blisters? Why would he have blisters?"

"I have no idea. I've never seen anything quite like them."

"Poor Pierce."

"I hear he was taking Spencer fishing."

She paused for a moment before responding. "We thought it would be good for Spencer to get away with Pierce. A change of scenery. It's hard to adjust. Everyone tells me we'll find a new normal. But nothing is normal. I feel like we're stumbling through every day without a clue where we're going. And now this. What on earth has happened to us?"

A doctor appeared in the doorway. "May I speak to you for a moment, please? We found the medical power of attorney Mr. Carver signed when he had surgery. It names you and appears to cover any eventuality."

Bobbie Sue stepped out into the hallway with him, but I could hear what they were saying.

"In layman's terms, please?" she asked.

"Sure. His heart rate slowed down dangerously. We thought we were losing him, but that seems to be stabilizing. The blisters on his hands and knees are a complete mystery. Has he been using any chemicals?"

"Not that I know of. He's a band director at a community

college. I wouldn't think he would come into contact with any chemicals."

"How about hiking or gardening?"

"Definitely not gardening! But he's very big on running. It wouldn't surprise me if he ran on paths or trails."

"Good to know. It seems unlikely but there's a possibility that he came into contact with a poisonous plant. We'll keep testing."

Bobbie Sue returned to the room. "I guess you heard that."

Before I could respond, Jo sidled into the room with us. "Mommy, it's already one o'clock."

"Honey, I think we're going to have to skip ballet today. I'm sorry, but Uncle Pierce is very sick, and no one knows why."

"I could take her," I said.

Bobbie Sue looked at me in surprise. "You *are* going that way. Are you sure you wouldn't mind? I feel obligated to stay here because he doesn't have anyone else. His mom isn't able to travel, and his sister died a year ago."

Jo tugged at her mom's dress. "Excuse me, but we're going now. I don't want to be late."

For a split second I saw hesitation in Bobbie Sue's eyes. But she forced a smile and hugged her daughter. "Behave and I'll see if you can spend the night with Esme. Okay?"

Jo nodded and fled the room.

"Don't worry. She'll be fine. Keep me posted about Pierce?"

"You bet."

Jo was an angel as we left the hospital. The minute we were in the car she turned into a nonstop gossip. "I'm sorry that Pierce is sick, but I wish he would go away and leave us alone. I don't like him hanging around all the time. All he cares about is Spencer and running. And he's not even my uncle. I don't know why I'm supposed to call him that. Did you know he's Spencer's father? My real uncles that are my father's brothers said Pierce is a gold-digger. Do you know what that is? It's someone who marries somebody for money. He is not marrying my mommy no matter what. Oh no! I don't have my costume. It's a dress rehearsal. I'm supposed to come in my costume."

I tried to sound super calm. She was agitated enough as it was. "We can stop by your house. Do you have a key?"

"No. But I know where we hide one outside. My dad was always worried that my mom would lose her keys. She has so many other things to think about. So he hid one outside and showed us where it was."

"Great!" We were already back in Old Town. I turned down the street to the Bodoin's house.

When I parked, Jo scrambled out of the car. I could barely keep up with her. That child had energy! She ran to a birdhouse, pulled down the bottom and slid a key out of it. Thankfully it fit the door and we were inside in a flash. If it hadn't worked, there's no telling what she might have done.

She ran up the stairs faster than the speed of light. "I'm going to put it on here."

"Okay. But bring your other clothes and a toothbrush along in case Esme's mom takes you to their house."

I didn't hear a response and reminded myself that she was just a kid. I walked upstairs to her room and knocked on the open door. I had expected a princess theme and was surprised to find white walls and white furniture with pink touches in the linens and accessories. It was simple and chic and still screamed *a little girl lives here.*

"Sophie? Could you help me pin up my hair?"

She was in the bathroom, wearing a glitzy white leotard with a blue tutu. After some instructions on what not to do, we had her hair pinned back, coiled into a bun, and sprayed so that a typhoon wouldn't move it.

"Jo, I think you should take a change of clothes and a toothbrush in case you stay over at Esme's tonight."

"Okay. I'd better hurry, though."

While she ran around her room throwing clothes and other items into a cream-colored backpack made of canvas and leather straps, I gazed around and that was when I saw it. On her desk, neatly standing in a stationery caddy, was lavender stationery and matching envelopes, exactly like the ones used by Worried in Old Town.

Chapter 29

Dear Natasha,
Does one still use stationery with one's monogram on
it? Or has that gone out of style?
    Old-Fashioned in Old Town, Alexandria, Virginia

Dear Old-Fashioned,
At best, monograms are now considered quaint. You
may date yourself if you persist in using them.
                         Natasha

Anyone could have them, I reminded myself. But the fact that they were so easily accessible by say, a big brother, was almost too convenient. Jo was too young to have written that letter. She was smart and observant, but even if she had discovered something about her father and his restaurant, I was one hundred percent certain she would have gone to her mom or asked her father about it. A laptop sat on her desk and connected to a printer. Still, it hadn't been the letter of a child. Spencer had to be Worried in Old Town. He had changed things around and used feminine stationery in an effort to disguise his true identity.

Jo stood before me, backpack in hand. "I'm ready to go."

We walked down the stairs and through the foyer. But when I opened the door, Coach stood on the stoop.

"We're just leaving," said Jo.

"Is your mom home?" asked Coach.

"No, she's at the hospital with Pierce. I'm running late." She stood her ground. The two of us effectively blocked him from entering.

"Whoa. Just a second. Is something wrong with Bobbie Sue?" asked Coach.

"Mommy is fine, but Pierce is sick." She looked at me. "And I'm not calling him uncle anymore."

"Where's Spencer?" he asked.

I was about to respond but Jo beat me to it. "They're all at the hospital. I have to go. You're holding me up!"

She pushed past him. I walked out and pulled the door closed behind me.

Jo shot me a worried look.

I held out my hand for the key and locked the door. "Sorry, Coach. Just bad timing. Is there anything I can help you with?"

"No. I came over to see if I could be of help."

"I'm sure Jo will tell Bobbie Sue you were here."

I walked to my car. Jo was already throwing her pack in the back.

We slid into our seats and closed the doors. Jo whispered to me, "What if Mommy and Spencer lose their keys? They won't be able to get in."

Coach still stood by the front door. He waved to us and slowly walked toward his car as if he were at a loss and didn't know what to do.

I turned on the ignition and pulled into the street. "It's all right. As soon as I drop you off, I'll come back and hide the key in the birdhouse. Okay?"

That seemed to placate her. She launched into a full description of Esme's family, including the elderly grandmother who lived with them and told the girls ghost stories.

In an effort to be super conscientious about delivering someone else's child to ballet, I parked the car and went inside with Jo. Besides, Jo was a little spitfire. I thought it wise to deliver her directly into the hands of her ballet teacher.

That done, I waved to her and left. But when I was on the sidewalk, I noticed the drugstore on the corner and strolled over to it. A little bell on the door clanged when I opened it and Sharon Beady appeared from the back.

"Hi, Sophie. What can I help you with today?"

"Do you carry creams for runners? For their aching muscles?"

"Sure do."

I followed her to an aisle with a huge assortment. "Do you put them on before you run or after?"

"Well, since the only running I've ever done was to be first in line at Ben and Jerry's, I really don't know."

They had at least fifty different kinds in tubes and jars. "Do they all have menthol?" I asked.

"I believe most of them do. It warms the area where it's applied. She picked up a jar and read the label. "It says right here, *Fast acting pain relief for cramping, tough workouts, and muscle strain.* It doesn't say when to use it, but it also acts as a decongestant. That's the menthol. I might have to try this on the arthritis in my left knee."

Her knee? Of course! Runners often had bad knees, didn't they? And one would rub the cream on with one's hands. Had that happened to Pierce? Was it possible that he had a reaction to something in his pain relief cream?

She'd been so nice that I felt obligated to buy a jar. And she had given me a possible clue to Pierce's odd medical situation. Maybe Mars would want the pain relief cream, though I couldn't ever remember him reeking of menthol. I returned to my car and drove back to Bobbie Sue's house.

I parked on the street and looked around for Coach's car. I didn't see it anywhere. He was probably at the hospital by now. Looking around furtively, lest anyone catch me, I opened the bottom of the birdhouse, slid the key in and closed it.

That done, I looked around and spied Pierce's Jeep in the Bodoin's driveway. The roof was off as usual. He'd left his running shoes in the back of the car, maybe that was also where he stashed his pain cream.

But I didn't want to touch it. If it had caused that blistering and his collapse, the last thing I wanted was to experience the same misery. I retrieved a box of tissues from my car and pulled out two wads at least an inch thick each. Thusly armed, I strode over to Pierce's Jeep and peered in the back. Sure enough, a bag lay there. Not a fancy gym bag but a simple bag with handles, the kind I took to the grocery store. Protecting my hands with the wads of tissues, I grasped the handles and peered inside. And there it was—pain cream in a plastic jar.

Feeling triumphant, I carefully carried it to my car and deposited it in the back. Then I drove to the hospital.

It was a long shot, for sure. But if there was even a chance that he had a reaction to the cream, I had to bring it to the doctors. Holding the handles with the thick bundles of tissues again, I returned to the floor where Pierce lay suffering. I went straight to the nurses' station and asked for his doctor.

Fortunately, he was nearby. I explained what I was thinking about the blisters on his knees and his palms. I held out the bag to him and separated the handles so he could see inside. "I found this in his car."

The doctor didn't laugh at me. He politely took the bag, also careful to grip it with the thick wads of tissues. "I can't say I hold out much hope, but I don't have anything else to go on." He thanked me and walked away.

I headed for Pierce's room. I hadn't thought it would be possible for him to look worse, but he did. He was shaking.

His face was the washed-out shade of someone who felt very cold. A nurse came in and deftly swapped his blankets for cozy, warm ones, straight from the heater.

His eyes were closed. I wasn't sure if he was asleep or under the effects of a medicine to keep him sedated.

On my way out, I peeked in the waiting room to see if Spencer was still there. Luckily, he was talking with Coach and Bobbie Sue.

"Sophie!" Bobbie Sue said in surprise. "What are you doing here? Is Jo all right?"

"She's fine. I helped her put her hair up and made sure she packed a bag in case she stays over with Esme tonight. Then I delivered her to her ballet class." And then I explained my theory about the blisters and a possible reaction to muscle cream. "I found some in the back of Pierce's Jeep and brought it over to be tested."

Bobbie Sue stared at me in silence, but her breath came faster, and she paled. "You went to the house?"

"I hope you don't mind. Jo knew where the key was, and she was desperate to put on her costume."

"Of course. Silly me. I should have known Jo would want her costume. Thanks for taking her to get it."

Coach snorted. "I use muscle pain cream all the time. I've never had a problem."

I edged closer to him and tried to look casual while unobtrusively sniffing in his direction. He reeked of heavily applied aftershave.

Bobbie Sue shot him a look of daggers. "Ignore him. Thank you, Sophie. That was very thoughtful of you." She gazed at her son. "You two better get going. I'll keep an eye on Pierce." She smiled at me. "Coach has agreed to take Spencer fishing now that Pierce can't go."

I blinked at her, smelling a rat. Spencer harbored a lot of resentment toward his biological dad, but would he really take off on a vacation when Pierce was deathly ill and the man who had treated him like a son had just died? And what had happened to the Bobbie Sue who had struggled and scraped by when Pierce left her in the lurch all those years ago? I could understand being compassionate to someone in need, but she had been quite bitter. "Could I have a quick word with Spencer before he goes?"

Bobbie Sue twitched. "About what? You can't believe anything Jo said."

I tried to make light of it. "Jo is darling. I did hear a lot about Esme's grandmother."

This was an interesting change. Why did I have the feeling that Bobbie Sue was hiding something? And Spencer, who had to be Worried in Old Town, knew what it was. It might even be what had concerned him sufficiently to write to me in the first place. But I couldn't ask him about being Worried in Old Town in front of Bobbie Sue. He would just deny it.

"Go on, you two," she said. "You want to set up camp in daylight and you'll need to stop for provisions on the way."

I desperately wanted to talk with Spencer, but I could tell Mama Bear wasn't going to let me near him.

I left, wondering what Bobbie Sue was hiding, and if Pierce would make it. I hoped so. Spencer didn't need to lose two dads in one week. I drove home, parked in my garage, and took a careful look around my backyard before dashing to the house.

I hung my purse in the closet and walked into the kitchen, thinking about the person who had attacked me the night before. When someone tapped on the window of my kitchen door, I screamed. I couldn't help it. My attacker had left me on edge.

Bernie gazed in the window at me. I was still angry with him, but I opened the door.

He held out a box of Krispy Kreme doughnuts. Chocolate iced, my favorite kind.

I took the box, and he came in.

"Thank you."

"Fresh from the shop. They're probably still warm."

If I hadn't been so mad at him, I might have cried. Not because of the Krispy Kremes, but because he had driven out of town to get them fresh. It wasn't a long trip, but he had taken the time to do it.

I could see his eyes studying the tiny mark on my neck.

"I'm so sorry." Bernie reached out and clutched me like we were parting forever. "This is all my fault," he whispered. "No one should ever have held a knife against your neck."

He drew back, his face a wretched wreck of sadness.

"It's not your fault at all," I said firmly.

"You would never have been attacked if you weren't helping me."

"You don't know that. But I am angry with you."

His eyes opened wide. "Maybe I should make you a cuppa while you try one of your fresh-from-the-bakery doughnuts?"

He hustled over to the stove and put the kettle on. "What have I done now?"

"You lied to me!"

Chapter 30

Dear Sophie,
I baked a cheesecake to enter in the County Fair but
it cracked! Is there any way to patch it?
Desperate in Fair Bluff, North Carolina

Dear Desperate,
It's very common for cheesecakes to crack. It will still
taste good. You can disguise the crack with an artful
dollop of whipped cream. If your cheesecake is Oreo
or some other cookie, then decorate it with cookies
over the crack. If it's a fruit cheesecake, pile berries
over the crack. Good luck!

Sophie

Bernie looked me straight in the eyes. "I have not! I would
never lie to you. I have no secrets. You know me better
than anyone except Mars. Well, I might lie about a gift. You
know, the good kind of secret."

"Really?" I sat down and bit into one of the sweet, pillowy
doughnuts. It was so good. But Bernie wasn't buying me off

with these doughnuts, even if they were unbelievably fresh. "You said you didn't know the beautiful, tall woman."

Bernie froze. "What makes you think I know her?"

"Oh, for pity's sake, Bernie. Even Daisy saw you two together behind The Laughing Hound."

"I see." He quietly poured hot water over tea in two mugs. After doctoring them with milk and sugar, he brought them to the table and sat down. "I wish I could tell you. For her safety, I can't reveal anything, not even her name. But I told Wolf. It's a complicated situation. This is one time you have to trust me, Soph."

"That's asking an awful lot after you lied to me."

He ran an uncomfortable hand through his hair, ruffling it. "You do believe that I did *not* murder Tate, don't you?"

I nodded and finished my doughnut. Even though he wouldn't tell me who she was, it didn't change what I knew of him. He was a great guy. However, that didn't prevent me from taking advantage of the situation. I asked what we had all wondered. "Who is the mysterious absentee owner of The Laughing Hound?"

Bernie winced. "I knew you would ask eventually. It's in a corporate name, but it belongs to me."

I honestly had not expected that! I must have shown my astonishment because he continued.

"When my mum's third husband died, he left everything to me. He had no children of his own, and we were quite close. He's the one who raised me. He was more of a parent to me than my own mum."

"And the mansion?"

Bernie's eyes met mine. "That belongs to me, too. I knew the house pretty well after the decorating competition. They dropped the price and I thought it was a good opportunity. Never really thought I'd stay there because it's so big, but it's home now."

"Bernie, why didn't you tell us?"

"Because I didn't want anything to change. I just wanted to be me. Not some fat cat that everyone kissed up to. I watched a couple of Mum's husbands fritter away everything they had. I didn't want that to happen to me. I thought it best to keep quiet about it. You'd be surprised how many people assume that I own the restaurant."

No wonder he didn't have trouble coughing up money for bail. "I guess Mars knows?"

Bernie grinned. "I blew it when I bought my one and only big extravagance."

"Allow me to guess. That gigantic TV with the two extra screens and speakers."

Bernie laughed. "I didn't want him yelling at me about saving my money every time I bought something nice, like the car." He grinned and held up a finger, "But it was used!"

I gazed at him in his worn jeans and simple button-down shirt. I admired him for taking his windfall in stride and being so sensible about it. It was up to him to choose when and if he wanted to reveal his private business. "I'll keep it under my hat."

"Thanks, Soph. You're the best. How about I bring dinner tonight? We'll get the gang together and catch up on developments in the case?"

"Sounds great. By the way, did you receive your invitation to the Hollingsworth-Smythe Fourth of July bash?"

He scowled at me. "How do you know about that?"

"I'm in charge of it. And Mrs. Hollingsworth-Smythe specifically asked me to make sure that you attend. It seems her daughter Dodie has her eyes on you."

Bernie turned slightly green. "She has told me at great length about her long-suffering husband. It's kind of humorous, actually, because the former husband is now a regular at the bar and very pleased to be rid of Dodie and her mom."

"Does that mean you won't come?"

"I wouldn't do it for anyone else but you."

He stood up and I followed him to the door. "I'll tell you all about the tall woman as soon as I can. I promise." He leaned over and pecked my cheek.

I closed the door behind him and locked it, pondering lies and secrets. Maybe there *were* valid reasons for keeping things quiet. I knew I didn't tell everything. And I truly did trust Bernie.

Trying to put Bernie, Pierce, and my attacker out of my mind, I forced myself to concentrate on the upcoming Fourth of July event. Fortunately, all seemed to be running on schedule for that.

By four o'clock, it wasn't really cool enough to walk Daisy but I was restless. Leaving her at home in the cool house, I retraced what I thought had been Tate's steps the night he died. I strolled over to Blackwell's Tavern. Would he have left through the front door or the back? I gazed around the front door. It was surprisingly busy even at that time of day, with diners coming and going. Not to mention the people who were picking up takeout meals. I decided he probably left through the back door and walked around the block.

The alley looked different loaded with parked cars. A large white van had stopped in the middle of the alley near the entrance to Blackwell's. The back doors were open. As I approached it, I stopped in my tracks.

Fortunately, I didn't think I had been seen yet, so I dodged behind a car and watched as Marsha flirted with a man I did not know. Could that be Eli? He had beautifully bronzed skin and dreamy brown eyes. He laughed at something she said and softly cupped her face in his hand. The next thing I knew, they were kissing.

That wasn't a timid we-just-met kiss! I felt a little creepy watching them. Hunched over like a rat, I prepared to scuttle out of the alley the way I had come in.

I heard something behind me but before I turned, a hand covered my mouth. "I have had about enough of you," a woman's voice whispered in my ear.

Chapter 31

Dear Natasha,
Is it appropriate to serve cheesecake at a tea? I am
hosting a tea party for my daughter's bridal shower
and she wants cheesecake. I can't ever recall seeing
cheesecake at a tea.
                    Proper Mother in Red Bud, Georgia

Dear Proper Mother,
Bite-sized cheesecakes may be served at tea. Cheese-
cake bars are also acceptable.
                                              Natasha

Fear rippled through me. I struggled to stay calm, but it
wasn't working. She gripped me firmly, but on the right
side, where her hand covered my mouth, my elbow was free.

I figured I had two choices. I could try to scream and get
Marsha's attention—but what if the woman was in cahoots
with Marsha? Or I could haul my elbow back into the
woman hard, catch her off guard and run for my life.

I chose the latter. With all my might, I yanked my elbow

into her ribs, twisted out of her grip, and ran like the dickens. I wasn't much of a runner, but I was determined to get away from her. My chest burned with every step I took. I was literally gasping for air as I sped down the street dodging tourists. I pulled open a shop door and ran up a flight of stairs. I didn't stop until I reached the landing.

I sat down on the top step and texted Wolf. **Was just attacked by a woman. Think I got away.**

He responded. **"Think" you got away? Where are you?**

The sad truth was that I didn't know. I had simply wanted an open door. Any door in a storm? From my perch, I peered out the glass door to the street. If she happened to walk by and look inside, I didn't think she would see me. She would have to make an effort to look up the stairs. I gazed around for a light switch. I found it and turned off the lights in the hallway and over the stairs.

Of course, now I was cornered. I would have to find a way out the back in case she did see me. But first, I needed to tell Wolf where I was.

The last thing I wanted to do was go downstairs and look for a street number. What if the woman happened by at that exact moment and saw me? I didn't even know what she looked like. In retrospect, I probably should have looked back. Too late now. If I saw her on the street, I wouldn't realize it was her.

My breathing was more normal. I stood up and looked at the glass door of a store. A sign hung there. MOVING SALE. COME ON IN TO OUR FABULOUS MESS.

A woman inside smiled at me and I realized it was Wanda, Natasha's mom! I couldn't have chosen a better place to hide.

I flung open the door and rushed into her arms.

"Goodness, child! What happened to you?"

"There's someone after me."

Griselda Smith, Wanda's business partner, and the woman who married Wanda's husband after he left her without benefit of divorce, emerged from the back. "Sophie! Is a man chasing you, honey?"

"It's a woman. But I don't know who she is. She came up behind me."

"What are you up to?" asked Wanda. "Does this have anything to do with that nice man who owned Blackwell's Tavern?"

"Yes. It does."

My phone buzzed repeatedly. I glanced at it. "What's the address here?"

Wanda told me and I texted it to Wolf along with, **I'm okay. Turns out I landed among friends.**

I looked around at the boxes. Fearing their business had failed, I asked timidly, "What's going on?"

"We can't keep up with demand for our CBD products. We've gone in with Charlene and we're renting a bigger place with a full-fledged commercial kitchen in the back."

"Is she giving up her dinner business?"

"No, ma'am. She's growing it! And baking CBD goodies for us, too."

Uh-oh. "Does Natasha know about this?"

"Not yet. She'll be very upset when she finds out we're still selling CBD products," said Wanda. "I think it will be easier if we just go ahead and do it. She didn't want us to rent this place, either, if you recall."

That was true. I hated to break it to them, but they would find out sooner or later. "She told me she was going to open a CBD bakery and call it CBDelicious."

Wanda and Griselda stared at me in shock.

"We didn't tell her our plans because, well, you know how she is. We knew she would make a big fuss," said Griselda. "This is quite a change of attitude on her part."

Wanda hastily said, "We'll just make her a partner."

Griselda groaned. "Oh no. I know you love her, Wanda, but your daughter is . . . difficult."

"There's Wolf now!" Wanda said with a huge smile. "Come on in, honey bunch. It's all legal!"

A sly smile crept onto Wolf's face. "I'm sure it is." He walked over to me. "She grabbed you pretty good. I can see red marks from her fingers. Any clue who it might have been?" he asked.

"I was in the alley in back of Blackwell's Tavern—"

"After what happened last night?" asked Wolf. "What could possibly have possessed you to go there?"

"There's nothing wrong with passing through that alley. Lots of people do it all day long. If you must know, I thought I would follow Tate's route the night he was murdered. I wasn't bugging anyone." I glanced at him. "But Marsha was locking lips with an extremely handsome man."

"Did this woman say anything?"

"As a matter of fact, she said, " 'I've had about enough of you.' "

Wanda and Griselda gasped.

"I've gotten too close to something. I still don't know what it is, though."

"There's an understatement," said Wolf. He checked his watch. "If I walk Tate's path with you, then will you go home and stay there?"

"Probably."

Wanda chuckled. "That's my girl! But you stay safe, Sophie!"

Accompanied by my own personal bodyguard, I returned to the alley.

Chapter 32

Dear Sophie,
I'm throwing a Fourth of July party. My first, actu-
ally. Do you have any advice?
                    Celebrating in Celebration, Florida

Dear Celebrating,
Make all your side dishes and desserts a day ahead of
time. Bribe a reliable friend to watch the grill. If you
run short on time, make an ice cream bar for dessert.
Fill it with several flavors of ice cream, whipped
cream, chocolate and caramel sauces, and fun top-
pings like crushed candy, cookies, and nuts. They'll
love it and you can relax.
                                              Sophie

I took deep breaths when I reached the spot where I had
been attacked.

"It didn't take Marsha long to overcome her sorrow about
the loss of Tate," I said. "Do you think she killed him?"

Wolf didn't respond. I couldn't blame him. He had a suspect. And at every turn, evidence continued to pile up against Bernie.

There were loads of possibilities where Marsha was involved. She could have killed Tate and already had the new guy lined up. Did she really need to murder Tate to move on? Maybe he was the jealous one. Or had she been manipulating Tate all along, pretending to be interested in him? Or had the handsome new guy done the dirty deed for Marsha?

We walked away from the restaurant and turned onto the cross street.

As we walked, the white truck turned right beside us. The good-looking driver was the man with whom Marsha had locked lips. He flashed his pearly whites at me in a big grin. There was something about him, high cheekbones and narrow jaw, that wasn't classically handsome, but it all worked together, and the guy was gorgeous.

We continued our walk over to Auguste's restaurant.

"There's nothing to see here," said Wolf.

But it prompted some thoughts. "Tate left the restaurant with the tall woman. Did they go their separate ways? Or did she go with him and bonk him over the head with a bottle of champagne? Why did they cut through the alley and where were they going?"

I hustled Wolf in that direction as possibilities raced through my head. And then it dawned on me. "We thought he and the tall woman were going somewhere to have champagne and cheesecake. But what if he intended to bring champagne to the race to celebrate what he hoped would be a victory for Spencer? Spencer is too young to drink it, but isn't it a tradition to spew it over the heads of the runners?"

"I think so," said Wolf. "Or maybe he was going to open it at home."

Wolf observed the people on the street.

"What are you looking for?"

"Anyone who might be watching you. Come on. I'll give you a ride home."

Wolf parked in front of my house and insisted on going inside with me. He did a quick sweep of the house while I played with Daisy and Mochie.

"Would you please stay home tonight?" he asked. "You've been attacked by two different people, and I still don't know why. Stay put!" He closed the kitchen door behind him and opened it immediately. "And lock the door."

I promptly locked the door. He was walking away when he heard the clank and without looking back, he raised his arm and gave me a thumbs-up.

I was glad Bernie had suggested dinner with our friends tonight. It was clear that I had gotten too close to uncovering Tate's killer and had unnerved someone or possibly two people.

Putting on the kettle, I wondered if the two attackers could have been the same person. They both approached me from behind. The first one had gripped me with more strength, I thought. And both of them whispered. Was that instinctive? Were the two of them connected? That would make sense. I knew one thing for sure. The woman hadn't been Marsha. She had been busy smooching.

I threw a fresh French tablecloth over my kitchen table. Cheerful sunflowers were printed in the middle, surrounded by a broad swath of cornflower blue. Stacking simple white plates on the table, I wondered why I hadn't had more moxie and found a way to speak with Spencer. Why hadn't I followed Spencer and Coach to the hospital parking garage and found a way to confront Spencer? It could be Eli's pocketing of money that he was worried about. But if that was the case, why hadn't he gone straight to Tate and reported it? Or maybe he had.

I made sure a couple of bottles of white wine were chilling

and was arranging a variety of glasses on the island when Daisy ran to the door, whining to go out.

It was unlike her, so I cautiously entered the sunroom that overlooked the backyard. I didn't see a squirrel or cat, either of which would have interested her. Maybe she just needed to go out? I had my hand on the door handle when I noticed that the door to the garage was open. Just a little bit.

It stopped me in my tracks. Had I forgotten to close it completely? Maybe Francie came over to borrow a garden tool? I could probably come up with a dozen completely plausible reasons for the door to be ajar. Part of me hated to call Wolf again. But another part of me reasoned that if I were watching a movie and a door was ajar, I would be yelling at the protagonist to call the police.

I jumped at sudden banging on my kitchen door. To be on the safe side, I darted through the hallway to the foyer and peered around the wall. Bernie was at the door.

Relief flooded through me. I dashed through the kitchen and opened the door for him.

He leaned toward me and kissed me on the cheek. "I'm running a little early, but I wanted to check on you."

I closed the door and locked it. "Someone might be in the garage. The door is ajar, and Daisy wants to go out there." While I spoke, I hurried to the foyer and retrieved the taser Mars had given me many years ago.

Bernie stood in the sunroom, staring at the garage.

"Um, before we venture out there, I should tell you that someone grabbed me from behind again this afternoon."

He swung around to look at me. "In broad daylight? Are you okay?"

"I'm fine. I managed to elbow her and get away. Would you rather that we call the police?"

"See if you can get hold of Wolf and have him on the line."

Lest Daisy get hurt, I insisted she remain in the house. She didn't appreciate that and howled pitifully in the sunroom. I followed Bernie outside, phoned Wolf, and told him what was happening. "It might be nothing," I said.

Bernie held the taser and kicked the garage door wide open.

Chapter 33

Dear Natasha,
Would you suggest a menu for a Fourth of July party?
You have such excellent taste and undeniable style. I
would love to know what you would serve.

Your Fan in Independence, Iowa

Dear Fan,
I am so glad that you asked. Stuffed jalapeños,
wrapped in bacon and grilled. Charred prosciutto-
wrapped melon. The main course would be grilled
mushroom, artichoke, and Chilean sea bass kebabs
with a homemade Tabasco and cayenne sauce. Roasted
broccolini salad with chopped cherry peppers and
feta, and Roquefort potatoes. And for dessert, an ele-
gant New York style cheesecake decorated with
whipped cream, strawberries, and blueberries.

Natasha

A figure moved in the shadows of the garage.
"Stop! Who's there?" yelled Bernie.
"Don't shoot!" cried a voice that I recognized.

"Spencer?"

He emerged from the shadows, holding his hands up in the air like he was in a movie.

I assured Wolf that everything was fine and disconnected the call. "What are you doing here? I thought you went fishing."

Bernie smiled at him. His voice was soft and reassuring when he said, "You can put your hands down."

Spencer walked out of the garage. "The trip fell through. Neither one of us wanted to go. Mom's gonna be really mad. I didn't want to go home. I knew she'd look for me at my friends' houses and"—he tilted his head and gazed away—"I don't know. You've been pretty nice. I thought you might not mind if I camped out in your backyard."

"I wouldn't mind at all. You're welcome to stay at my house, but I think your mom will flip out if she can't find you. Let's go inside and call her."

He followed us in, and Daisy went bananas over him. He rubbed her ears and crouched to pet her. I thought it was the first time I had seen him look happy.

"Would you like some iced tea? It's hot out there."

"Sure. That would be awesome." Spencer sat down in one of the chairs by the fireplace and focused on Daisy and Mochie.

"They like you," I said, pouring the tea into tall glasses filled with ice cubes.

"I like dogs and cats. I've always wanted one."

I handed him and Bernie tea and sat down opposite Spencer.

He stared at Bernie. Frowning, he asked, "Aren't you the dude that killed my dad?"

"No. I'm the one they arrested for killing your dad, but I didn't kill him." Bernie, to his credit, appeared composed.

Spencer gazed at me. "Is that true? My mom said they had caught the murderer."

"I'm afraid not."

He took a long drink and seemed to be considering the situation. "But what about the blood on your car?"

Bernie remained cool and collected. He sat in a chair with his legs stretched out in front of him. "Someone took my car keys and the car. But here's the thing—other than a little blood, your dad's DNA isn't inside my car. They found Sophie's DNA, they even found Daisy's DNA, but there's no evidence that your dad was actually in the back of my car. The blood in the front is only on the driver's seat. It's Tate's blood, but no one thinks he was driving the car."

"Then the killer must have had a tarp or something."

Bernie grinned. "Tate would be proud of you. But where's the tarp?"

Spencer shifted uneasily and licked his lips. "I believe you. Someone else killed Dad." His lower lip trembled. "I played in some of those games between the restaurants. My dad liked you. I don't think I was wrong about that. We had fun." His forehead wrinkled. "I rehearsed what I was going to say on the way over here but now I don't know where to start." Suddenly he blurted, "I'm the reason my dad was murdered."

Chills ran through me. He'd said *the reason*, not that he murdered Tate. I asked gently, "Are you *Worried in Old Town?*"

His eyes widened with recognition. "How'd you figure that out?"

"I saw the stationery in Jo's bedroom. She's not old enough to write a note like that. Is this about what you saw at the restaurant?"

He nodded and shifted uneasily. "I hope it's okay that I came here. My girlfriend and best friend are away. Jo is too young to understand. Mom has been flipping out since Dad died. I can't talk to her about anything. I couldn't talk to

Pierce about Dad because it annoyed him. I guess it makes him feel bad that he wasn't the father to me that Tate was. And now he might die, too."

"You could always call your aunt Belinda."

"Blabbermouth Belinda? No, thanks! And I'm not being mean. Even my dad called her that behind her back. She can't stop talking."

I smiled. "There's at least one in every family."

"I'm not a restaurant genius or anything. Dad had me going in early before everybody else to check and accept food deliveries. There's a whole routine, picking up the top vegetables to make sure rotten ones aren't hidden underneath. Checking the bottoms of the boxes to be sure they're not wet, stuff like that."

Bernie smiled at him and nodded.

"Then I was supposed put them away. For the most part, it went okay. I was usually the first one there, and Marsha came in after me. She was supposed to be training me about meat and fish. I'm pretty good at picking fruits and vegetables, stuff like that, but meat and fish are a little different. I got my food handling certificate and everything, but if you don't know what you're doing, it's easy to accept the wrong cuts of meat."

He took a long sip of his iced tea, and I refilled his glass.

"When I started, I just went along with whatever Marsha said. But after a while, I noticed that she always sent me to do something else when the fish delivery came. She let me accept the beef and pork. She didn't even double-check it. But every day when the fresh fish came, she sent me somewhere. 'Go upstairs and see if your dad is here yet. Go check to see if all the bathrooms were cleaned. Refill all the salt and pepper shakers.' I'm not saying that stuff didn't need to be done, but the timing was weird." He leaned his head forward and looked up at us. "I started spying on her. I know that's wrong, but I had this feeling that she was up to no good. Like a sixth sense or something. I guess I should have done things differently. But I didn't know it would turn out like this!"

"It's okay," I said as soothingly as I could. "What happened?"

"You've been there. You know how it is in the alley where the trucks stop to unload their deliveries. There's no place you can hide, unless it fills up with cars, so I went upstairs to Marsha's office because there's a window that overlooks the alley. I opened it just a little bit so I could hear what was going on. The window creaked and I was afraid they would hear me, but I guess they didn't. At least, I didn't see them look up at me or anything. He handed her money. Cash. A lot of it. And he said very clearly, 'Nice haul. Those fish specials of yours are paying off.' And then he kissed her!"

"So she's getting a kickback," said Bernie. "They probably bill high, and then they give her part of the extra profit."

Spencer nodded. "That's what I guess."

So that was what I had seen earlier. "You think your dad got wind of it and that's why he was murdered?" I asked.

Spencer groaned. "He didn't get wind of it. I *told* him." He winced. "I told him the day he died. I think he must have confronted Marsha and that's why he was murdered. I don't know if it was Marsha or the fish guy or some henchmen that they paid."

Unfortunately for Spencer, it was the most plausible theory yet.

"You have to tell Wolf," I said, reaching for my phone.

"No!" Spencer looked at me in horror. "I can't do that."

"Why not?" asked Bernie.

"Because I'm not supposed to talk to him."

"He *is* underage," I pointed out.

"Mom told me not to say a word to Wolf or any cops unless our lawyer was present. Did . . . did I mess up by telling you?"

"No, Spencer. You did the right thing. Wolf will probably need to talk with you, but we'll make sure your lawyer is with you when it happens." I took a deep breath. "Now, about camping out. You are welcome to stay here but only if it's okay with your mom."

Spencer cringed. "You know what she'll say."

"What about camping in Pierce's room overnight? I bet Bobbie Sue could use a break."

He nodded and pulled out his phone. "I could do that." When Bobbie Sue answered, we heard her shriek, "Where *are* you?" Spencer held the phone away from his ear. Bobbie Sue didn't stop. "Your father was just murdered and then you go and disappear? I thought he had killed you, too. I'm sending Coach to pick you up. Where are you?"

Spencer said calmly, "I'll meet him at the house in half an hour."

"Spencer! That is not acceptable. Where—" Spencer stared at the phone and disconnected the call.

"A little trick my dad taught me," he said. "Makes her mad, but she's already mad so it doesn't really make a difference."

Bernie and I exchanged a glance. I didn't blame Bobbie Sue. She had loved Tate. He was obviously her rock. With his death, her life had gone haywire. The last thing she needed was for her children to disappear.

Spencer collected his things. "I guess it was a good thing Mom wouldn't let me go back to work, huh? Now we have to be on the lookout for Marsha and that fish guy."

Bernie and I accompanied him to the door. "Are you sure you're okay walking home?"

He grinned. "I can outrun Marsha and that guy any day."

"What did he look like?" I asked, wondering if he was the same fellow I had seen.

"Tall, trim, black hair, kind of tanned skin," he said.

I just nodded. It sounded like the same guy all right.

Bernie shook hands with him. "For the record, your dad and I were mates. I'm going to miss him."

Spencer murmured, "Thanks."

As he walked away, I said, "Be safe!"

He passed Humphrey, Francie, and Duke, who walked up just as a gentleman delivered Chinese takeout. Bernie had ordered enough Chinese dishes to feed a dozen people.

I whispered to him, "We don't mention that it's Spencer who saw Marsha taking a kickback?"

Bernie nodded. "I think that's wise. I don't want anyone after him. But we will tell Wolf, right?"

"I'll call him."

Bernie wasted no time setting the food on my kitchen table. "Moo shu pork, lemon chicken, General Tso's chicken, beef with snow peas, Peking duck, Szechuan green beans and broccoli, and double shrimp lo mein," he announced.

Nina, Muppet, and Mars arrived simultaneously.

I hurried to put out knives and forks, but Bernie stopped me. "It's all chopsticks tonight!"

Nina got to work making piña coladas and pouring wine. Bernie poured sparkling water for the two of us.

I slipped away to my office to phone Wolf. His cell rolled over to voicemail. Good thing it wasn't an emergency. I left a message. "Call me. There's been a development you need to know about."

I hurried back to the kitchen. When we sat down to eat, Bernie lifted his glass and said, "To my friends, who have stood behind me and never doubted me."

Lifting my glass, I felt a little guilty about my moments of doubt when I found out Bernie had lied to me. But even then, I couldn't truly imagine that he had murdered Tate.

Everyone spoke at once and started passing around the food that Bernie had ordered.

Francie asked, "Was that Bobbie Sue's son I saw leaving your house?"

I assured her that it was. Skipping the part about the dreadful blisters, Nina and I told them what happened to Pierce.

And then Bernie and I filled them in about Marsha taking kickback money from the fish guy.

Just as I had gotten a good grip on some lo mein and was lifting it to my mouth, a sad face looked in the kitchen door. Natasha stood there like she was posing for a neglected orphan photo. All she needed was rain.

I opened the door. "Come in and join us, Natasha." I handed her a plate. "The moo shu pork is delicious."

"You're all here together? Without me?"

My heart went out to her until she said, "I see you're dining with Tate's killer."

Chapter 34

Dear Natasha,
I watch your show all the time. I love that you're not like everyone else and that you are willing to take food to new levels for gourmands. What do you see coming up?

Epicure in Vinegar Bend, Alabama

Dear Epicure,
I love fans like you! Charcoal and artificial sweeteners are so yesterday. Look for lots of charred food, especially veggies and burnt sugar. There will be more wonderful sweet and salty pairings like butterscotch fish sauces and salted caramel potatoes.

Natasha

"Natasha!" cried Mars.

"You needn't scold me, Mars. I've had a terrible day. Week. Month. Actually, the whole year has been dreadful."

"You cannot move in with me," said Francie, helping herself to more lemon chicken.

"I'd have to redecorate first," said Natasha.

"What happened to your business plans?" I asked, pretending not to know.

"My own mother, half-sister, and her mother have stolen my idea. Not only that, but they stole the storefront I was going to use. They have stabbed me in the back," she wailed. "I refuse to have anything to do with their plans."

"I thought your mother and Griselda had a store of their own," said Mars.

"They do. They ran out of room, so they're moving to a larger space in a better location. They never tell me anything."

"Gee, I wonder why," said Nina wryly.

"What happened to your bakery space?" I asked.

"That's the one they stole. The three of them are renting it and the place next door for their store. There's a huge commercial kitchen in back where Charlene can cook for her clients. All they can talk about is expanding and their success."

Humphrey set his chopsticks down. "It sounds like you should go to work for them if they're doing that well."

Natasha gasped and clasped a hand just below her neck. "Never! But now I'm back to square one."

I hoped to cheer her up when I asked, "How's the new beau?"

"You're seeing someone?" asked Mars.

"Are you jealous?" Natasha flirted.

"Nope. Just happy for you." He smiled at her.

"He's scrumptious," she said. "I've invited him to Marjorie Hollingsworth-Smythe's Fourth of July bash." She preened and purred, "Only the crème de la crème have been invited."

"Terrific. You'll have to introduce us," said Mars.

"Marjorie is as pompous as you are, Natasha," said Francie, "but she throws a great party!"

"Am I the only one not invited?" asked Humphrey.

Francie piped up immediately, "Then you *must* be my plus-one. My girlfriends will be envious when I arrive on the arm of a handsome young buck!"

"So who is this guy?" asked Nina.

"Harrison Grant. The epitome of tall, dark, and handsome. Honestly, he could be a movie star. He has the looks and manners of Cary Grant."

"Wow," said Francie. "I can't wait to meet this gentleman!"

"Now, Francie," teased Natasha, "he's all mine."

Although Natasha had simply pushed a few noodles around her plate, I didn't think she had eaten a bite. The rest of us had eaten too much.

We adjourned to the sunroom and sat under the fairy lights, surrounded by the dark of night outside the glass. Nina refilled everyone's drinks and I brought Mars a pad and pen.

"I suspected Marsha all along," said Nina. "But now that I know she and her bartender boyfriend, Eli, were stealing from Blackwell's Tavern and cheating Tate, I'm certain that they killed him."

Natasha, who had been busy planning her CBD business and had been out of the loop, gasped. "I thought for sure that Bernie knocked him off."

"Thank you for your confidence in my character, Natasha." Bernie gave her a little mock salute.

Mars scribbled on the pad. "I'm in total agreement. It's the first decent motivation I've heard. They would have lost their jobs and gone to prison for that."

"Well," said Natasha, "be that as it may, if it's not Bernie, I would put money on Bobbie Sue's ex-husband, Pierce."

"Why?" asked Humphrey.

"He looks like a murderer. And he has plenty of motive." She rubbed her fingers together indicating money. "There's a man who must be really sorry he dumped his wife. He probably never imagined she would be so successful."

"Has anyone considered that Coach fellow who has been hanging around Bobbie Sue?" asked Humphrey. "When she came in to select a casket, he seemed sort of proprietary."

Bernie gazed up at the lights. "Diners at the restaurant have thrown all sorts of names out there. Most have absolutely no logical basis. But one keeps coming up—Bobbie Sue. After all, she's the one who inherits everything. Does anyone know if the expansion of her company might be costing more than expected? Maybe she's not as successful as we all think."

"Aha!" Natasha shouted. "That's a very good point. Everyone fawns over her like she's really a queen. Calling yourself a queen does not make you one."

"We don't know where she went when she left her party," Nina pointed out. "Her daughter was conveniently at a slumber party. And her son ran in the 5K, so he was probably out late partying that night."

"I'm still thinking Marsha and Eli." Mars tapped the paper with the pen. "They had a lot to gain. If Bobbie Sue allowed Marsha to run the restaurant after Tate's death, then they could have robbed her blind. And they also had a lot to lose. The best that could happen after Tate knew of their thievery was that they would be fired and wouldn't have references from their previous employer. The worst would be prison. That's a lot of motivation."

"The only thing that bothers me about them is that I was attacked by a woman today," I said. "And when it happened, Marsha was standing in my line of sight. That means someone else is involved."

That came as news to all of them except for Bernie. In the middle of their questions, I asked, "Who feels like sampling a Japanese cheesecake?"

Happily, and rather remarkably considering how much we'd eaten for dinner, everyone was interested, even Natasha.

I returned to the kitchen and pulled the cheesecake out of

the fridge. It looked fairly plain, so I washed some strawberries to dress it up.

Nina followed me to the kitchen and opened the refrigerator door. "Do you have any of the chocolate cheesecake left over?"

"I do."

"I don't see it." She stepped aside and I searched for it.

When I removed it from the fridge, I stared at it. Why had there been chocolate cheesecake at the murder scene?

"Hey, hey, hey! That's mine, remember? I knew something was up with Tate when he didn't show on Midsummer Night."

"That's right," I murmured. "You won the bet."

"I wouldn't have minded a mom who served me chocolate cheesecake for breakfast."

That was it! That was what had been bothering me. My throat tightened. Spencer. Bobbie Sue had called herself a bad mother for giving her son chocolate cheesecake for breakfast.

Chapter 35

Dear Sophie,
I tried making cheesecake in my food processor. It seems so logical. Like a dump cake, just throw everything in and let it rip. But it definitely wasn't the creamy cheesecake I had imagined. What went wrong?
                    Creative Baker in Bakersfield, California

Dear Creative Baker,
It works for some recipes but generally, cream cheese doesn't like being beaten. Even in a mixer, it's best to beat cream cheese as little as possible.
                                        Sophie

The cheesecake at the murder scene had thrown me off. Tate didn't have the cheesecake with him, his killer did!

"Sophie! What's with you?" asked Nina.

I was still a little stunned at the thought that Spencer might have killed Tate. I cut slices of the Japanese cheesecake and placed them on white dessert plates rimmed in gold. I used my immersion blender to whip cream, added a dollop on each plate, and garnished each with a couple of fresh strawberries. Nina carried them into the sunroom two at a time.

I preferred a cup of hot tea with dessert and felt like I needed one, now that Spencer might be the murderer after all. Could he be the one who warned me to stop looking into Tate's murder? Had he come here to frighten me or worse, but when he was caught and Bernie was present, did he fib and make up that story about Marsha?

When Nina came through for more plates, I asked, "Do you think anyone wants coffee? I'm putting on water for tea."

She reported back a few minutes later. Five decaf coffees and Bernie would like tea.

I pulled seven mugs out of the cupboard. Only two of them matched, but the wonderful thing about white and gold was they all seemed to go together anyway. Plus, my guests would know which one was theirs if they set their mugs down. I poured tea into the matching ones for Bernie and me and loaded a coffeepot for the rest.

Nina and I carried everything into the sunroom, including sugar and cream.

And then, we tested the Japanese version of cheesecake. I noted that even Natasha tried more than one forkful. After everyone had taken a bite and rendered their amazed verdicts, I said, "I think we overlooked something. At least I did. I kept thinking that it was Tate who had cheesecake with him the night he was killed."

"Right," said Humphrey. "Daisy found it."

"What if it was the killer who brought the cheesecake?"

"Ohh," said Francie. "Symbolism. Which would mean Bobbie Sue was somehow involved? Like retribution for something she did?"

"Or something much more simple. Like someone who took chocolate cheesecake to work that day. Maybe he didn't eat it. Maybe he ate some but not all. And when he killed

Tate, whatever remained fell out of a bag. He tried to clean it up, but on the uneven surfaces of the alley and the backyard, bits of it remained."

I had their full attention.

"You're saying this like you know who it was," said Bernie.

I didn't want to say it. I didn't even want to think it. I winced when I spoke. "I now believe it could have been Spencer."

Mars stared at the pad where he had made notes. "He did have an argument with Tate the night before the murder."

"And Bobbie Sue told us she gave him chocolate cheesecake to take to work for breakfast," murmured Nina.

"Is he old enough to drive?" asked Humphrey.

"Probably," said Bernie. "But now I feel like a dolt for being nice to him. What does he have against me?"

"He also knew that his girlfriend and her family were away," I pointed out, still feeling horrified that Spencer had fooled me. "He's been very upset. Everyone was chalking it up to Tate's death, but now I have to wonder if it was because Spencer murdered Tate."

Nina fluttered her hand in my direction. "Plus, he had a key to the restaurant and knew about the cellar."

"Bobbie Sue will be devastated when she finds out," said Mars.

Natasha nodded. "Imagine your child murdering a member of the family."

"I have a feeling she already knows," I said. "She wouldn't let him go back to work. Pierce was supposed to take him fishing. When he collapsed and that fell through, she enlisted Coach to fill in for Pierce. Spencer was totally unenthusiastic about it."

"Maybe she just wanted to get him away from everything," said Francie. "Give him a break to come to terms with Tate's death."

"Or she wanted to get him out of town and away from the police!" said Natasha.

Our dinner party broke up after that. I shooed everyone home, but Bernie produced a toothbrush. "I'll sleep down here, just in case. It's the least I can do for you."

The two of us were washing and drying dishes when we heard someone at the door. Wolf waved at us and Bernie opened the door for him.

Wolf said, "I thought you were going to stop nosing around Tate's case."

"Decaf coffee?" I asked.

"Sophie," he growled.

I took that as a yes and poured him a cup. Handing it to him, I said, "To be honest, I really haven't done anything objectionable today."

Wolf sat down at my banquette and grumbled, "Pierce Carver."

"Oh, I'm sorry. The next time someone starts stumbling and falls *into the street* right in front of me, I'll ignore him and keep on walking."

"Not funny."

"It really wasn't. And Wolf, you should have seen those blisters. They were scary!"

"I suppose poking around in his personal belongings wasn't being nosy?"

This was ridiculous. I explained about the smell of menthol and muscle cream. "It was a long shot that he had rubbed it on his knees and had a reaction to it, but give me another good reason for his hands and knees to blister. I had to try. You would have, too."

In a completely ordinary tone, like he was telling us the time, he said, "Pierce was poisoned."

I gasped. "What?"

Bernie and I sat down at the banquette.

"Someone put poison in his muscle cream?" I guessed.

Wolf nodded. "It will be on the news tomorrow morning because we don't know if it was only in his cream or if someone poisoned a bunch of them. It's from a plant called American false hellebore."

"Never heard of it."

"I hadn't, either. Apparently it has slowly been invading Virginia. Most of the plants are removed immediately because they're so toxic. They grow tall and have a flower that looks like Queen Anne's lace. If you even brush against it, you can be poisoned because it can be absorbed by the skin. It's deadly to humans and livestock."

"They're sure it's in the cream? No chance that he rubbed against one on a trail?" asked Bernie.

"They tested the cream that Sophie brought to the hospital. Someone blended it into the cream."

"Wow. What's the prognosis for Pierce?" I asked.

"Guarded. They really don't know what will happen yet. There *are* some cases of people who cooked it and ate it. Let's just say they were very sorry and lucky they survived. But the doctors haven't seen a case like this before."

"Does Bobbie Sue know?" I asked.

"I have no idea. I was called in because it's attempted murder."

"That's why you're here," I said. "Clearly I had no way of knowing that! I just helped Pierce because he collapsed in front of me."

Wolf tried hard to suppress a grin. "I have to say it was a shock when I saw your name in the paperwork as a witness."

"I thought maybe he had a reaction to something in the cream."

Wolf finally snickered. "You okay being by yourself tonight?"

"I'll be fine. I dreaded the onset of darkness, but Bernie is staying over with me."

"Stay inside and call me if either of you hear anything."

Wolf rose and walked to the door. "And Sophie, try to keep out of trouble."

Bernie and I were beat. I said goodnight and walked upstairs, Daisy and Mochie racing ahead of me. It was a beautiful night. I raised the window for some fresh air and decided to sleep with it open. The cool night air wafted in and as I drifted off, I thought I even heard an owl calling into the night.

I woke to the scents of bacon and cinnamon. Daisy and Mochie, who had slept with me, had abandoned me for the delicious smells that wafted up the stairs. I slung on a bathrobe and hurried to the kitchen, where Bernie was hard at work.

He poured me a mug of tea and placed it on the table. "Good morning! Fried or scrambled?"

"Fried?"

"Oh good. Mars always wants scrambled."

"Can I help?"

"You timed it perfectly." He slid a platter of blueberry pastries onto the table and looked at his watch. "Should we phone Nina or—"

"Here she comes."

Bernie looked out the bay window and laughed. "I don't know how she does it."

He unlocked the door and opened it wide.

Clad in a lavender bathrobe and slippers with little faux marabou feathers on them, Nina hurried into the house. Muppet trotted in at her feet.

Nina headed straight for the platter of bacon strips, plucked one, and munched before saying, "Morning, all. Hope I'm not late."

Bernie and I laughed at her.

While we ate our breakfast, Bernie kept checking the time.

"Are you in a hurry?" I asked.

"I just need to be at work early this morning. There are a few things I would like to resolve before everyone else arrives and the day gets crazy busy."

"You fixed such a lovely breakfast. This is a real treat! Nina and I will clean up."

"Are you sure? It's my mess."

"I'm sure." Bernie planted kisses on our cheeks and fled out the door.

"Wow. He was in a hurry!" said Nina.

"Yes, he was. Something is up with him."

"You don't mean that he murdered Tate? Do you?"

"Of course not. But he's up to something." I gazed at her. "Nina, I'm going over to Bobbie Sue's this morning. She has to know that Marsha and Eli have been stealing from Black-well's. The problem is that she's relying so heavily on Marsha, that I'm not sure she'll believe it unless she sees it with her own eyes."

"I'm in. Give me half an hour to change."

We met on the sidewalk in front of her house and walked over to Bobbie Sue's.

"What if Spencer is there?" asked Nina.

"I don't think he'll kill us, because we're not trying to make him take AP classes."

"Ha ha. Do you really think that's why he murdered Tate?"

"Nina, I have trouble believing that Spencer is the killer. It's kind of the way I feel about Bernie. We know him well, so it's impossible for us to imagine that he could do something like that. I get the same sort of vibes from Spencer. Yet too many pieces fit into place about Spencer."

From the outside, no one would have guessed the turmoil inside Bobbie Sue's home. It looked as perfect as the other houses on the street. Pierce's Jeep was still in the driveway.

I knocked on the door and Bobbie Sue opened it. She wore a fluffy bathrobe, her hair was wet, and she didn't have on a stitch of makeup. She looked younger and more vulnerable.

She seemed pained when she saw us. "Come on in."

We followed her to the kitchen.

"Coffee?" she asked.

We declined.

"Bobbie Sue, there's something I need to talk to you about." Tears welled in her eyes. "Please. Please don't. I . . . I've been trying so hard to—" She stopped and wiped her eyes with a tissue. "Don't do this," she whispered. "I beg of you."

Chapter 36

Dear Sophie,
I hate to trouble you, but the strangest thing is hap-
pening. My birdfeeders are disappearing. I'm not up
on the latest silly things kids do. Is there a birdfeeder
nabbing gang? If not, then I suspect my daughter-in-
law may be taking them. How can I find out?
                    Leery in Ravenswood, West Virginia

Dear Leery,
I am unaware of a birdfeeder nabbing gang. In your
shoes, I would set up a camera that will be triggered
by anyone walking toward your birdfeeders. Let me
know what happens!
                                            Sophie

"Mom!" Spencer's voice came from upstairs. "I can't find my team T-shirt. All the guys are going to wear them today."

"Excuse me," said Bobbie Sue.

She had only taken a few steps when Spencer bounded into

the kitchen wearing a plain gray T-shirt. "Hi. Sorry, I didn't mean to interrupt."

"Sweetheart, I don't know where it is. My purse is upstairs, just take what you need from my wallet, okay? Buy a new one and when we locate the old one, you'll have two."

Spencer loped to the banister, where a cream-colored canvas backpack with leather straps hung. He picked it up and struggled to open it. "I hate this backpack," he griped.

"Give it a chance to break in," Bobbie Sue said in the knowing voice of a mom.

"Hey, Spencer," I said, "what time does the fish delivery usually come?"

He pulled a T-shirt out of the backpack, shot me a horrified look and said, "In about an hour." Then he hurried up the stairs.

Bobbie Sue sat down and forced a wan smile.

She had a lot going on so I thought I'd better get right to the point. "I have reason to believe that Marsha is taking kickbacks in cash from your fish supplier."

Her entire expression changed. The tiredness in her face was gone. "Marsha? Are you sure?"

"She's dating Eli and I'm told he's shorting you when he sells drinks."

Bobbie Sue's mouth gaped. "Good grief! What will be next?" She sighed. "I can't just walk up to them and make that kind of accusation."

"I agree. I thought the three of us could hide and watch the fish delivery from the window in her office."

Nina nodded vigorously.

"Marsha? Seriously? I can hardly believe it. I trusted her. Now that Tate's gone, she's stabbing me in the back?"

"My sources indicate that it's been going on for some time."

"It's true, Mom," Spencer said quietly from the stairs.

I didn't realize that he had returned and been listening.

"You knew about this, Spencer?" asked Bobbie Sue.

"I saw Marsha take money."

"That's why you're here?" Bobbie Sue asked me.

"Yes. Go get dressed."

Bobbie Sue nodded. "That, that witch!" She took off up the stairs.

Nina leaned over and whispered, "She knows about Spencer."

I thought so, too. Bobbie Sue thought we had come to accuse him of murdering Tate. There was no question in my mind about that. But I couldn't quite accept that Spencer had plotted Tate's murder over advanced placement classes. Had something else been going on between them? Did Tate forbid Spencer from seeing his girlfriend, perhaps?

Bobbie Sue returned in short order with her hair damp and pulled back into a bun. With makeup, she appeared more like the Bobbie Sue I knew. Her dress was perfect for a hot summer day but still looked professional. "They're judging cheesecake recipe entries this week, Nina," she said. "I can get you in as a taster if you like."

Nina swooned. "I'm your gal. Bring on the cheesecake!"

We walked over to Blackwell's Tavern. Bobbie Sue unlocked the back entrance. As soon as we were inside the cool, empty restaurant, she locked the door behind us.

"Marsha will probably go straight up to her office to put away her purse or whatever. We'll need a place to hide while she does that," said Bobbie Sue.

"We can crouch behind the bar," said Nina.

I was worried that she might go back there. "What if we hid in Tate's office? If she doesn't notice us, that would be great. If she does see us, then you can always say you were looking for documents or the lease or something," I suggested.

They nodded and we trooped up the stairs and into Tate's

office. Ten minutes later, we heard the key unlocking the door. We positioned ourselves so she wouldn't spot us as she walked by. It worked beautifully. She deposited her belongings in her office and quickly went back down the stairs.

We hurried into her office and raised the window ever so slowly so it wouldn't screech. Spencer had been correct. It was a perfect view of the alley and the back door to the restaurant.

Time ticked by slowly as we waited for the fish delivery to arrive. When the white delivery van drove into the alley, we stepped back from the window. Marsha was on the ball. We could hear her talking. She wanted her money. I angled my phone out the window and managed to take several photos when the driver handed over cash to her.

Bobbie Sue was furious and immediately texted Wolf.

I noticed that it was a younger driver this time. In fact, he looked vaguely familiar, but I couldn't quite place him. I gasped when it came to me. It was Austin Sinclair, the guy who had dumped sweet Liddy, the girl who hung an angel on Tate's photograph.

Working for a congressman, my foot. What a liar! I was glad she wasn't seeing him anymore.

He drove away and we waited for Wolf. When he texted that he was at the front door, the three of us walked down and opened the door. We showed him the photos.

"You'll need to back this up with invoices," said Wolf.

At that moment, Marsha walked out of the kitchen. "Hi. What's going on here?" Her expression was innocent as a baby's.

Bobbie Sue faced her. "It appears that we have an employee taking kickbacks. How could you, Marsha? Tate thought so highly of you. Do you know how disappointed he must have been in you?"

"I don't know what you're talking about," Marsha replied, edging backward toward the rear door as she spoke.

Could I run around the block fast enough to prevent her from escaping? I doubted it.

"Unbelievable," said Bobbie Sue. "I thought you liked Tate. Actually, I thought you were in love with him."

"Fool!" Marsha snarled. "The two of you just collected money hand over fist. I deserved what I took. I was here all the time. No one cared if I had a life or not. Everyone thought I should be devoted to *wonderful* Tate. I kissed up to him because I needed this job. I knew he wouldn't leave you. He told me right up front that he did not date employees." She laughed. "And he advised me to do the same! Well, Queen of Cheesecake, this restaurant is all yours now. You go ahead and see how easy my job is. I quit!"

Marsha turned on her heel and opened the back door.

But Wong was waiting for her. In a matter of minutes, Marsha was handcuffed and taken away in the back of a waiting squad car.

Nina and I left Wolf and Bobbie Sue to sort everything out. We treated ourselves to icy strawberry frappé drinks and walked home by way of the alley where Tate was murdered.

We paused at the Eklunds' gate. "He had dinner with a beautiful woman," I said. "Then, someone carrying cheese-cake—"

"Most likely Marsha or Spencer," Nina interjected.

"—crashed a bottle of champagne on his head. That person had Bernie's car keys and his car."

"Nope," said Nina in between slurps. "There was cheese-cake and champagne out here, right? And inside the Eklunds' backyard."

"Right."

"Something unexpected happened. Either someone came along or the killer was in a hurry. Don't you see? If the killer had the car here, then why drag Tate around? He would have put him in the car and driven away. Instead, the killer dragged him inside the fence to hide him."

"Or he killed him inside and dragged him out to place him in the car."

"Mmm, could be," said Nina.

"Where is Spencer's T-shirt? And why does he have a new backpack?" I asked.

"T-shirt is in the laundry because Bobbie Sue hasn't had a minute to do laundry. And the backpack busted because he's a kid and he stuffs too much junk in it."

"You're probably right," I conceded. "Between the time it would have taken to get Bernie's car and the time it probably took to tail and murder Tate, there's no way Bobbie Sue could have done it."

"Plus, she would have had blood on her dress, but when she came back, she was wearing the same dress," Nina pointed out.

"She is officially off the list," I said.

"But she could have worked in conjunction with Spencer. Remember how she kept looking at her watch? She seemed nervous about something, didn't she?"

Nina was right. "You're saying Bobbie Sue arranged to meet Tate. She hit him over the head with the bottle and waited for Spencer to help her lift him into a car"—I waved my hands—"and that's why Tate's blood isn't in the back of Bernie's car! They transported him in a different car."

"Exactly!"

"But she would have had blood on her," I protested. "There would have been cheesecake and champagne on her shoes. I don't know . . ."

"Are you kidding? They prepared for that. She probably had two identical dresses."

We started walking home. "Where's the bloody one?" I asked.

And then the two of us said simultaneously, "With Spencer's missing T-shirt."

"Well, they're long gone then," I said. "She's no dummy. She would have burned them."

"Where?" asked Nina.

"Loads of people have fire pits. What about Pierce or her buddy Coach?"

"You're now involving the whole town in Tate's murder," said Nina.

"Hey, how is your husband doing? Any more weird packages?" I asked.

"Come inside and see." Nina trotted up the stairs to her house and unlocked the door. She pointed to a large box in the foyer. "We have here bacon-flavored lip balm, this lovely can of dehydrated water—"

"What?" I picked it up and read the label. "*Just add water.* Very funny."

Nina continued. "—a computer microphone that doesn't work with any of our computers, these lovely cat pajamas, and finally, a reptile habitat light. They just keep coming."

"Oh, Nina. I'm so sorry. Does he sound confused when you talk with him on the phone?"

"Not a bit. If he's lost his mind, how could he continue to work? Seems like they would stop hiring him, but he's still busy."

"It's very strange. Could someone be pulling a prank on him?"

"I've considered that. It's definitely possible. I keep hoping one of our friends will call and have a good laugh about it."

"When is he coming home?"

"Next week. The big confrontation is coming."

My heart broke for her. I said goodbye and walked across the street to my house.

Daisy was thrilled to go outside for five minutes. When she returned, she was panting and stretched out on the cool floor. Mochie accompanied me to my office, where I tried to focus on work.

A couple of hours later, I heard someone knock and found Bobbie Sue at my kitchen door.

I invited her in. "Who's minding the restaurant?"

"An employee who has filled in for Marsha in the past. There's a nice young woman, Liddy, whom Tate said was a terrible waitress, but he had high hopes that she might be exceptionally good at management. I phoned her and she was excited about the prospect of being trained."

Bobbie Sue massaged her forehead. "I don't know what to do about the restaurant. It's so much work. It might be smarter to sell it and be done with it."

"Would you care for iced tea?"

"Yes, please. It's hot out there."

I poured tea for her and she guzzled it, then didn't say anything for what seemed an awfully long time. I refilled her glass.

Finally, she asked, "Why hasn't Spencer been arrested?"

Chapter 37

Dear Natasha,
I haven't seen your color prediction for this year. Are
you making one? I need to know. I'm redecorating!
Done with Gray in East Orange, New Jersey

Dear Done with Gray,
You're not the only one who feels that way. This
year's color is sea-glass aqua. It will play nicely with
corals and bold yellows.

Natasha

I hadn't expected that! "Should he be?"

"Oh, Sophie," she wailed, "please don't make me say it. I know that you know. I don't understand what's happening. Are you giving him a pass? Sophie, I've been doing my best to get him out of town."

"I noticed that. Hasn't worked out very well for you. Has it?"

"He's flying out this evening. He'll be somewhere safe, where he's loved. In the fall, I'll make sure he gets into a good boarding school. Someplace where he can get therapy. I'll make sure nothing like this ever happens again. He's a good boy, Sophie. Truly he is."

"Are you telling me that Spencer killed Tate? Did he confess to you?" I really hated to think it, and there remained a hair of doubt in my mind. Had he helped her and now she needed to pass off a good story, placing the blame on him and getting him out of town?

"The day we found Tate's body, everything was a blur," she said. "Just trying to wrap my head around the fact that Tate was gone was overwhelming. I was numb. Then there were the EMTs, and being questioned by Wolf, and people calling to ask if it was true. It was like a house of mirrors, with another nightmare no matter which way I turned. When Wolf left our house, there was a brief period of quiet. Pierce pulled me aside and showed me Spencer's backpack." Bobbie Sue swallowed hard. "Tate and I had bought the kids planet-friendly packs. They're a natural color, sort of off-white because they haven't been dyed. There was blood on it. It was unmistakable. And then he opened it and pulled out a team T-shirt that the kids wear. And there was blood on it, too. So much blood." Bobbie Sue buried her head in her hands. "I couldn't believe it. My sweet little boy!"

I patted her shoulder. "I thought Spencer ran in the 5K."

"Coach said something about how well he did. Came in second, I think."

"Where was the backpack while he was running? Wasn't the finish line at Market Square? There are plenty of lights at night. Wouldn't someone have noticed a bloody backpack?"

Bobbie Sue raised her head slowly and looked into my eyes. Relief washed over her face. "Yes. Yes, they would have noticed! And Spencer wouldn't have run with it on his back. How could I have overlooked that?"

"Where did Pierce find the backpack?"

"In Spencer's room, I think. I don't really know."

"You didn't ask Spencer about it?" I stared at her.

"No! We were in a panic. The bloody backpack, the bloody shirt. It was so obvious to us. What were we supposed to think?"

"Where is it now?"

"Pierce destroyed it. We couldn't have the police find it. He meant well, Sophie. We had to protect our boy."

An awful thought crossed my mind. What if Bobbie Sue was worried about Pierce blabbing? "Did you poison Pierce?"

"No! How could you even suggest such a thing? Granted, I hated the miserable lug. There were times when I'd have liked to wring his neck. But I didn't. I wouldn't! Besides, I had never heard of that plant. Do you really think I would have had the time to go out and find one? I wouldn't know where to begin."

She made a very good point. It had to be someone who ran along trails and would have run across one. "Coach," I said.

Bobbie Sue blinked at me. "Why him?"

"I guess it could have been someone else, but I know of two runners who have been hanging around Pierce. Coach and Spencer. I could be wrong, but doesn't Spencer run mostly around town? That leaves Coach."

"Why on earth would Coach poison Pierce? Oh, dear heaven! What if Spencer poisoned Pierce?" Bobbie Sue slid off her chair onto the floor in a dead faint.

I knelt next to her, gently tapping her cheeks and thinking that Spencer had been right. It was all too much for Bobbie Sue to take.

I retrieved a paper towel and wet it slightly with cold water. Kneeling again, I laid it across her forehead. "Bobbie Sue?"

She groaned and opened her eyes briefly before mashing them closed again.

"Maybe you should get some rest. Would you like to nap here or would you rather go home?"

She looked at me wearily and struggled to get up. "I'm so embarrassed."

"You've been through a lot, Bobbie Sue. You need to take some time for yourself."

She plopped into a chair. "I was afraid that you would discover that Spencer had killed Tate. I paced the house at night. I've hardly had any sleep. I should have come to you instead of hiding it like a dirty little secret. How stupid could I be? I need to see Pierce."

"How about I drive you home to get some rest and *I* will go see Pierce?"

"No, I'm fine." She stood up and swayed. Grabbing the table to steady herself, Bobbie Sue said, "Okay. Maybe that's not such a bad idea."

I grabbed my purse and walked her out to my car, staying very close lest she fall again. I drove her home and helped her to a sofa. When Bobbie Sue was comfortably sprawled out with a light throw over her, I asked, "Where would Spencer be about now?"

"They like to hang out around Jones Point Park. I think there are basketball hoops or something."

"Thanks, Bobbie Sue. Get some rest." I headed for the door.

"Wait! I thought Spencer was in the clear! Why are you looking for him?"

"Just for information on when and where he last saw his backpack. Get some sleep."

"You will report back to me, won't you?" she called.

"I promise." I made certain the door was locked and pulled it closed behind me.

I drove over to the park and spotted Spencer right away.

He saw me as I approached and ran toward me. "Is Mom okay?"

"She's exhausted. She's taking a nap."

"Whew! Seeing you here scared me."

"I wanted to ask you some questions. Do you mind?"

"Yeah, it's fine." He pointed at a bench.

We sat down and I asked, "How did you lose your backpack?"

"I was working on Midsummer Night's Day." He snorted. "Is that a thing? Anyway, I took my running clothes and shoes with me to work in the backpack so I wouldn't have to go home. I changed my clothes at the restaurant and met up with a bunch of my friends. After the fireworks, I wanted to run a little to warm up, so I left the backpack with them. When I came back, it was gone. I thought Moe Millhouse had taken it and we got into sort of a tussle."

"A tussle?"

"Yelling and pushing each other. Nothing major."

"Why would he take it?"

"As a prank. Moe's a jerk. He knew I could beat him, and I thought he wanted to throw me off by taking my backpack."

"Did you ever see it again?"

"Nope. Is that important?"

"I don't know. Did Pierce or Coach run in the 5K?"

"Naw. Coach is past his competitive days. Pierce wanted to run, but I didn't see him. Typical."

"What does that mean?"

"Ask anybody. Pierce is always late."

"Coach was there when you finished?"

"Yeah."

"Did you see Pierce before you ran?"

"No."

One-word answers. Oy. Teenagers! "Do you recall what Coach was wearing?"

"Seriously?"

"Try," I said.

"I don't know." Spencer smiled. "Yes, I do. Coach wore his team shirt. I thought it was nice of him to show up to support the guys he coaches."

"A team shirt like the one you couldn't find this morning?"

"Yeah. Some of the guys are wearing one." He pointed at his friends. They were typical. A cartoony mascot on blue and gold, which I presumed were the school colors.

A couple of his friends motioned for him to join them. "One last thing, Spencer. Did you see Coach anywhere that night?"

"Sure. He was at the play. I remember that because he was really nice to Jo, telling her what a great job she did. And I could tell Mom appreciated it, especially since Dad wasn't there."

Spencer went back to playing basketball with his friends and I sat on the bench for a few minutes watching them. Anyone could have taken Spencer's backpack. I eyed the boys as they played. They were old enough to wear a size large or even extra-large in a T-shirt.

The disappearing and reappearing backpack was very odd. If an ordinary thief had taken it, then it would not have turned up in Spencer's bedroom. It had to have been taken and returned by someone who knew that it belonged to Spencer. It had blood on it, so it was most likely at the scene of Tate's murder. And since Tate was dead, the only person who could return it would be the killer. And that pointed directly to Pierce, who showed the backpack to Bobbie Sue.

Thoughts were swirling through my head. What if Pierce wanted to be Tate? Maybe he envied what Tate and Bobbie Sue had and he wanted to step into Tate's place. He murdered Tate and then came to the rescue by making up the story about Spencer's backpack so he and Bobbie Sue would have a new bond. A twisted one, but a joint desire to protect Spencer would unite them. *Had* united them.

I waved at the kids when I left the park and then drove to the hospital to see how Pierce was doing. If he was better, he might be able to talk to me. He would probably lie, of course. Especially if he murdered Tate.

Chapter 38

Dear Sophie,
I have a cheesecake recipe that requires a water bath.
What does that mean?

Clueless in Bath, Illinois

Dear Clueless,
It's really very easy. When the cheesecake is ready to
bake, wrap the bottom in aluminum foil about three-
fourths of the way up. Then place the whole thing in
a roasting pan. Fill the pan with hot water halfway
up the cheesecake pan. Place the roasting pan in the
oven. It will steam and create moist air so the cheese-
cake will bake more evenly and gently.

Sophie

Pierce was sitting up in bed. I made a point of propping the door open in case I needed to beat a hasty retreat. "You look better," I said.

"The doctors tell me I'm lucky. Hard to imagine given how rotten I felt." He looked at his hands, which were no longer bound in gauze but looked raw and extremely painful.

"I haven't had a chance to thank you. I remember running toward you and Nina and then stumbling. The last thing I saw before I passed out was you telling me I would be okay. I appreciate that. You can't imagine how reassuring it was."

"Anyone would have done the same."

"Are you kidding? Most people would have videoed me on their phones and it would be all over the Internet." He looked askance at me. "You . . . didn't do that, did you?"

"No. I never understand how people can video someone in the middle of an emergency. Put the phone down and help that person already!"

Pierce chuckled. "Exactly!"

"Are you up to talking about the night Tate died?" I asked.

He looked like I had offered to smear more of the poisonous cream on him.

"It's okay. I know about Spencer and the backpack," I said.

"How did you find out?" It was only a whisper.

I skipped answering that and asked, "Where did you get the backpack?"

He raised his scabby hands, palm out. "I did not murder Tate. I swear."

That was an interesting response. What did that imply? If he had taken the backpack while Spencer was allegedly warming up, then it would not have been bloody. I went out on a limb. "But you saw Tate that night."

"Are you going to turn Spencer in?"

I was able to answer honestly since I didn't think Spencer had killed Tate. "No. Where did you see Tate?"

"He was already dead."

Pierce looked miserable. "I meant to get there in time to see the fireworks, but I missed them. I found a parking spot near the alley and was jogging through it to find Spencer when I saw the backpack. I knew who it belonged to. How many kids have"—he spoke sarcastically—"natural fiber, environmentally friendly, white backpacks? White, for pity's sake. They're kids. They'll stay white for ten minutes." He collected himself. "It had blood on it. A lot. And the alley was wet. I couldn't tell what it was, but I had a very bad feeling about it. I opened the gate and Tate was lying just inside to the right."

Either he was telling the truth, or he had murdered Tate. How else could he know Tate was lying on the right side of the gate?

"I checked his pulse. He was dead." Pierce sniffled and closed his eyes while he talked. "I knew Spencer had done it because his bloody backpack was there." He opened his eyes and shook his head. "I had to save him."

"Save Spencer?"

"He would have been tried as an adult. What's the punishment for murder? Life in prison? Twenty or thirty years in prison? That's longer than he's been alive." His head fell forward. "I wasn't there for him as a kid. Of all the things I have done in my life, it's the one thing I wish I could take back. I should have been a dad to him, but I was too selfish. Too absorbed in my own fun, running around, playing in bands, out all night. But this was something I could do to help him. I raced back to my car—"

"The Jeep?"

"Yes. I drove it down the alley and hoisted Tate into the back. He was way heavier than I thought. I threw the backpack in and took off. It was a nightmare. I didn't have a tarp or anything. I was scared to death someone might see blood on my car or see Tate in the back. I drove home and parked in my garage. After I showered, it was close to midnight. I found the key to the restaurant in his pocket, covered him with a blanket, and drove back to Old Town. It was quiet when I got there. Not a soul was around. I carried him into the basement of the restaurant, laid him facedown, broke a couple other bottles to make it look like an accident, and left. The next day I showed Bobbie Sue the backpack. You know what's worse than your husband being murdered? Finding out that your son killed him. I'm not sure she'll ever recover."

"Why didn't you hide the backpack and call the police?"

Pierce looked me in the eyes. "I had to save him. He's my son."

Part of me believed him. According to Spencer, Pierce was always late. That part rang true. And Tate was lying face-down in the cellar. "Did you ask Spencer about it?"

"I didn't have to. I knew what had happened. Bobbie Sue and I agreed that we needed to get him out of town as soon as possible."

I wondered if he realized that moving a corpse was against the law. He might feel better getting it off his chest, but there was a good chance he would do time for it.

"I was *going* to take him camping when I collapsed." He pointed at his knees.

"How do you think that happened?" I asked.

"I think some idiot thought it would be funny to mix that poison into jars of cream. I hope he ended up with it all over him!"

"You think someone did that in the store or the factory?"

"You bet! I'm filing a lawsuit, too. They should have better safety measures in place."

He could be right, but I didn't think so. The real question was who hated him enough to want to poison him?

I thanked Pierce and was about to leave his room when he asked me if I could hand him a book someone had left across the room. I retrieved it for him and when he stretched out his left hand to take it, the sleeve of his gown pulled back, showing four distinct claw marks.

My blood ran cold. In that moment, I could feel the cold blade against my throat.

His eyes locked on mine. "I'm sorry, Sophie. I feel really

guilty. You were so kind to me when I thought I was dying on the street. I guess I *was* dying, they said my heart nearly gave out. But the point is that you saved me when I had been so awful to you."

"I don't understand. Why? Why would you do that to me?"

He touched his throat. "I was frantic to save Spencer and you were getting way too close to the truth. Lying in this bed, I can't get it out of my mind. Wouldn't it be the ultimate irony to incapacitate the very person who would save my own life the next day?"

I left the hospital reeling. Pierce had had a big scare, and now the truth was tumbling out of him. I believed every word of it. He knew how Tate had lain in the Eklunds' backyard and in the cellar of the restaurant. And he had the mark I had left on his arm. He knew about the attack on me and where the knife had left a line on my throat.

Best of all, maybe when the police tested his Jeep, Bernie would be exonerated. But one problem still remained. Assuming Pierce was telling the truth, now it looked as if Spencer had indeed murdered Tate. He must have planned to move Tate in Bernie's car.

I was both relieved to have it over with and truly broken about Spencer being the murderer. I parked at home, let Daisy out and back in, and called Wolf to let him know about Pierce's confession.

While it wasn't a done deal yet, since that was up to Wolf, I walked over to The Laughing Hound to tell Bernie. On the way, I passed the location Natasha had wanted for her bakery. I recognized the man standing outside. He was the fishmonger who had been kissing Marsha so passionately.

"Hellooo, doll," he said in an appallingly saccharine manner.

Did he think we were in the 1940s? Who talked like that? I gave him a nod and kept going but he fell in stride with me.

"I've seen you around."

I tried to ignore him and picked up my speed.

"Could I buy you a drink?"

I stopped walking and faced him. "In the first place, I have seen you smooching with Marsha. And in the second place, it's only noon."

He grinned, flashing those ridiculously white teeth. "I like a girl who's feisty."

Eww. Eww. Eww. "Excuse me, please." I didn't dare give him any satisfaction by running, and my run was pathetic anyway. It would probably only make him laugh. But I picked up my walking speed to put some distance between us. I didn't dare look back out of fear he would interpret that as interest.

Fortunately, the restaurant was around the corner. I shot inside, out of breath.

Being accused of murder hadn't hurt business, that was for sure. People waited to be seated and the bar was packed. Was this the "there's no such thing as bad news" effect? Had people come in hopes of seeing the accused murderer? Or were they showing their support? The latter, I hoped.

A motion near the stairs caught my eye. Mars was waving at me. I darted between people and dashed up the steps.

"Where have you been?" asked Mars.

"You will not believe what happened. Pierce confessed to moving Tate's body. I had to tell Bernie right away."

"He's waiting for us in a private room." Mars led the way.

I was pleased to find Bernie, Francie, and Humphrey gathered around a table. "Where's Nina?" I asked.

"Tasting cheesecakes," said Francie. "That lucky dog!"

"After this, she may not ever want to eat another cheesecake," I joked.

"While she's sampling cheesecake, you're eating healthy," said Bernie. "There's a restaurant in Texas that made a big name for itself by serving incredible vegetable platters. We've done our own take on that idea by incorporating nine vegetables and fruits on each platter. Feedback cards are to everyone's right with a pen."

We started sampling right away. I bit into roasted asparagus, always one of my favorites. Then I ever so casually said, "Wolf is over at the hospital getting ready to question Pierce about Tate's murder."

That got their attention.

"It's true," I said, and told them about Pierce's confession. "He never said he killed Tate. He blamed that on Spencer. And if that's not enough, Pierce was the one who held a knife against my throat. I saw the marks on his arm where I clawed him."

Francie hit the table with her fist. "I told you that guy was the one who murdered poor Tate. I knew it."

Bernie scowled. "I haven't heard anything from Wolf or my lawyer yet."

"It's only been a few hours. I imagine they'll need some time."

"Let me get this straight," said Mars. "Pierce admits to finding Spencer's bloody backpack in the alley. That prompted him to open the Eklunds' gate, where he found Tate dead. He then loaded Tate and the backpack into his Jeep, drove home and waited until midnight, then returned and placed Tate's body in the cellar of his restaurant."

"That about sums it up."

Bernie still didn't look happy. "They're going to claim that I murdered Tate, went to get my car and got the blood on it, but by the time I returned, Tate's body was gone."

Chapter 39

Dear Natasha,
I read your menu for an elegant Fourth of July. I'm
using blue placemats. How do you suggest bringing
red and white on the tablescape?
                              Fireworks Fan in Fire Island, New York

Dear Fireworks Fan,
I grow weak at the mere thought of placemats at an
elegant dinner. Please use a tablecloth. I admit that I
do like red, white, and blue for the Fourth of July. It's
easy to bring all the colors in on plates, glassware,
napkins, candles, flowers, and lanterns. But please,
no paper plates! Buy a stack of inexpensive white
plates. You'll find them much more elegant.
                                                      Natasha

My news didn't seem quite so special anymore. "If they
find blood or Tate's DNA in Pierce's car, then who's to
say that he didn't drive your car and get it bloody to throw
suspicion on you?"

It sounded lame when I said it and I knew it.

"Or that his story is true," said Humphrey, "and it was Spencer who planned it? The backpack is key. Why would you pick up Spencer's backpack and leave it at the scene of the crime? Spencer had to have been there. What a convenient excuse. *My backpack was stolen.*"

We all tried to spin the news in a positive way, but the gloomy current underneath couldn't be completely hidden. Happily, Bernie's new fruit and veggie entrées were delicious. Still, we left knowing Bernie's situation hadn't been resolved.

I went to bed early, feeling more secure that night, in the knowledge that Pierce was the one who threatened me, and the police had him in their sights now. I still didn't know who the woman was who had grabbed me. Had Pierce had a female accomplice? I sat bolt upright in bed. The tall woman! It was hard to imagine anyone so chic grabbing me from behind, but stranger things had happened.

At three in the morning, Daisy pawed at me, whining. At first, I thought she needed to go outside to relieve herself, but then I caught the dull rumble of a truck in the street.

I rolled out of bed and looked out the window. A Humvee blocked the street. Six people in helmets and vests carrying rifles ran down the street away from my house.

Stumbling over my own feet in my hurry, I grabbed a robe and pulled it on as I raced downstairs to look out the bay window.

Nina raced across the street in her nightgown with Muppet at her feet.

I unlocked the door for them, and they dashed inside.

"What's going on?" she asked. "There are armed people outside. Like we're being attacked!"

"I'm calling Wolf. He must know."

The door opened again as Bernie and Mars darted in.

"I'm borrowing one of your bathrobes," said Nina.

"Help yourself."

But before I could call Wolf, we heard a voice over a loud-speaker. "All residents of 2249 Duchess Street, come out of the house with your hands in the air and empty!"

Mars shouted, "That's Natasha's house!"

Everyone except me ran to the front door. I swept up Mochie and Muppet, and called to Daisy. She followed me to my home office, where I closed the doors so they wouldn't escape in whatever mayhem might ensue.

When I returned, Mars and Bernie were standing outside, just feet from the door. Nina remained inside, but was whispering, "What's happening? Can you see anything?"

I wondered about Francie. Was she afraid? I didn't want to wake her if she was asleep, but I could hear Duke barking.

My phone rang and I picked it up fast. Francie sounded grumpy. "What in blazes is going on out there? Have you called the police?"

"It's the FBI, Francie. They've surrounded Natasha's house."

After a pause, Francie said, "Uh-oh. Maybe that's not CBD they're putting in their goodies."

"Are you okay? Do you want to come through the back fence and join us?" I asked.

"Nah. I'm fine. I just wish I could see more of what's happening. Call me if you hear anything of interest."

She disconnected the call.

"Can you see anything?" I asked.

"Looks like they've lined up some people in the street," said Mars. "I imagine it's Natasha, Wanda, Griselda, and Charlene."

"There's a fifth person now," said Bernie.

"That's probably their tenant," said Nina. "Seriously, what on earth can they have done?"

Bernie stepped inside and sent a text to someone.

"I'm sure that person will appreciate being awakened," said Nina.

Bernie grinned at her. But a moment later, we heard the ding of a response on his phone. He looked up at my house number and sent another text.

Lights were on in all the houses on our block. None of the neighbors dared leave their premises, though. Who wanted to be caught up in an FBI raid?

Two hours later, we had consumed countless cups of coffee and tea, all of the Krispy Kreme doughnuts, the leftover Japanese cheesecake, and the leftover triple chocolate cheesecake. The Hummer finally unblocked the road and drove away. We exchanged fearful glances when there was a knock at the door.

Everyone followed me to the foyer. I peered out the peephole. The tall woman gazed patiently at my door.

Chapter 40

Dear Sophie,
I heard you are a friend of Bobbie Sue Bodoin, the
Queen of Cheesecake. Can you get me her recipe for
Oreo Cheesecake?"
       Cheesecake Girl in Hungry Hill, New York

Dear Cheesecake Girl,
I don't think Bobbie Sue gives her recipes away to
anyone!
          Sophie

I swung the door open.

"You!" barked the tall woman in dismay.

She was more than a head taller than me. "Who are you?" I asked.

Bernie cleared his throat. "Morgan Newhouse, this is Sophie Winston."

Morgan stared at me with cold annoyance. "You have been a pain in my side. Literally." She winced.

"So it was you who grabbed me!" I blurted. "Sorry, but I

think you deserved that bruise. Why did you do that? You scared the daylights out of me."

"Because you keep getting in the way. Why do you think we're here now?" She flashed an angry look at Bernie. "I can't believe you told her."

He shook his head. "I said nothing."

Against my better judgment, I asked, "Would you like to come in?"

"No, thanks. I don't have time. I just wanted to thank Bernie and let him know it's over. We raided the vessels and nabbed quite a few people. The only one who is missing now is Eddie Bigelow."

"I don't understand, Morgan. Why did you raid Natasha's house?" asked Bernie.

"For starters, she rented the apartment over her garage to Austin Sinclair, whom we arrested, and as if that's not enough, she's dating Eddie."

"What?" asked Nina. "I don't understand any of this."

Morgan glared at me. "I'm glad to be done with you. Nice working with you, Bernie." She turned and walked away, ever elegant in a black business suit and heels.

I closed the door. Everyone was glaring at Bernie.

"You knew all along what they were doing out there and you didn't tell us?"

"Actually, I did not know. I knew about the sting against illegal fishing, but I didn't know about the raid and I couldn't imagine why they would be at Natasha's house. I thought it had to be something else."

We returned to the table. "So who is Morgan?" I asked.

"An FBI agent. She was in charge of an investigation into illegal fishing. It's a huge problem," said Bernie. "Did you know that one out of five fish sold in the US is illegally caught?"

"Zzzzz." Nina feigned a snore.

"Hey!" Bernie objected. "We're talking about millions of

dollars of losses each year. And they're fishing where licensed fishermen aren't allowed to fish. They're depleting the waters."

"So what did FBI agent Morgan Newhouse want with Tate?" I asked.

"Tate and I were cooperating with them. Eddie Bigelow is the mastermind behind this illegal fishing scheme. But you kept getting in the way, Soph. Then this morning when you nailed Marsha for getting a kickback, they had to move fast before she had a chance to warn them," Bernie explained.

"This Eddie that Natasha's seeing. Tall, handsome, big brown eyes, kind of slimy guy?" I asked.

"I'd say that's an accurate description." Bernie nodded.

"I can't believe how desperate we women are. Both Marsha and Natasha are involved with him. Unbelievable!"

Dawn had broken and we were all exhausted. I let Mochie, Daisy, and Muppet out of my office and my friends left for home. I crawled back in bed. I couldn't sleep, though. The revelation of the illegal fishing scheme explained so many things. I understood why Bernie had to lie to me about Morgan, the tall woman. I would have done the same. If information leaked out about the sting, it would have ruined their chances of catching those guys. Wolf obviously knew about it, too, which is why he was so worried. FBI agents weren't perfect people, either, but Morgan probably had a decent alibi about where she went after she parted ways with Tate that night.

But we still didn't know who had killed Tate. The backpack and Bernie's car seemed key to me. If Pierce wasn't lying, it meant that the killer dragged Tate into the Eklunds' backyard and then went to retrieve Bernie's car. I couldn't help laughing at the thought of the killer returning, only to find Tate's body gone! That must have been a shock!

But why did the killer have Spencer's backpack? Was there something in it that he wanted? I would have thought that he planned to frame Spencer, but he had gone to all the trouble of framing Bernie. It didn't make sense.

I gave up on sleep, took a long, hot shower and dressed. I hated to admit it, but Natasha's scolding about my attire had wormed its way into my head. I dressed in a summery turquoise sheath.

It surprised me when my door knocker clanked. I wasn't expecting anyone. I ran down the stairs and swung the door open to find Jo on my stoop.

"Jo! What are you doing here? Come on in." I looked outside for Bobbie Sue but didn't see anyone.

"Hi, Sophie. I would like to hire you to find a murderer."

"Another one? Who died?"

"The same one. The killer of my father."

I didn't understand at all. But since she was being so formal, I thought I should treat her like an adult and showed her into the living room. Jo sat primly on the sofa and petted Daisy.

"What's going on, Jo?"

"They're going to arrest Spencer!" She burst into tears.

I brought her tissues and sat down beside her. Wrapping my arm around her, I asked, "Where did you hear that?"

"Mommy and Coach were talking about it last night. Spencer can be really annoying, especially when he teases me. But he's the only brother I have!" She bawled into my shoulder.

I stroked her hair until she calmed down. "Jo, did you hear the fight Spencer had with your father?"

"Yes. It was lame. Daddy said that Spencer needed to get a better attitude about school if he wanted to go to a good college."

"Did they mention Spencer's girlfriend?"

"I don't think so. It was about spending more time on schoolwork."

"Does your mom know you're here?" I asked.

"No. I walked over. She thinks I went to Esme's house. I'll go there when I leave."

She most certainly would because I was taking her.

"Mommy said you don't charge for finding killers."

I tried to hide my grin. "That's correct. But I believe the police are wrapping up that case."

"They have the wrong man. Pierce shouldn't have moved Daddy, but we don't think he killed him. I don't like Pierce, but isn't justice important?"

This child had been eavesdropping on too many adult conversations.

"Justice *is* important. I'll see what I can find out."

Jo hugged me. "Thank you, Sophie!"

"Now, how about I walk over to Esme's house with you?"

"Okay. Can you come to my ballet recital tonight?"

"I wouldn't miss it."

At noon, I met with representatives of the Organization of Research Chefs to discuss their plans for a national conference. They are an interesting and diverse group of people who come up with new menu items, evaluate ingredients, and ensure food safety for restaurants, among other things. On their insistence and against my better judgment, we ate at Blackwell's Tavern.

I recognized the two servers Mars and I had talked with. And I spied Liddy walking through and thought I heard her talking to someone about his work schedule. To the average diner, I was certain nothing seemed amiss.

When our lunches arrived, I gazed at my plate and instead of thinking about how beautifully arranged it was or being eager to taste it, my thoughts wandered to who had selected and accepted the shrimp on my plate. Spencer wasn't working and Marsha had been sacked. No matter. The shrimp were beautiful and delicious.

I should have been listening to my clients, but my mind wandered to the morning we discovered Tate's body. When the EMT was cleaning up Bobbie Sue's face and hands and Marsha arrived for work. And in that moment, a shiver ran through me. Wasn't Spencer supposed to be the first to arrive at the restaurant? Why hadn't he been there that morning?

I couldn't believe that Nina and I had overlooked that detail.

I forced myself to focus on my clients. Lunch went well and I promised to send them a detailed schedule of events along with other options. I walked home thinking about where Spencer might be. I took a chance, got in my car, and drove to Jones Point.

Spencer was there with friends, kicking a soccer ball around. I waved at him and he jogged over to me.

"Hi, Sophie."

"Looks like fun. I hope I'm not interrupting a game."

He shrugged. "We're just fooling around."

"Spencer, on the morning that we found Tate's body, Marsha was the first to arrive at the restaurant."

He nodded.

"I thought it was your job to be there first and accept the food deliveries."

Spencer didn't look one bit perturbed that he had been caught skipping work. He said, "It was my day off." His tone was as calm and confident as if he were telling me the sun was shining. He frowned at me. "You thought I didn't go to work because I had murdered Dad?"

That was embarrassing and insulting to him. "No," I lied. "I just can't figure out why your backpack was there."

His eyebrows rose. "Are you kidding? To frame me."

I shook my head. "I don't think so. If the killer wanted to frame you, why did he go to the trouble of using Bernie's car? That took a lot of planning and effort."

Spencer chewed on his lip. "I don't mean to be a jerk, but did you ever consider that Bernie killed my dad? He was really nice to me, but maybe he wants to buy Blackwell's Tavern or something."

"Then why did he have your backpack? How did he know it was *your* backpack?"

Spencer stared at me as though that had never crossed his mind. He turned slowly and looked at his friends on the field. "You don't think . . ."

"All I know is that your backpack being at the scene of the crime was not a coincidence. Clearly, the obvious inference is that you left it there." I didn't spell it out, but he could have forgotten it in his panic over having murdered someone.

"But I didn't. I wasn't there. I swear. I loved my dad."

I honestly believed that was true. "Then we have to go to the next step. Who knew it was your backpack, took it, and killed Tate? Was there anything in it someone might have wanted?"

"My shoes? The shirt I wore at work?" He shrugged. "It was probably Pierce. Then he lied to my mom about me being the killer. Nice father, huh?"

"I'm sorry, Spencer. This must be so hard for you."

He raised his thumb and pointed it over his shoulder. "I'm gonna get back."

He turned and ran. For a moment, I thought he might run past his friends and keep going. Instead, he kicked the soccer ball with such force that it slammed into the goal.

Chapter 41

Dear Sophie,
I wrote to you earlier about my disappearing bird-feeders. Well! The camera caught my daughter-in-law sneaking one away. When I confronted her, she had the gall to inform me that I had too many birdfeeders. I told her my birdfeeders were none of her business and if I ever caught her taking one, I would call the authorities. She hasn't been to visit since. My son tells me she thinks the feeders make too much of a mess on the ground. But this is my house, and those birds make me happy!
     Happy as a Bird in Ravenswood, West Virginia

Dear Happy as a Bird,
If you are troubled by the mess under the feeders, then you can do something about it. There are trays made exclusively for this purpose. They go under the feeders to catch loose seeds. You can also buy hull-free seeds. Most of what drops is the hull. Some bargain seeds are packed with seeds birds won't eat. If you spend a little more for hull-less seeds that birds like, there will be less waste.

     Sophie

I drove home, convinced that I had overlooked something important. I must have.

I was working on the plan for the research chefs when the door knocker sounded. Expecting to see Jo or her mom, I opened the door with a smile. But it was Wolf who stood on my stoop.

"You look beat," I said.

"I hear you finally met Morgan."

"I don't think we'll be besties. Would you like to come in?"

Putting on a pot of coffee, I asked, "Would you care to try my no-bake cheesecake?"

Wolf grimaced. "Do I want to try it?"

I laughed at him, cut slices for both of us, and poured the coffee. "What kept you up all night?"

"Pierce Carver. He's being released from the hospital today."

"Are you going to charge him with Tate's murder?"

"Most likely. We used luminol on his Jeep. Looks like he tried hard to scrub something with bleach. We found a few drops of blood that he probably missed and a little bit of hair that matches Tate's. But best of all, there's the glass neck of a bottle of champagne that exactly matches the brand used to kill Tate. Hey, this is pretty good!"

I thought it was, too. Nicely refreshing with the fruit in it. "Then how do you explain the blood on and in Bernie's car? And the clamshell that held the cheesecake?"

"We suspect that he saw Spencer's backpack and took it to convince Bobbie Sue that Spencer had killed his dad."

"That didn't answer my question about Bernie's car."

Wolf sat back, holding his coffee mug between his hands. "I don't have an answer for that. All I can imagine is that he planned to use Bernie's car, thus implicating him, but something happened that made him use his own car instead. We'll get it out of him."

"So Bernie is off the hook?"

Wolf released a big sigh. "Almost. The problem for us is *beyond a reasonable doubt.* Unless we can explain the blood in and on Bernie's car, you can bet Pierce's lawyer will make a very big stink about it, and it would probably be enough for a couple of jurors to have a reasonable doubt about Pierce's guilt."

"At least you can get some sleep tonight," I said.

"And he won't be threatening you, or worse." Wolf got to his feet. "It was good seeing you, Sophie."

"It was good seeing you, too, Wolf."

He pecked me on the cheek and left.

I walked Daisy down to my favorite florist and bought a dozen red roses for Jo. I could remember the thrill of being presented roses when I was a kid.

It was still light outside when I drove over to Jo's ballet recital. I could have walked, but I hadn't napped in the afternoon, and with so little sleep last night, I wasn't sure I wanted to take a longish walk home.

Bobbie Sue beckoned to me from her seat when I entered. I slid in next to Spencer and said hi to Spencer and Coach. Coach seemed to be turning up everywhere they went. But it had always been that way. Hadn't he said that he coached the kids in their informal games when Spencer was little? Before Bobbie Sue was the Queen of Cheesecake and before she married Tate.

The lights were lowered, the curtain opened, and live music began.

Jo and her friends danced to Pharrell Williams's "Happy," which lived up to its name and left everyone smiling. Coach excused himself, saying he'd left their flowers in the car and they might wilt in the heat. He returned with gorgeous pink and white lilies. After the recital, parents rushed the stage, and I was pleased to see that Jo wasn't the only child receiving flowers.

Darkness had fallen while we were inside. We said good-night and I told Jo one last time how fabulous she was. Bobbie Sue was taking them to Jo's favorite place for ice cream and invited me along. I declined, citing exhaustion. All I wanted was to crawl into bed and sleep.

The parking lot emptied fast as families left with their dancers. I turned on my ignition and the car started, then coughed and sputtered. I tried again and it simply refused to turn on. I slumped in my seat, telling myself to wait a minute and try again. I pumped the gas pedal and pressed the ignition button. It just wouldn't respond.

It was entirely too late to call the shop that had repaired it. I phoned Nina but my call rolled over to voicemail. I hated to bother Mars again, but I called him because it was that or walk home. His phone rolled over to voicemail, too. Poor Bernie, he picked me up last time. Still, I called his cell phone but he didn't answer. What were they all doing tonight? I left a message and tried to start the car one more time.

After three more attempts I had to face facts. The car was not going to start. No problem. I could walk. It wasn't *that* far.

I screamed when someone tapped on my window. When I saw that it was Coach, I rolled the window down. "You wouldn't by chance be a wizard with cars that don't start?"

He smiled at me and in that moment, I remembered the first words he ever said to me. *I was supposed to give Spencer a ride to work this morning and Bobbie Sue told me what happened.* That was what I had missed. It had been a bold lie. Spencer was off that day. On the morning that Tate was discovered, Spencer had called Pierce, but not Coach. He had shown up on his own to find out if Tate was dead or alive.

And now, I was looking into the eyes of Tate's murderer. My only way out was to keep my cool and pretend that I didn't know he had killed Tate.

"Pop the hood and I'll have a look," he said.

I pulled the lever that opened the hood and glanced around the parking lot. It was empty except for a lone car on the other side that probably belonged to Coach.

Was it safer to stay in my car or to get out? I rolled the window up. Could I slam the hood on him and run? Or was he happy and thinking he got away with murdering Tate? Maybe he wasn't planning to harm me. But then why was he still here? Why, when everyone else had left, was he still in the parking lot waiting for me? Fear struck my heart. Had he disabled my car intentionally when he left to retrieve the flowers?

He returned to my window. I rolled it down just two inches so it would seem like I was being friendly.

"No luck, I'm afraid. Can I give you a ride?"

I knew better than to get into his car. Not a chance! They would never find my body. He would drive out into the countryside somewhere and dump me in the woods.

"Thanks!" I said cheerily, but I called a friend and he's on the way to pick me up. I appreciate your offer, but I'd better wait for him."

He smiled at me again. Why hadn't I noticed that horrible sinister smile when I first met him?

"No problem," he said. "I'll wait with you. Make sure you're safe."

Oh no! It was a no-lose proposition for him. Now I couldn't walk home because he would grab me if I left the car. And if Mars or Nina showed up, Coach would look like the good guy for protecting me. And if no one showed up, which was highly likely, then . . . then what? Why was I being so stupid? I quickly pressed 911.

"Alexandria Police Department," said a woman's voice. "What is the nature of your emergency?"

"My car conked out and there's a man here who is scaring me."

"Is he threatening you?"

How to answer that? "I'm afraid of him," I whispered.

"Ma'am, just call an Uber. We're not here to give people rides home."

At that moment, Coach slammed a rock into the driver's side window. I screamed as glass shattered all over me. He reached a hand through the hole and tried to grab my neck. I seized his hand in both of mine and chomped down on his fingers as hard as I could.

He yowled in pain and jerked his hand back. He yanked at the door handle repeatedly in an effort to open the car door. His bloody right hand returned through the broken window in a minute, trying to locate the buttons that unlocked the doors. Why didn't I have a knife or any kind of weapon in my car?

I pressed 911 again. This time I screamed, "Help!" and rattled off the address.

The woman's voice asked calmly, "What is the nature of your emergency?"

I had lost every fiber of politeness and self-control. "A man is trying to kill me!"

The click of the car doors unlocking shot terror through me and propelled me into a complete panic.

"Why?" I screamed at him as I scrambled to the passenger seat. "Why me?"

"Because you figured it out. You asked Spencer if he was working that day. It was one of my two mistakes."

I had to keep him talking. I unlatched the passenger door but didn't open it. "You lied to me. But you did it well. I didn't realize it for a long time. What was the other mistake?"

"Leaving Tate's body while I went to get Bernie's car."

He was inside the car now and reaching for me. I squished against the passenger-side door as far away as I could without opening it. I needed him to follow me.

"You must have been surprised when you returned, and Tate was gone."

"Big mistake. Big bad mistake. I spent a night thinking I blew it and expecting the police to show up. I thought maybe he wasn't dead after all. I planned it so well. So precisely. And then to have that happen—"

He lunged at me as I expected he would. I pushed the door open and jumped out of the car, positioning myself toward the door to the back seat. He reached for me, fumbling as he crossed the center console, his arms and hands going for my throat. I managed to evade them and slammed the car door on his arms. He bellowed like a wounded animal. The window was closed and intact. I leaned against the door, digging my heels into the pavement and using my body like a lever to hold the door closed.

He was stronger than me, but his arms were pinned. And heaven help me for being so horrible, but I hoped they might even be broken.

I heard a siren in the distance, but I didn't dare relax or run. What if it was on the way to another emergency? Running was my next option. But he would catch me. He was a runner, and I most certainly wasn't. I couldn't let that happen. If it did, I would have to be clever and take cover, hiding wherever I could. I glanced around, choosing the road that had the most homes. Where people might hear me, might help me. We were only two blocks from King Street. If I could make it that far, there would be a lot of traffic.

My heart sank when the siren faded. I had to keep this up as long as possible. I needed to buy time.

But then he managed to yank his arms inside the door, and I knew time was up.

I ran across the street and down the middle of the road. He would be behind me soon. He was so much faster than I could ever be. I darted to the right and ran along the sidewalk to King Street.

"Sophie!"

For a moment, I thought Coach was calling me.

"Sophie! Over here!" I recognized Bernie's voice. Mars's car pulled up to the curb and Bernie hopped out of the driver's seat. He ran to me and I grabbed him in a fierce hug.

"Are you okay?" he asked.

"I am now," I said into the cotton fabric of his shirt.

Chapter 42

Dear Natasha,
I am your biggest fan. When I'm not sure about something, I ask myself, what would Natasha do? So now I have to ask: What is your favorite kind of cheesecake?

FanGirl Crush in Fancy Gap, Virginia

Dear FanGirl Crush,
My absolute favorite is a recipe I developed and entered in the Queen of Cheesecake contest. It's a savory cheesecake that is served as an appetizer. It contains cream cheese, sour cream, chopped dates, fresh rosemary, and chopped jalapenos. And it's topped with a spicy onion relish! Yum!

Natasha

Safely ensconced in Mars's car, I phoned Wolf. He surprised me by actually answering his phone.

"You're not going to let me get to bed at a decent hour, are you?" he asked.

"It's Coach," I blurted. "Coach murdered Tate."

"And how do you happen to know this?"

"Because he just tried to murder me."

"Where are you?"

"Bernie came to pick me up. I'm okay. However, Coach, if he's not still in the parking lot, may be going to an emergency room. I bit his fingers, and they were bleeding like crazy, and then I slammed the car door on his arms."

"Ouch!" Bernie, who was listening, said. "Remind me never to anger you."

Wolf groaned, thanked me, and disconnected the call.

Bernie parked in front of my house. "Do you want me to stay over in case Coach eludes the police?"

"Thanks for the offer, but I don't think he'll get very far. And thanks for rescuing me."

"Anything for a damsel in distress."

I hit the sack early and when I woke to a beautiful blue sky, I was terribly sad for Tate. He'd had so much to live for.

After a shower, I moseyed down to the kitchen and let Daisy out. She returned with Muppet, Duke, Francie, and Nina. I put on coffee and was pondering what to make for breakfast when Bernie and Mars arrived.

While breakfast was discussed, I called to have my car towed to the dealership again.

They decided on pancakes, which suited me perfectly. Everyone pitched in and we were soon seated at my kitchen table, enjoying blueberry pancakes, bacon, and a colorful fruit salad.

I filled them in on what had happened the night before.

Nina huffed when she realized that both of us had missed the most important clue—Coach's lie about taking Spencer to work. "I cannot believe that slipped by us."

Francie scowled. "Let me get this straight. Coach grabbed Spencer's backpack, followed Tate, and slammed him over the head with a champagne bottle. Then he hides Tate's body in the Eklunds' backyard. He goes to get Bernie's car but when he comes back, Tate is gone because Pierce saw the backpack and Tate's body, so he thought incorrectly that Spencer had murdered Tate. He drives Tate to the restaurant, leaves him in the cellar, and destroys the backpack."

"That about sums it up," I said.

"Wait"—Mars picked up another slice of bacon—"that leaves so many questions unanswered."

Wolf knocked on the door and opened it. "Am I too late for breakfast?"

Bernie and I set him up with coffee and pancakes.

"You're just in time," said Mars. "Do you know yet why Coach murdered Tate?"

Wolf groaned. "He has been in love with Bobbie Sue for over a decade. He saw the family together at games, and Bobbie Sue was always nice to him, including him in their plans, dinner, picnics, things like that. He was a family friend, but none of them realized how much he wanted to be part of their family. And then he convinced himself that Tate was the only thing stopping him. He had to get rid of Tate."

"He lost his mind," said Nina.

"He was obsessed with Bobbie Sue," said Francie.

"Why did he take Spencer's backpack?" I asked.

"According to him, he saw the backpack lying in the grass. He figured Spencer had forgotten it and he would give it back to him after the race. Initially, he had planned to kill Tate after the race, when everyone broke up to go home. But then he saw Tate cutting through the alley. He was ready. He had the champagne bottle. The fireworks were going off. They weren't noisy but everyone was focused on them. He caught up to Tate and swung the bottle. Then he dragged Tate into the Eklunds' backyard. He could feel blood on his shirt, so he dug in Spencer's backpack and found a shirt. He put that on and stuffed his bloody shirt into the backpack. In the process, the clamshell with the chocolate cheesecake that was in the backpack fell to the ground and opened. He went to get Bernie's car, not realizing there was blood on his pants. He didn't even know he left a smear on the car door. When he came back, Tate and the backpack were gone. The only thing that remained was the clamshell, so he threw that into Bernie's car and drove it back to Bernie's garage."

"And that was where Pierce came in," said Nina. "Did you really find a piece of the champagne bottle in his Jeep?"

Wolf nodded. "Pierce wiped the back of his Jeep clean with bleach. But what he didn't realize was that the more time he spent with Bobbie Sue, the more he was pushing Coach out of the way. Pierce was trying hard to be a dad to Spencer, so he was the one who was always around the family. And that made Coach mad. He'd heard about this deadly plant and seen one near a trail where he runs. He mixed it with Pierce's muscle cream, and that landed Pierce in the hospital but fortunately didn't kill him. But when Coach heard Pierce confess to Sophie about moving Tate's body—"

"Coach was there?" I asked.

Wolf nodded. "Listening, out in the hallway. He decided to frame Pierce. He took some hair out of a brush that he thought belonged to Tate, and he bought a bottle of the same champagne he used to kill Tate. He left them in Pierce's Jeep and sure enough, our crime scene techs found them."

"Coach seemed like a nice bloke," said Bernie, "but that man is dangerous. He really thought everything through very carefully."

"And I'm afraid he did *not* like you, Bernie." Wolf sipped his coffee. "Apparently, you threw him out of The Laughing Hound once when he was drunk."

"Hah! There's a good reason to frame someone for murder," Mars said sarcastically.

My phone rang and I excused myself to answer it. When I came back to the table, I reported, "My car wouldn't run because someone put water in my gas tank."

"Coach?" asked Bernie.

"I have to think so. He left the recital last night for a few minutes. I bet that's exactly when he did it."

"We found him in the parking lot where you left him last night," said Wolf. "He has two broken arms. His fingers are all right. They'll be scarred, though. But you're alive. That's the important thing. We'll be bringing additional charges of attempted murder. Think you're up to testifying?" asked Wolf.

"You bet!"

Nina lingered when everyone left. "You're not going to believe this. You know all the packages we've been receiving? It's a scam!"

"I don't understand. Your husband fell for a scam but was ashamed and didn't tell you?"

"No! The seller of the product sends them out to people, then makes up fake names and leaves five-star reviews. If they aren't actually purchased and sent to someone, the program doesn't allow them to leave reviews. We get to keep everything, though I don't know why we would want most of it. I'm taking a huge load down to the thrift shop."

"So your husband is well. He doesn't have anything wrong with him."

"Nothing except being away too much!"

Chapter 43

Dear Sophie,
My grandmother says there are two ways to make
cheesecake. One is with sour cream and one is with
heavy cream. Is that true? Which one is better?
                    Grannie's Girl in Grand Rapids, Michigan

Dear Grannie's Girl,
It is true. Some people even substitute cottage cheese,
but those are the two most common ingredients.
Heavy cream makes for a richer, more silky cheese-
cake. Sour cream is also delicious, but it results in a
slightly more dense cheesecake.
                                                    Sophie

On the Fourth of July, I heard Marjorie Hollingsworth-Smythe utter, "Now that's a stunning man, Dodie."

Naturally I had to look up and see who she meant. It was Eddie Bigalow, the man who had followed me down the street, the same one I had seen kissing Marsha during a fish delivery. The mastermind of the illegal fishing scam. What was he doing at Marjorie Hollingsworth-Smythe's party? He stood next to Natasha, cooing, "Natasha. My beautiful Natasha. You must forgive me. Please!"

Her mother, Wanda, stood next to her. "Give him a break, Natasha. I haven't had a handsome man burst into my bedroom in the middle of the night in years! And never an FBI agent before!"

"Mother, please."

Griselda beamed. "He's lovely, Natasha. Not everyone has their houses raided by the FBI in the middle of the night. I say we all forgive him. If I were your age, I would grab him and run."

I reached for my phone and texted Wolf to let him know the mastermind of the illegal fishing deal was at Marjorie's party.

Natasha gazed at him adoringly.

Had she lost her mind?

She curled a finger at him, coaxing him slowly to the display of gorgeous cheesecakes. "Which flavor is your favorite, darling?"

I heard Mars groan, "Oh, give me a break!"

Eddie didn't act like a fugitive from the FBI. He smiled at Natasha. "Perhaps this one with all the luscious berries piled on top?"

In an amazingly swift move, Natasha slid her right hand under the cheesecake, turned around and smashed it in Eddie's face so hard that he stumbled backward and fell to the ground on his back. The cheesecake was so dense we couldn't even see his eyes. Berries rolled off his face to the ground.

Natasha stood over him and spoke in an even tone. "I have been disappointed by men all my life. And *you* have the distinction of being the very worst of the bunch."

She walked away, her head high, as though she was through with him and was moving on to another chapter of her life.

Bernie and Mars grabbed him. I handed them plastic wrap.

Mars gazed at me in horror. "Won't this suffocate him?"

"Use it to wrap his hands and feet, not his head." I laughed at them. Anyone who has ever used plastic wrap knows that pulling on it only tightens the silly stuff into an impenetrable mess.

I glanced at Marjorie Hollingsworth-Smythe, thinking that she would be appalled by a crook invading her party, not to mention having a cheesecake slammed in his face, and now tied up.

But she merely gave him a glance, and said, "Pity. He's so beautiful."

He was, alas, a bit incongruous lying in the grass tied up next to the beautiful dessert table.

The sun was setting, sending golden and rosy hues through the sky. I had ordered blue French tablecloths as bases and covered them with white tablecloths bearing red and blue stars on an angle. Vases burst with fresh daisies as well as colorful gerbera daisies, whose beautiful blooms were reminiscent of bursting fireworks.

A string quartet played and guests mingled with drinks in their hands. Marjorie had insisted on an open bar, but I noticed that most were trying her watermelon margaritas. Some sat at tables on the lawn, others roamed and filled their plates with goodies. Unlike Bobbie Sue's party, this dessert table was loaded with cheesecakes to try.

Morgan Newhouse, the tall, stunning FBI agent, showed up and graciously thanked Marjorie Hollingsworth-Smythe for allowing a scumbag like Eddie Bigalow to attend her party so they could arrest him. She handcuffed him and cut off the plastic wrap with a minimum of fuss, then escorted him to a waiting van.

Bobbie Sue had told me in confidence how delighted she was that a single mother with a toddler had won her cheesecake contest. She could relate all too well with the woman's circumstances and had offered her a job.

She stood now with Spencer and Jo, looking at the Potomac and probably thinking about Tate watching his family from above. Spencer would be staying home and continuing at his regular school and would definitely be taking advanced placement classes in the fall.

The three of them were leaving town for a much deserved two-week vacation at the beach. Bobbie Sue said Pierce was not invited. He still faced charges for moving Tate and hiding him in the cellar of the restaurant, but Bobbie Sue had paid to bail him out until his trial. His lawyer was optimistic that the charges would be reduced because he had a clean record otherwise.

The evidence against Coach had been so overwhelming that the judge denied bail. He would be in prison for decades to come.

Darkness had fallen and all the lanterns and fairy lights sprang to life. Minutes later, a crackle in the sky let us know the fireworks were about to begin. They reflected on the water, doubling the explosions of color.

By ten thirty, the party was over. The guests had left. The caterers were gone. Bobbie Sue had departed with her children.

Marjorie Hollingsworth-Smythe had rescued leftovers and cheesecakes, pressing them on me. "I've paid for them. Someone better eat them." She tore her daughter, Dodie, away from Bernie and they departed with stacks of cheesecakes. The tables and chairs and food had been removed, and the fireworks were now just a memory.

We sat on blankets under the stars, bathed by the light of the moon. I had borrowed forks from the caterer and handed them out. We tried the various cheesecakes, passing them around. We had no plates and simply ate like heathens, dipping our forks into the cheesecakes. Charlene fussed at Natasha and insisted that from now on, she would interview potential tenants. Wanda told her not to be so hard on Natasha because being raided was the most exciting thing that had happened to her in ages. Francie and Griselda discussed whether the amaretto cheesecake was better than the raspberry chocolate cheesecake. Nina was telling Mars and Bernie all about the shipping scam. The rubber chicken slingshot had evidently escaped the trip to the thrift shop because she pulled it out of her purse, which broke them into gales of laughter.

And I looked up at the sky and thanked my lucky stars for such great friends.

Recipes

Krista's notes on baking cheesecakes.

- Always bake it the day before serving. Cheesecake needs time to set up properly.
- Some cheesecakes will crack. They still taste great. If necessary, hide the crack with whipped cream or berries.
- The water bath will be *very* hot when you remove it from the oven. Make sure no children or pets are underfoot in case you spill some.
- When using a water bath, do not skimp on aluminum foil. Wrap it very tight so water cannot seep in.

Egg Muffins

Oil for greasing the cupcake pan
8 eggs
½ teaspoon salt
½ teaspoon garlic powder
¼ teaspoon pepper
1 cup Gruyère cheese, shredded
½ cup red pepper, cut fine

Preheat oven to 375° F. Grease the cupcake wells generously with oil.

Break the eggs into a bowl.* Add the salt, garlic powder, and pepper and whisk well. Stir in the cheese and red pepper. Divide between the 12 cupcake wells. Bake 8–10 minutes or until the centers begin to set. They should not brown. They will inflate in the oven and collapse as they cool.

*Krista's hint: Use a bowl with a spout (like a 4-cup Pyrex measuring cup) instead of a plain bowl. Then you can *pour* the egg mixture into the cupcake wells. Use a spoon to distribute any remaining cheese or red pepper.

Baked Potatoes on the Grill

These are the easiest thing in the world.

Russet potatoes
Unsalted Butter
Salt

Wash and dry russet potatoes. Rub generously with unsalted butter. Sprinkle with salt. Wrap in aluminum foil. Grill 55–60 minutes. Remove with a potholder or tongs and allow to rest for a few minutes. They're hot! Unwrap and serve with your favorite baked potato toppings.

Veggie Kabobs

2 cloves of garlic
1 teaspoon salt
½ cup olive oil
¼ cup balsamic vinegar
1 tablespoon prepared yellow mustard (not powder)
½ teaspoon dried thyme
½ teaspoon dried sage
¼ teaspoon black pepper
1 small or average size yellow summer squash
1 red pepper
1 cup cremini mushrooms
6 stalks of asparagus

If using wood skewers, soak them.

Crush and peel the garlic. In a bowl large enough to accommodate your vegetables, combine the olive oil, balsamic vinegar, mustard, thyme, sage, salt and pepper. Whisk together and add the garlic. Try to cut the vegetables the same size. Slice rounds of the squash. Snap off the tough ends of the asparagus and discard. Slice the remaining pieces about 1½ inches long. Cut the red pepper into 1½-inch squares, and snap the stems off the mushrooms. Lay squash, red pepper, mushrooms, and asparagus in bowl of marinade and toss. Marinate for a minimum of half an hour. Thread soaked skewers with pieces of squash, red pepper, mushrooms, and asparagus. Grill until tender, roughly 15 minutes depending on the heat and placement.

Alternatively, you can roast them in the oven. Preheat to 400° F. Place the skewers in a pan and slide into the oven. You can also skip the skewers and spread the vegetables in a single layer on a pan. Roast about 25–30 minutes or until tender.

Very Berry Coolers

4 cups water
½ cup sugar
½ cup fresh lemon juice
4 ounces vodka
4 ounces peach schnapps
Blueberries
Blackberries
Strawberries

Place water, sugar and lemon juice in a pot and bring to a boil to dissolve the sugar. Allow to cool. Place eight blueberries and eight blackberries (note that you can swap berries depending on what is available) in a bowl and crush. (If you want, you can put them through a sieve.) Then place them in a pitcher and add the sugar water, vodka, and peach schnapps. Add a few more berries to each glass and pour the lemonade over them. Garnish with a split strawberry on the rim of each glass.

Mushroom & Havarti Cheese Omelet

(Ingredients are for one omelet.)

Canola oil
3 large eggs
⅓ cup shredded Havarti cheese
1 cooked mushroom, sliced

Use an immersion blender to whisk the eggs (or whisk very vigorously in a bowl).

Pour oil into a 9-inch skillet. Heat on medium-high until the oil shimmers. Pour the eggs into the pan and rotate the pan in a circle. Keep rotating the pan to spread the eggs. When the edges set, flip the omelet and cook for 30 seconds. Flip again and fill with the Havarti and mushrooms. Fold one side of the omelet over and serve.

Chocolate Cheesecake with Mousse

Make this a day before you plan to serve it.

You will need:
1 9- or 10-inch springform pan.
1 roasting/baking pan in which the springform pan fits.
Aluminum foil.

Chocolate Crust

8 honey graham crackers
1 tablespoon unsweetened cocoa powder
¼ cup sugar
5 tablespoons unsalted butter

Preheat the oven to 350° F. Butter the bottom and sides of the springform pan.

Melt the butter. Place graham crackers in the bowl of a food processor and pulse until fine. Add cocoa powder and sugar and blend. While running, add the butter. Remove and press into the bottom of the springform pan. Bake 10–12 minutes.

Chocolate Cheesecake Filling

1¼ cups granulated sugar
¼ cup cornstarch
3 tablespoons unsweetened cocoa powder
2 8-ounce packs of cream cheese (full fat), room temperature
1 large egg
1 tablespoon vanilla
⅓ cup heavy whipping cream

Whisk together the sugar, cornstarch, and cocoa powder. If you have any lumps, then put the mixture through a sieve.

In a mixing bowl, beat the cream cheese until creamy, then on low, add the sugar mixture and beat, scraping the bowl as necessary.

On medium speed, beat in the egg, the vanilla, and the cream until nicely blended. But do not overmix.

Tightly wrap the bottom and side of the springform pan in aluminum foil so no water will leak into the cheesecake. Pour the mixture into the springform pan. Place the foil-wrapped springform pan in the roasting pan. Fill the roasting pan with hot water halfway up the side of the springform pan. Slide into the oven and bake about 70 minutes. The center should barely jiggle. Take it out of the oven and remove from the water bath. It's okay if it cracked. Place on a wire rack and allow to cool completely.

Chocolate Mousse Layer

2 large egg yolks
1 cup heavy cream
½ cup semisweet chocolate chips
½ teaspoon vanilla

Whisk together the egg yolks. Heat ½ cup of the cream to a simmer. Spoon a tablespoon of the hot cream into the egg yolks while whisking, to temper them. Add another spoon of the hot cream and continue to whisk. Add the yolks to the remainder of the hot cream and, whisking constantly, bring the mixture to 160 degrees. It should have thickened. Take off the heat and stir in the chocolate chips until they are melted. Cool completely.

When the chocolate mixture is completely cool, beat the remaining ½ cup of heavy cream until it begins to take shape.

Add the vanilla and beat. Fold into the chocolate mixture and spread on the cheesecake.

Refrigerate cheesecake overnight.

Optional:
Nuts
Sweetened whipped cream
Decorate by sprinkling chopped nuts around the edge of the top. If you like, you can pipe 12 whipped cream rosettes evenly spaced on top of the nuts.

Blackberry No-Bake Cheesecake

This is a lovely, creamy, not overly sweet cheesecake for hot days.

9 graham crackers (one pack)
¼ cup butter, melted + 1 tablespoon for greasing the pan
2 cups (around 12 ounces) blackberries, plus some for decorating
⅔ cup + 1 tablespoon sugar
2 tablespoons cornstarch
2 tablespoons water
2 8-ounce packs) cream cheese
1 cup heavy (whipping) cream

Butter the bottom and sides of a 9- or 10-inch springform pan. You can use parchment paper around the sides if you like.

Place the graham crackers in a food processor and pulse until fine. While it's running, pour in the melted butter. Press the mixture into the bottom of the springform pan and set aside. Wipe the bowl and blade of the food processor clean.

Cut cream cheese into 8 chunks and place in food processor.

Place sugar and cornstarch in a heavy bottomed pot and stir with a whisk to blend and get rid of chunks. Do not heat yet. Add 2 tablespoons of water and whisk to combine.

Wash the blackberries and pour them onto double paper towels so they won't be soggy. Add to the pot with the sugar mixture. Cook on medium high, stirring constantly, until they bubble. Turn the heat down and simmer, stirring, for 1½ minutes. Pour through a sieve into the food processor on top of the cream cheese. Pulse four or five times, then push on and mix together until no white spots show.

Whip the cream until it begins to take shape. Beat to a soft peak.

Fold the whipped cream into the cream cheese $\frac{1}{3}$ at a time until mixed. Pour into prepared springform pan and refrigerate overnight. To serve, loosen the sides with a slim knife if necessary, and remove from the pan. Decorate with blackberries.

Cream Cheese Pumpkin Pie with Caramel Sauce

Use 9.5 or 10-inch pie pan.

I bake this once a year at Thanksgiving. The top will crack, but that's okay. You will hide it with whipped cream and caramel sauce.

Graham Cracker Pie Crust

1½ cups graham cracker crumbs (about 9–10 sheets)
⅓ cup light brown sugar
¼ teaspoon cinnamon
6 tablespoons melted butter

Preheat oven to 350° F. In a food processor, pulse together the graham crackers, sugar, and cinnamon until fine. Add the butter and pulse. Pat into the pie pan. Bake for 10–15 minutes. Cool on a rack.

Cream Cheese Pumpkin Pie Filling

16 ounces cream cheese, room temperature or softened
4 eggs, room temperature
1 cup dark brown sugar
2 teaspoons cinnamon
½ teaspoon nutmeg
⅛ teaspoon cloves
2 cups pumpkin puree (not pie filling)
1 teaspoon vanilla

Preheat the oven to 275° F. Beat the cream cheese until smooth. Add the eggs one at a time and beat well. Add the sugar. Mix together the cinnamon, nutmeg, and cloves in a bowl and stir with a fork to mix and eliminate any lumps.

Mix into the filling. Add the pumpkin and the vanilla. Beat. Scrape down the sides and beat one more time. Pour into prepared pie crust. Bake one and one-half hours until the middle doesn't wobble.

Caramel Sauce

¼ cup heavy cream
2 tablespoons butter
¼ cup white sugar
¼ cup dark brown sugar, packed

Place ingredients in a microwave safe bowl. (I use a Pyrex 2-cup measuring cup.) Microwave in short bursts from 20–50 seconds, stirring each time until it bubbles up and is hot. Set aside to cool.

Sweetened Whipped Cream

1 cup heavy cream
⅓ cup powdered sugar
1 teaspoon vanilla

Beat the cream. When it begins to take shape, add the sugar and the vanilla. Beat until it holds a soft peak.

Assembly:

Slice the pie. Place a dollop of whipped cream on each piece. Drizzle with caramel sauce.

Strawberry Butter

Use this on pancakes, French toast, biscuits, or plain toast for a morning treat.

½ cup large strawberries
¾ cup confectioners' sugar
½ cup unsalted butter, softened

Using a food processor or an immersion blender, crush the strawberries. Add the sugar and mix. Add the butter and mix.

Store in the refrigerator for up to one week in a jar. It can also be frozen.

Japanese Cheesecake

Makes one 8-inch cheesecake.

Japanese Cheesecake is quite different from American cheesecakes. It is more like a very light cake with a cream cheese flavor. It is not difficult to make, however, as you will notice, it requires several reductions of heat so make sure you carve out enough time to baby it.

You will need:
8-inch springform pan
Parchment paper
A roasting/baking pan in which the springform pan fits
Aluminum foil

For the cheesecake:

8 ounces cream cheese
¼ cup (½ stick) unsalted butter, plus enough to grease the springform pan
½ cup whole or 2% milk
⅓ cup sugar
⅓ cup flour
3 tablespoons cornstarch
4 egg yolks

For meringue:

4 egg whites
¼ teaspoon cream of tartar
⅓ cup sugar
Powdered sugar or whipped cream and fruit to decorate (optional)

Grease the springform pan with butter. Line the bottom with parchment paper. Wrap tightly in aluminum foil so water will not leak into it. Have a large baking pan ready for the water bath. Preheat the oven to 325° F.

Pour water in the bottom of a double boiler and bring to a boil. Cut the cream cheese into 8 pieces and melt in the top of the double boiler, whisking until it is creamy. Add the butter and whisk it into the cream cheese while it melts. Remove the pan from the heat.

Adding one ingredient at a time, whisk in the milk, ⅓ cup sugar, flour, cornstarch, and four egg yolks. Set aside.

Whip the egg whites slowly at first. When they foam, add the cream of tartar. Continue whipping at a higher speed. When they begin to take shape, add the ⅓ cup sugar a little at a time. Whip until you get soft peaks. Do not overbeat.

Gently fold ⅓ of the cream cheese mixture into the egg whites. When they are combined, fold in the next ⅓ of the cream cheese mixture. When they are combined, fold in the final third.

Pour into the prepared springform pan. Rap the pan on the counter to get rid of any air bubbles. Place the springform pan in the baking pan and add hot water to ½ the height of the springform pan.

Bake at 325° F. for 20 minutes.

Lower the heat to 285° F. and bake for 40 minutes.

Turn the oven off. Leave door closed for 30 minutes.

Using a cake tester, test near the center. If the tester comes out clean—yay! If not, then bake 15 minutes longer at 285° F.

Take the cake pan out of the water bath and allow to rest for 20 minutes. Remove the cheesecake from the springform pan to cool down. Refrigerate overnight and serve the following day. Serve plain, with whipped cream and fruit, or dust with powdered sugar.

Pear Helene

Makes four servings.

Using the right pears is one of the difficult parts of this recipe. They have to be soft, but still firm enough to cut out the core. Hard pears simply will not work. Leave the stems intact and if you are lucky enough to have a leaf, leave it on the stem and treat it well.

The other difficult part is carving the core out of the bottom of the pear. The softer the pear, the easier this task will be. I found it useful to use a poultry knife and a very slender grapefruit spoon.

Select a pot in which your pears just fit standing up. If your pot is too large you will have to use more simmering liquid.

Originally, I planned this as an authentic French Pear Helene in which the pear is simmered in lemon water and served with a dark chocolate sauce. But my taster hated it! So this is my version of a Pear Helene, and it's quite tasty. If this is too much work but you want some of the flavor and concept, you can create a mock Pear Helene by using canned pear halves and store-bought chocolate sauce.

For the pears:

4 Bosc or red pears
2 cups Triple Sec
water

For chocolate sauce:

½ cup heavy cream
½ cup semisweet chocolate chips
¼ teaspoon vanilla
½ tablespoon butter

For serving:

Vanilla ice cream

Pears:

Peel the pears but do not remove the stem. They are meant to stand up. Cut off the very bottom so they can stand on their own. Then, using a small spoon and a thin knife, remove the seeds and the core through the bottom.

Place the pears in the pan (I used one with a 6–7 inch diameter). Add the triple sec and a bit of water as needed to cover them to just below the stem. Simmer until they can be pierced easily with a fork or a thin knife. Do not overcook! They need to remain intact.

They should be refrigerated in the poaching liquid until you are ready to serve them. They can easily stay overnight in the liquid and be served the next day.

Chocolate sauce:

Place cream, chocolate chips, and pinch of salt in a small pan but do not bring to a boil! Stirring constantly, melt the chocolate chips over medium heat. Add the vanilla and butter. Stir until the butter has melted and all is combined.

Assembly:

To serve, place a pear on the dessert plate. Next to it, place a scoop of vanilla ice cream. Ladle the chocolate sauce over the pear.